BLOOD OF THE TEMPLAR

D.H. Nations

BLOOD OF THE TEMPLAR

DOUBLE DRAGON

Dedication

For Gene

CHAPTER ONE

Palestine, 1192

They were still chasing her. Josephine felt them just as she felt the horse's heartbeat echoing through galloping hooves. Her lungs clutched at every breath, sucking at the rushing wind; fear lodged in her throat.

She stole a glance behind her. A vision of dark men on angry horses flashed in the moonlight. They were gaining on her. Clutching the reins in her trembling hands, she pressed her knees against the sides of the horse, urging it onward. She had never liked horses, but tonight she blessed her father for teaching her to ride.

Father. Tears welled up in her eyes. She could see him standing over mother's fallen body. He raised his sword, challenging the murderers, and his eyes urged her to run. She obeyed, dashing to the stables and saddling the mare, leaving him there to die.

Josephine leaned down low like he taught her, and the ground flew by beneath her. At the corner of her vision, she spotted a black stain in the darkness of the night, but when she looked directly at it, the shadow disappeared. She might have thought it a trick of the moon's light if not for the way her heart trembled. Clenching her teeth, she bit into her lip and blood filled her mouth with the taste of her fear.

Was it one of them left on the road to guard against escape? It was no matter. She was past him now. Steam rose from the horse's breath, and lather dripped from its lips. It could not travel much further. She spurred the horse onward, praying it would outlast the assassins.

Why? It was a question that burned in her soul. Her father was a simple merchant. Her sisters were younger than her, and she used to play hide and seek with them in the hills behind their house. Her mother would sometimes bake a pie and put it in the window to cool, a soothing scent that welcomed them home from their play. Why would anyone want them dead? Why would the murderers turn their blades on innocent children?

The riders were gaining on her, and in the pounding of the hooves, she could hear her sister's scream. The scream awoke her to murder, and she could smell death approaching in the stench of blood and urine. Again, she saw her father raising his sword in challenge, buying time for his daughter to escape. And this time, she heard the scream of his death as she rode from the estate.

She must escape these men. Father had given his life for her, and she would not fail him. She scanned the hills looking for something, anything that would give her hope. Just past where the road bent around a large hill, she spotted a twinkle of light. She thought it might be a star hanging low on the horizon, but it burned orange, not white. Torchlight! It revitalized muscles drained from fear, and she urged the mare onward. The riders were close now. Turning her head, she could make out the faces that glared back at her.

The horse galloped around the bend in the road, and she saw the old monastery. Josephine gasped.

8

Even under the sparse light of the moon, the signs of ruin overshadowed the building. Had it not been for the lit torches perched on either side of the entrance, she would have thought the monastery closed, long since abandoned. Her horse burst toward the monastery with renewed strength.

Thankfully, the iron gate was open. The horse flew through the gate and down the path. The men were very close now. She only had a few precious seconds. She jumped from her horse, her ankle twisting when she hit the ground, but she ignored the pain in a wild dash up the stairs.

"Help!" she screamed, her voice barely audible over her fists pounding against the wooden doors. "Please help me!"

The riders were through the gate now. The horses slowed as they approached, their riders wary. She continued to slam her fists against the wood with her head half-turned to stare at the riders in horror. Would they cut her down right here, so close to sanctuary?

They flowed off their horses, hands drifting to the long, curved swords at their belts. They were clad in darkness, black cloaks cradling their bodies and black scarves covering their mouths. The flickering torchlight reflected a dire warning in their eyes.

"Please!" Josephine slammed both fists against the door with all her might. Tears streamed down her face, and her body quaked with fear. The last of her strength ebbed from her body. "Please..."

The doors opened, and she fell to the feet of a man. She looked up into a face cloaked in shadows and could make out nothing save two eyes that glowed red in the torchlight. A chill ran through her. She trembled in pure terror, and then the darkness took her.

***

Geoffrey Furnivall spared the young woman a quick glance before stepping over her collapsed form to face the riders. He folded his arms across a wide chest, the worn hilt of a great broadsword sticking up from his waist. He drew back the hood of his cloak, revealing a scarred face, devoid of emotion. The man stared at the riders, daring them to approach.

The black riders paused, glancing at each other in silent communication. Their prey was in sight, but Geoffrey could see doubt crack their confidence. He drew his broadsword. The iron blade scratched against the leather scabbard, hissing out a dire warning.

"You dare stand before the Templar?"

The black riders turned their eyes to one man in the center. The knight, standing protectively over the collapsed woman, knew this one was different from the others. There was no fear in this one's eyes, only annoyance. He watched the leader's hands hover near the two blades hanging at his waist, his fingers dancing across the hilts. A tense moment passed and the man's lips cracked into a smile. He nodded to the knight, and signaled to his companions.

Geoffrey watched the assassins retreat into the night. "Micah?" he whispered, feeling an unseen presence in the darkness of the monastery.

A young monk in plain, brown robes stepped through the doorway. The monk's mousy brown hair matched his robes and his eyes. He ran a nervous hand over the neat bald spot cut in a perfect circle at the top of his head. "I heard a noise and came to investigate."

"Very good." Geoffrey slid the broadsword back into its scabbard and took a step toward the unconscious woman lying on the steps of the temple. He contemplated the woman, his thick mustache twitching with his thoughts. "We will need a room readied for our unexpected guest."

"Yes, sir," Micah said, scurrying back into the temple.

"Is that wise, Geoffrey?" came a soft, musical voice.

The voice held the faint trace of a French accent, and Geoffrey recognized it at once. He turned his head and watched his friend materialize from the night. "What else are we to do, Gerard?" he asked. "You saw the men?" He motioned his head in the direction of their retreat.

"Yes," Gerard de St. Amand replied. His long, black hair danced in the wind and he ran a hand through it, sweeping it out of his face. He pulled it into a tight ponytail and bound it with a strip of leather. "I spotted the chase on the south road."

"You know who they are?"

"Isma'ilites." Gerard hissed the word with disdain.

11

"The Old Man's assassins." Geoffrey nodded. "We must know what interest he has in the girl. He has been very active as of late. We must know more of his plans."

"But..."

Geoffrey shook his head cutting off his friend's objection. He knew what Gerard would say. The woman represented danger, not of assassins, but another danger they could ill afford. Yet, this was their duty, and they were sworn to it. He bent down and took the girl in his arms, lifting her with ease, as if she weighed no more than the flowers patterned on her dress. "She will come to no harm," he said, stepping into the temple. "At least, not on this night. See to her horse and meet me in the study."

He entered the monastery, and Micah met him on the stairs. "The guest chambers in the northeast wing." Geoffrey carried the woman into the room and laid her gently on the bed. He wrapped the blankets around her and bowed his head. "Lord, protect her," he whispered, "And deliver her from evil so that she may know your glory."

He backed out of the room and closed the door, and heard a growl down the hall. "Fresh meat?" The thick, burly voice of Edward Conyers spoke malice. The big man raised a hairy arm to scratch roughly at his cheek.

Geoffrey Furnivall glared a warning at Edward. "What?"

"She is not to be harmed," Geoffrey said.

"Your private play thing?"

Geoffrey raised his arm and put his hand on the taller man's chest. "She is not to be harmed." He

12

pushed, sending the man stumbling backward into the wall. Staring at Edward, he dared the larger man to disobey.

Edward's stare met his in defiance. Geoffrey recognized the lust, and he held the stare until it faded. Edward snarled and looked away.

"Follow me," Geoffrey said. He turned and walked down the hall, Micah trailing after him. With a final, aggravated glance at the closed door, Edward followed in their footsteps.

"Sit," he beckoned when they reached the private study. Gerard was already there, and Geoffrey remained standing while the two knights took their seats at the table. Micah hovered at the doorway caught between wanting to stay and knowing he should leave. Geoffrey gave him a quick smile and indicated with a nod that he could remain.

"The men chasing her, as Gerard noted, were Isma'ilites," Geoffrey said. "We do not know what they want from her, but they chased her some distance. The nearest village is two leagues south of here. It must have been a valuable prize for them to have followed her that great a distance."

"How do we know they didn't jump her somewhere on the road?" Edward interrupted, still scowling from their earlier altercation. His hands rested on top of the table, his fingers tapping out a rhythm against the wood. "She could have been traveling to any number of places."

"There were no bags on her horse, no supplies of any kind. She was not traveling. Her dress is made of a fine material and well stitched. She is not

13

of noble blood, but also not poor. Her father is, perhaps, a prominent citizen of the village, or even a minor merchant of a nearby city, though I doubt she could have evaded them that long."

"It is a wonder she evaded them at all," Gerard said. "The Isma'ilites are not known for their incompetence."

"Aye." Geoffrey nodded. "Two leagues is too great a distance for one girl to have evaded them, which leads me to believe they did not want to catch her."

"That makes no sense," Edward said. "If they did not want her, why would they chase her?"

"Perhaps they wanted something else," Micah whispered.

The others turned to look in the direction of the monk and Geoffrey could see the shy monk become uncomfortable under the weight of their stares. "Go on," he said.

"Perhaps they wanted to see where she would lead them," Micah said. "Though I doubt they expected it to be here."

"Yes." Geoffrey smiled his approval at the monk. "There was blood on her dress, fresh blood, though she had no cuts on her body. The girl fled from foul murder, I suspect. Not finding what they sought on the murdered, the assassins followed her in hopes it would lead to their prize. Instead, she led them here."

"What could the girl have that would interest the Old Man of the Mountain?" Edward asked.

"Not the girl, the family," Gerard corrected. "It is her family's blood on her dress. She alone

14

escaped, and the assassins, not finding their prize, followed her."

"Still, what does this have to do with us?" Edward asked. "She's a peasant, after all, and her concerns are not our own."

"If it has to do with the Old Man, it has to do with us," Geoffrey replied. "Don't be daft, man. You'd think you were still a bandit preying on the weak in England. You are of the Inner Circle now. Learn to use your mind."

"You are no better than I," Edward returned, his fist pounding down on the table emphasizing his words. "You were not higher born. You were excommunicated and had to beg forgiveness from the Bishop the same as I."

Geoffrey's eyes glittered dangerously. Like many knights, he had once led a sinful life that had caused his excommunication from the church. It was common practice to allow those of noble birth the chance to redeem past sins by taking up the cause of the knights.

"I have atoned for my sins," he said. "I now fight for the glory of God. What do you fight for, Edward?"

"I fight for blood, the same as you," Edward said. "Only I am not too blind to admit it."

"Enough!" Geoffrey said. "I am your superior, do not forget that, Edward. You live by my grace and by my grace alone. Do not challenge me."

Edward shot up from the table, his chair crashing to the ground behind him. "Do not talk down to me. I am not some peasant boy that can be pushed around."

"Gentlemen," Gerard said, moving to stand between them. "We are all three stuck in this dreadful outpost away from the civilized world. We each know the price we paid on our road here. Whether we be angels or devils, let us, at least, keep enough of our humanity not to come to blows over so petty a thing."

Edward growled at him, but grabbed the chair and set it back in its place. With a furious glance at the others, he sat. "I'm thirsty," he said.

"Is..." Micah whispered, his voice wavering and his cheeks flushed red with fear. "Is there anything I can do?"

"No, Micah," Geoffrey said. "I would not ask that of you. You are here to serve, yes, but not in that fashion."

"Thank you, milord," Micah said. He lowered his head and trembled in relief.

"We must learn what the Old Man seeks," Geoffrey said. "I have heard rumor that the Hospitaller have allied with the Isma'ilites. There is no love lost between our brother-knights and us. If the girl has knowledge of something the Old Man wants, then it may very well be something the Hospitaller want as well. We must find out what it is they seek."

"But, she can't stay here" Edward said.

"Why not?" Geoffrey asked.

"Because..."

"She need never find out, brother," Geoffrey said. "Micah will keep her occupied during the daylight hours. We will question her at sundown on

16

the morrow and decide then what our next step will be."

"Very well," Edward said. "Just make sure she knows nothing when she leaves here. I will not let her knowledge doom us all, Geoffrey. That, too, is our sacred oath."

CHAPTER TWO

Josephine woke early the next morning. The bedchamber lacked windows, so she did not know if the sun had already risen. Her first thoughts were those of confusion, until she remembered the mad dash to the monastery. She remembered pounding on the doors and the riders coming up behind her. She also remembered the dark figure that came to the doors, and the chill she felt deep in her soul when she gazed into those eyes.

With the memories came tears. The dark shadow plunging a blade into the body of her sister, the hollow scream of her mother, her father hopelessly outmatched. The murderers spoke in Arabic, a language Josephine knew only a little. She recognized a few words, but in the chaos of the moment, they were lost.

Why? The question still burned in her soul. Her father was a fair man, a merchant by trade, and he dealt as fairly with the Saracens as he did with his own kind. He was not the kind of man to have enemies. He was not the kind of man to be murdered in his own house with his wife and his daughters.

Finally, exhausted but unwilling to stay in bed, she ventured out into the halls of the monastery. Those halls were strangely silent, and she almost jumped at the sound of her own footsteps echoing back at her. She made her way down the stairs, past the altar, and to the great doors of the building without seeing anyone. It was strange how the building held no windows to let in the sun. It must be mid-morning, but the hallways loomed in darkness. She needed the sun, needed its light to banish the darkness haunting her mind, so she went through the doors and out into the courtyard.

She closed her eyes, opened her arms wide and let the warm rays of the sun cascade across her face. The lingering terror of the night receded in the light of day. The fear faded, but not the sadness. It rose up again threatening to overcome her.

"I hope the lady is feeling well this morning."

The voice startled her. She spun, one hand on her breast and the other raised to ward off any danger. But the man standing before her was not dressed in black. His robes were brown. Instead of the black cloth masking his face, he wore a crucifix hanging from his neck. "Yes," she said.

"I am Brother Micah," he said. "I am a monk serving this small outpost of the Templar."

"I am Josephine Mowbray," she said. "I..." her eyes dropped to the ground, "I arrived here last night."

"I know," Micah said. "I helped prepare the room where you slept. I hope the chamber was to your satisfaction? We do not have the lavish guestrooms of other monasteries."

"It was fine."

"Are you hungry? We have bread, cheese, and fresh eggs inside if you would like to break your fast with me."

"Yes, I would. Thank you, Brother Micah."

"Just Micah," he said, smiling. Micah led her through the monastery to a humble room with a small table surrounded by chairs. He fixed them

19

each a plate of food and whispered a brief prayer of thankfulness. Silence descended on the pair while they ate, but Josephine, lost in her thoughts, did not notice.

The silence remained unbroken until Josephine finished the last morsel on her plate. "You live here at the temple?" she asked.

"Yes," Micah responded, grabbing their plates. "For the past six years now." He disappeared into the other room to dispose of the dishes and then returned. "Before that, I was in the Holy City."

"The Holy City." She breathed the words in awe. "What was it like?"

"It was beautiful. Every day I could slip away I spent in deep mediation in front of the Dome of the Rock. The years have not eroded the holiness of that place, and even now, the spirit calms in its presence. It has been six years since the city fell to the Sultan, and every day I miss the peacefulness of that place."

"I would like to visit the Holy City some day." Josephine sighed, looking off into the distance.

"You have never been?" Micah asked.

"No," she replied. "My father intended to take us, but he was always too busy with his work."

"What did he do?"

"He was a merchant. He collected old, valuable objects and sold them to those making the pilgrimage and to the church. He frequently dealt with the people here and was well liked. I cannot believe anyone would wish him such harm." A tear blurred her vision and as she spoke it began to trail down the side of her cheek. The talk of her father brought back the memories. "He was a good man, an honest man. Why would anyone do such a thing to him?"

"There, there, child," Micah said, placing a hand on top of hers.

"Why would God allow such a thing to happen?" she asked.

Micah squeezed her hand. "Now is not the time to turn from God. Now is the time to embrace him. We know not what the Lord has planned for us in this life, but we do know that, in the end, he will gather us to him and all will be right. Your father was a good man? A Christian man?"

"Yes." She sniffed. Father had been strict, but fair and oftentimes generous. A winter did not pass without Father giving aid to a distressed family of the village helping them to put food on the table.

"I am sure he and your family are in Heaven now. They feel no pain, only joy, and they wait patiently for the day you will join them there."

The words sounded cold and distant next to the pain in her heart, but the tone was soothing. "I suppose," she said, wiping her eyes with the sleeve of her dress. They drifted into silence again, but this time it was the comforting silence of healing. Micah stayed with her, his hand clasping hers. Slowly, her grief faded, though she knew it would come again. Her wounds were not the type to heal overnight.

"Where is everyone?" she asked. "The halls seem so empty this day."

"Your arrival caused quite a stir," Micah replied. "The others spent most of the night searching the countryside to be certain the men who chased you would not come again. I suspect they were up late in council as well. I imagine it will be late evening before we see them."

"Do you think those men will be back?"

"I am not wise in these things. On that, you must ask the knights. But you are with the Templar now, and you are safe, of that you can be certain."

"When I arrived last night, a man came to the door. He seemed, at the time, to be a sinister man, at least that is what I felt when I first glimpsed him, but I suppose he was one of the knights."

"That would be Geoffrey. He can seem like a hard man with a dark cloud hanging over him, but it is just the difficulties of his job weighing upon him. He is a just and fair knight. He leads the other knights who reside here."

"How many knights are here?"

"Just three. They have no retainers, not at the moment at least. They rely on me to keep up the monastery." He smiled at her. "I don't do much of a job which is why the place is in such a ruin."

"I think it looks fine," she replied.

"You are too kind." He patted her hand. "I know it looks poor. You should have seen it years ago, though. The walls shined with the good work we did here. The stables were full, and knights and their retainers bustled through with never-ending activity."

"What happened?"

"Most of them were called back to the Holy City, and many were lost in its defense. You would have to ask Sir Geoffrey for the details. But with the men went most of the monks, leaving just me to tend to the garden and keep up with the monastery."

"Don't you get lonely?"

"Sometimes," Micah admitted. "But I have my garden to keep me company. We don't get many visitors these days, so I spend much of my time outside with my flowers."

"Would you show me your garden?"

"Certainly," he replied.

He led her out into the garden, pointing at his adored flowers and naming them for her. When they were finished, he listened to her speak of her family. She told him more of her father, her mother, and her sisters. Tears streamed down her face on several occasions, but on others, her face beamed with pleasure at a memory. He was patient, allowing her to do most of the talking.

When the sun finally began its descent behind the horizon and the shadows grew long in the courtyard, he led her back into the monastery. Her stomach grumbled in displeasure at having skipped the midday meal, but she wore a smile on her face. Micah boiled some water and used some vegetables to cook a stew, and they continued to talk lightly over dinner.

They were just finishing up with the meal when Josephine felt a chill drift through her body. Small bumps rose on her skin, and her body shook with an uncontrollable shiver. She put her hands up around her chest, wishing she had a shawl to cover her shoulders, and looked over into Micah's eyes. A strangled look passed over his face.

"Good evening," a deep, rumbling voice came from behind her. Her heart twitched within her chest.

"Sir Geoffrey Furnivall," Micah said, rising to his feet. "May I present to you Josephine Mowbray."

"Sir," Josephine said, standing up and turning to the newcomer. Her breath caught in her throat at the sight of him. His black hair, flecked with gray, fell limp over two deep-set brown eyes that seemed to look straight through her. She had not seen his face the night before, but knew he had been the one to come to her rescue. She bowed her head. "I would like to thank you for your kindness last night."

"Think nothing of it, child." The knight brushed his hand lightly over hers to comfort her. That hand, strong and powerful, felt like a cool breeze and left hairs standing up on her skin. "The Knights Templar are at your service."

She nodded and sat back in her chair. Staring down at her now-empty plate, she wished there remained some small morsel she could pick at instead of facing him once again. There was something about him, about his eyes, that made her feel very uncomfortable.

He sat down next to her but remained silent for some time. Micah picked up the dishes and vanished into the nearby room. More time passed, and Josephine realized Micah was not coming back. Hesitantly, she looked over at the knight. She stared into his face, noticing the small wrinkles around the eyes, a sign that time was catching up with him. There was an old scar on his chin that ran halfway across his left cheek, just under the end of his thick, black mustache.

As she stared, her fear went away. He was not a villain. He was a knight far from his home sent to protect people like her. He was a man who had done that duty, suffered wounds in battle protecting good Christians from harm. She looked into his eyes and realized that her fear was a childish reaction.

"I'm sorry," she said. "For staring, that is," she added, though she was, in truth, apologizing for her earlier feelings.

"It's quite alright." The right side of his lip rose in a partial smile, and his eyes stared off into the distance. "We are a mystery to some, and coming face to face with a mystery leads to curiosity. Am I what you expected from a knight?"

"I don't know," she said. "I don't know what to expect."

He smiled at her reply, but the smile dropped suddenly. Josephine felt the chill enter her soul again, but this time it was different. The chill was coupled with dread, and she knew what he was about to ask.

"I need to find out more about last night, child," he said. "Do you think you are ready to speak of it?"

"I'm not a child!" she said. "I turned seventeen last spring, old enough to wed by most standards."

"Am I interrupting something?" a new voice floated across the room. There was a melody within the voice, and she was somehow calmed by it.

"I'm sorry," she said. "I don't know why I reacted that way." She turned a shy stare on the newcomer and watched him flow across the room and sit next to Geoffrey. He was a tall man with a slim mustache and just a touch of a beard that danced when he smiled.

"I am Gerard de St. Amand." His English had a hint of a French accent. "Do you mind if I sit with you?"

"Of course not," she replied.

"Geoffrey?" he asked.

"Sit, Gerard, and be welcome," Geoffrey said. "Where is our friend on this night?"

"Edward had some business," Gerard said. "Urgent business he was unable to resolve last night."

"Ah." He nodded at Gerard and turned his attention back to Josephine. "Do you know who attacked you last night?"

Josephine shook her head.

"Isma'ilites," Geoffrey replied. "Do you know who they are?"

"No," she whispered.

"They are assassins," Geoffrey said. "They are the protectors of the Ismaeli people and, in ways, they are not that much different than us knights. They are divided into lasiq, who are workers and laymen, fidais, who are diplomatic agents and skilled assassins, and rafiq, who are chief among the assassins. The Isma'ilites control much of the land to the north and east of us."

"Why would they be after me?" she asked, looking back up at Geoffrey.

"That is what we must find out," Geoffrey said. "Do you think you can tell me what happened last night?"

"I..." She sniffed and tried to talk around the lump forming in her throat. "I had gone to my bed later than usual. My sisters were already asleep. I made my preparations as quietly as possible and slipped into bed. I think I drifted off to sleep, I'm not sure, but the next thing I knew..."

The words faltered on her lips while the terror of the memory took hold of her. Again, she saw the dark form hovering near the beds and blood splashed against the wall. Tears welled up in her eyes, and she couldn't go on. The knights were patient, remaining silent and allowing her to come to terms with the memory in her head.

When she was finally able to speak, her voice trembled. "I heard a terrified scream. It was my mother's scream. I looked up to see a shadow hovering over my sister's bed. At first, I thought I was dreaming, but then I saw a strange light between the shadow's hands. It was a sword. He plunged it into her body and she tried to scream, but it came out garbled.

"I screamed for her. I screamed and rose up in my bed, dashing to the door. I opened it, but just before I went into the next room, I glanced back. The man, for it was a man, I could see that now, was ignoring me. He descended on where my littlest sister lay in her bed. She was awake, but I could tell by the look in her eyes she was too afraid to move. I..." Tears streamed from her eyes. "I left her there..."

She collapsed on the table, her cries more violent than before. Gerard reached his hand over and placed it on the back of her head, stroking her hair. "It's all right. You did the right thing. There was nothing you could do."

Josephine squeezed her eyes shut, trying to block out the pain of that memory and the guilt in her conscience. After a time, the pain and guilt receded, and she became aware of the gentle hand brushing through her hair. The knight whispered to her in French. She did not understand the words, but the voice was soothing. Finally, she was able to lift her head from the table.

"Can you tell us what happened next?" Gerard asked.

"I..." She swallowed, hard, trying to control the tremor in her body. "I ran into the living area. There were two more there. My mother, she..." Josephine shook her head, trying to banish the image of her mother's body lying in a pool of blood, her hand reaching out, as if with her last breath she tried to reach her daughters.

"Father had taken down grandfather's sword and fought with one of them. His eyes told me to run, so I did. I ran to the stables and saddled a horse. I rode off, but they chased me. They chased me for what seemed hours until, finally, I saw the torches burning outside of this place and hoped I might be safe."

"You ran out and saddled a horse," Gerard said, his voice gentle and soft. "Do you know what the men were doing in the house while you saddled it?"

"Searching, I think."

"They were looking for something?"

"I don't know," she said. "But, when I first came into the room, the man fighting with my father

28

was speaking in Arabic. I couldn't understand much of what he was saying, but I did pick out two words."

"What two words?"

"Holy Book."

CHAPTER THREE

"So, you have failed."

The words echoed through the great hall of al-Kahf, and Zain ul-Baqir bowed his head before his master. Rashid-al-din Sinan, the Old Man of the Mountain, had little patience for failure. Those who failed him were quick to feel his displeasure. And those who failed him too often found their head on a spike, their dishonor mounted on the battlements for all to see.

"Tell me, my young rafiq, how does a young girl evade the most lethal of my men?"

"My orders were to find the book," Zain said. "After the infidel merchant was dead, we searched his home and found nothing. We followed the girl in hopes she would lead us to the book, but instead she led us to those demons."

"The Templar." Rashid-al-din spat the name like a curse. "So the merchant was in league with the dark ones."

"I'm not sure, master." Zain lifted his head to look the Old Man in the eyes. "The girl's route was haphazard, the chaotic path of one who knows not where she goes. She seemed as much surprised by the monastery as we were. But, once there, the knights were honor-bound to protect her."

"And you let one knight stand between you and the girl?"

"No," Zain said. "As powerful as they are, there were four of us against just the one. His blood would have stained the grass."

"Then tell me, young one, why is his blood still flowing within his veins?"

"His death would not have gained us the prize. The girl is worthless to us dead, but alive, she may still possess some value. Killing the knight would have only set the Templar against us."

"The Templar are already aligned against us," Rashid-al-din said. "Left alive, the knights know of our part in the scheme and will be wary of us in the future."

"Wary, yes," Zain said. "And, will not they investigate this further? They will question the girl, find out about the prize and seek it for themselves. I have left two of my men in the hills near the monastery. Even now, they watch the sanctuary. When the knights move to take the prize, we will be close behind."

Rashid-al-din raised his hand and stroked a long beard graying with age. "Yes," he said. "That will work. You have done well, Zain. It was wise to leave the girl alive."

Zain bowed.

Rashid-al-din reached for a nearby pipe and filled it. "Will you share some pleasure with me, young one?"

"If I might be excused, master?" Zain asked. "I cannot stay long, and I have many preparations to make."

Rashid-al-din's eyes glittered dangerously at the refusal, but he waved his hand. "Go, then, young one."

Zain turned on his heel and marched from the hall. Nizam al-Qadmus, silent during the discussion,

31

walked beside him. Zain could tell from his friend's pursed lips he was not happy. They left the hall. "What is it, Nizam?"

"You upset the master," Nizam replied. "He offers you great honor in sharing his pipe with you."

"I will not touch the hashish." Zain shook his head in disgust. "It stains the body, the mind, and the spirit. It brings disgrace to our order."

"But it has always been so," Nizam said. "Through it we glimpse the realm of paradise and know what awaits us upon death."

"That is exactly what he wants you to think," Zain said. "But it has not always been as such. The great al-Hassan ibn-al-Sabbah never allowed the sin of the hashish to stain his body. It is a great lie used to control the fidais, and it tarnishes the great one's memory."

Nizam glanced around. "You speak heresy, Zain. You must keep your words low when you talk of such!"

"I speak the truth," Zain said, though he lowered his voice.

"Our lord is a great man. He has done much to further our cause. Under his guidance, we have grown in power while the power of the infidel cracks and grows weak."

"Our lord *was* a great man," Zain said. "He has succumbed to the temptations of the world, and his soul is now tainted with the hashish he breathes into his body. The body must be pure, as does the mind, or else the spirit rots."

Zain stopped walking and turned to his friend. "Did not their king, the Lion..."

"Richard Coer del Lion," Nizam said.

"Did he not defeat our brothers at Argut? The murdering Christians now hold Joppa. We grew in power under our master, true, but now we stagnate and the demons rise from the shadows."

"You speak as if..."

Zain grabbed his friend's arm and led him to his private quarters. "Nizam, you have been with my company the longest of any," he whispered. "You, better than any, know my heart and my soul. I am a true follower of Muhammad and al-Hassan, and I would do nothing to dishonor their memories. But our great leader brings shame to their memory with his actions."

He placed a hand on Nizam's shoulder in a rare sign of affection. "There will come a time, my friend, when action will be needed to preserve the true path of the Isma'ilites. When that time is upon us, I intend to act. You, my friend, will need to decide what action you will take at that time."

"I am with you, Zain," Nizam replied. "As always. But let us take care in this. If others were to suspect, we would not live to see the next rising of the sun."

"Good," Zain said. He had been certain he could count on his friend, else he would have never mentioned the plan growing in the back of his mind, but it was good to hear his friend's loyalty spill from his lips. "I rest easy knowing I can trust in your support. There are others, too, that have grown uncomfortable with the direction our leader takes us. This pact with the infidels has angered more than a few within these halls."

"We turn one against the other," Nizam said. "The Hospitaller and the Templar have always had distrust between them. We only brew that distrust to the boiling point, and when one goes down, we will cover the other in our shadow."

"That is fine," Zain said. "But must we invite their unclean souls into this holy place? They stain the ground they walk on with every step of their foul boots. They poison the air we breathe with their sick lies. Drive a wedge between them, yes, but do so from afar, else we risk drowning our own souls in their defeat."

"If we obtain the book, we won't have to suffer them much longer," Nizam said. "The Templar will be damned. Their church will be unable to back them when the words of the book become known and they are unveiled as demons."

"But where is the book?" Zain asked. "It was not in the house, and all my senses tell me the girl does not know what we sought."

"Whether she knows or not, we will soon find out," Nizam said. "As you said, the Templar will recognize the danger it presents and will lead us to the prize. If the girl knows, they will pry it from her."

"And then we strike," Zain said. "We cannot stay here long. It will take a great many of us to overtake them. They are a powerful enemy. Be ready on the morrow. We will gather more forces and meet back up with those we left behind."

A soft knock on the door interrupted their hushed conversation. Nizam looked alarmed, and Zain knew his friend feared their treasonous words had been overheard. Zain smiled, reassuring his friend, and walked to the door. He did not fear discovery, just as he did not fear his own death. He would, however, regret discovery. The honor of Allah faltered in the halls of his master, and it was his duty to restore that honor.

He opened the door and was relieved to see a familiar face, but his ease faded when he saw the blood staining his friend's clothes. "Ahmed, what has happened?" he asked, helping the fidais into the room and pulling out a chair for him.

"A foul demon sprang on us in the night," Ahmed said, putting his hand to his head where crusted flakes of blood covered a large, swelling bump.

"Where is Nassar?" Zain asked, growing alarmed.

"I fear he is dead." A look of terror filled Ahmed's eyes. "The demon bested us. He swept Nassar over his shoulder and carried him off just as I drifted into darkness."

"Wait," Zain said. "Here, sit." He beckoned to the chair.

Nizam brought a wet cloth and washed the blood from their friend's forehead while Zain examined the wound. It was a shallow cut, but powerfully delivered. The surrounding skin was swelled and had taken on a purplish tint. It appeared to be a minor wound, but Zain was familiar with wounds to the head. They could be dangerous despite appearances. He tucked a hand under his friend's jaw and raised his head to look deeply into

Ahmed's eyes. He saw fear there, but not the disorientation that could be such a danger.

Zain smiled and patted his friend's shoulder. "Now, start at the beginning."

"We were watching the round temple," Ahmed said, his voice quivering. "For most of the night all was silent, and we thought the knights had gone to bed. Nassar was about to sleep when we spotted a shadow moving through the darkness. It was strange. The shadow seemed a part of the night, flickering in and out like a star. We would spot it, and before our eyes, it would disappear, only to appear again some minutes later.

"We asked Allah for courage, but the fear of that shadow bound us. For most of an hour we stood watch, keeping a wary eye on the temple and watching for that shadow.

"Dawn came, and with it, the shadow left us. We watched the temple through the day. The woman came out into the courtyard in the morning and met up with one of the monks. They disappeared for a time into the temple, but then came back outside and walked through the yards outside for most of the day. We were careful, staying close enough to watch, but far enough away not to be seen.

"Our thoughts, and fears, of the strange shadow were dismissed as foolish superstition under the light of the sun. Just before dusk, the monk and the woman entered the temple again. Nassar and I crept closer to keep a better eye on the temple in case any decided to leave during the night.

"Just after the sun set, the shadow returned. We had circled the temple during the day and were certain the door in front was the only way in or out of the building, and we had seen no one leave the temple but the woman and the monk. Still, the shadow appeared. But, this time, it did not play with us, blinking in and out of our vision. This time, it struck.

"It was a foul demon. It looked like a man, one of the knights perhaps, but it moved faster than a horse in full stride and struck with the strength of ten men. The thing carried a huge sword that a normal man might have difficulty lifting with both hands, but it swung the sword with one hand like it was made of air.

"It came at me with the speed of a wolf, lunging at me with that sword. I beat back the blade with all my strength, but the demon knight merely smiled at me as if I were no more than an ant crawling on the ground waiting to be squashed. It jumped into the air, higher than I thought possible, and its boot came crashing into my temple.

"I fell to the ground and lay there for several minutes, my eyes blurry, but my mind fighting the darkness. I watched the demon knight dispatch Nassar just as quickly. The knight swung the sword overhand. Nassar raised his blade to block it, but his scimitar broke under the power of that blow. The knight dealt a blow to Nassar's skull with his gauntlet, catching our brother's body in his arms before it hit the ground. The beast then lifted him up over his shoulder and, without even a glance at me, slipped into the shadows of the night.

"I'm not sure if he left me for dead, or knew I still lived," Ahmed said, his eyes still wide. "I slipped into the dark of sleep, and when I awoke, the full light of day was shining down on me. Nassar was nowhere to be seen."

Ahmed let his head sink into his hands. "I know I have failed, Zain. I was told to watch the temple, and I abandoned my orders. I didn't know what to do. If I stayed, I knew I would not survive another night, but if I left..."

"It is fine, Ahmed," Zain said, putting his hand on the man's shoulder. "You did the best you could do. As you can see, what we fight are not men like you or I, they are foul demons raised from the hells to test our strength and tempt our faith. They look like men, but they are drinkers of blood who survive on our death."

"How can we hope to defeat them?" Nizam asked, his voice betraying doubt.

"There are ways," Zain reassured. "They are powerful, it is true, but they have weaknesses and can be bested. They are fast, so we must be faster. They are strong, and thus we must gather the strength of our faith. Do not fear them. They are our test, and we will be martyred before we shrink from this task. Take strength in the paradise that awaits us upon death and the fires that await them.

"Rest here, Ahmed," Zain said, helping the fidais out of the chair and over to his bed. He could see the exhaustion in the man's form and knew his quarters were on the far side of the hall. Zain would not have him walk there in his condition when he

38

could rest here. They waited in silence until Ahmed drifted into sleep.

"What are we going to do, Zain?" Nizam asked.

"We must watch that temple," Zain replied. "The book is too important. We will gather a dozen men to watch the monastery. The knights may be powerful, but we can counter them with numbers."

Zain grabbed a piece of parchment and began scratching down orders. His right hand flowed across the parchment, creating the precise letters of his handwriting. He finished and reached for a seal.

"How far from the monastery should they make camp?" Nizam asked. "The knights may grow wary if they are too close."

Keeping his right hand on the seal, Zain grabbed the pen with his left hand, dipped it in the ink, and revised the orders. "Have them make camp around the hill at the base of the road."

Finished, Zain handed the orders to Nizam. "We will *not* fail in this."

CHAPTER FOUR

"The merchant stayed at the palace for some months during that summer," Sir Francisco said. The knight sat back in his seat and stroked the curve of his mustache.

Sir Jonathan Alderson nodded to the Spanish knight though, in truth, he was barely listening. His thoughts were preoccupied these days, his focus bent entirely to the secret mission whose outcome might have already been decided. He fidgeted and forced himself to pay more attention to his fellow knight.

"His wife left the palace after a few weeks," Sir Francisco said. "She complained of hearing ghosts in the night and went to stay with friends. The merchant stayed behind but admitted he often heard odd noises sounding out during the dead of night. He would often investigate the noises and came to believe the Templar were digging for something beneath the palace."

"Digging?" Jonathan asked. He leaned forward and put his elbows on the table, glancing from Sir Francisco to Sir Lothar. "What were they digging for?"

"The son of the merchant claimed his father didn't know," Sir Francisco replied. "He reported his father often had a tale on his lips about the Knights Templar. Some of the tales were meaningless babble, others, though, were dark and chilling indeed."

There was a knock at the door. "Come in," Jonathan called, irritated. He wanted to hear more about the digging.

A nervous squire peeked his head into the room, licked his lips, and said, "My good sirs, a messenger from the Old Man has arrived and requested an audience with Sir Jonathan."

"You have done well, squire," Jonathan replied, easing the squire's nerves. "You may leave us."

"Very good, sir." The squire bowed and rushed from the room.

The messenger was dressed in black and wore a curved sword at his waist. "Well, well, Master Messenger." Jonathan rose from the table. "Let me make introductions so that you may know us by name. I am Sir Jonathan Alderson, Knight-Captain of the Hospitaller. To my right is Sir Lothar Malle, Knight-Sergeant, and to my left is Sir Francisco Narvaez, Knight-Sergeant."

"Umar bi Amrih." His voice was low, but powerful. He bowed stiffly to the knights before continuing in a thick accent. "I bring words of greeting from the devout one, Rashid-al-din Sinan, Old Man of the Mountain."

"I hope you bring words of success," Lothar said, chuckling.

"Yes, what of your mission?" Jonathan asked. "Has the Old Man succeeded in retrieving the book?"

"My master brings his regret that he has, thus far, been unsuccessful in obtaining the holy book, but hopes to bring you word of his success in the near future."

41

"What?" Jonathan said. "Were our sources not correct? Wasn't the book in the hands of the merchant?"

"From the information we have gathered, it appears the merchant did indeed have the book," Umar replied.

"So why hasn't the Old Man retrieved it?" Jonathan asked. "Was a lowly merchant too much trouble for the old man? Or is his mind too dulled by hash to take care of a pot-bellied old merchant?"

"You would do well to speak of my master in a tone of respect," Umar said.

"Bah," Jonathan said, pushing himself back in his chair. "We will hold him in respect when he deserves it. If he is cowed by a merchant, we will afford him the deference that brings."

"Then my business here is done," Umar said. The assassin stared at the knight, his eyes hinting that his business might not be entirely finished.

"Sit down," Jonathan ordered. Anger flashed across the messenger's eyes. "Please," Jonathan added, realizing his mistake in showing the Old Man disrespect in his follower's presence. The Old Man's shadow reached long and far, and those who found his displeasure often found themselves lying face down in an alley -- be they noble, knight, or commoner. Outwardly, Jonathan remained calm and in control, but inwardly he cursed himself for a fool.

"I apologize for my earlier disrespect," he said. "This business with the book is most urgent, and I am eager to have it completed. My eagerness led me to brash speech."

42

"Very well," Umar said, taking a seat in the chair opposite Jonathan. His face bore no expression the knight could read. "You Christians often seem to speak before you think, and act out of the heart instead of the mind."

"I am sure that is why we hold so many cities in the land of Palestine," said Lothar. He stared at the assassin and smiled.

"Tell me of the mission," Jonathan said, eager to change the subject back to the business at hand. "What troubles have kept the Old Man from retrieving the book?"

"The merchant was disposed of as was his family," Umar said, still staring at Lothar. The assassin's lips twitched into a tiny smile and Lothar looked away. "The book was not in the house," Umar continued, turning his attention back to Jonathan. "A girl, his daughter, was allowed to escape in hopes that she would lead us to the book, but, instead, she ran to those demon-knights, the Templar."

"The Templar!" Jonathan clenched his fist and bit his tongue, forcing himself to calm down before continuing. "How did you manage to let the girl fall into the hands of our enemy?"

Sir Francisco coughed at these words.

"I know where we are," Jonathan said. "The plan against our brother-knights has sanction in the highest circles of the Hospitaller. The Isma'ilites know of our plans and, I daresay, the Templar now know too."

He turned back to Umar. "So, the girl ran straight to the Templar. The knights she seeks

43

sanctuary with must be destroyed. We cannot allow word of our plans to find its way to Rome, or else the Mother Church will be turning on us and not them."

"The monastery is being watched," Umar said. "My master hopes the knights will be able to glean information from the girl that would not be forthcoming with threats or torture. He believes it possible she holds clues to the location of the book, but may not be aware of the information."

"So you will watch and follow then kill and snatch?" Jonathan smiled. "Yes, that might work, but the knights will not be so easy to dispatch. They have drank the devil's blood and hold powers unlike a normal man."

"We have ways of dealing with the dark ones," Umar said, a strange light coming into his eyes. "We will deal with them, but my master asks if there are some knights of your order that would be willing to help. A few blooded warriors of your house might be beneficial."

"Yes," Jonathan nodded. "We will make arrangements to have a detachment of knights ready in case there is need."

"Very good," Umar replied. "We risk much in this venture. My master wishes assurances that this book you seek will prove the downfall of the infidel Knights Templar."

"I assure you, once the holy Mother Church in Rome reads the words of that book, the destruction of the Knights Templar will soon follow."

"What are these words that would destroy the knights?" Umar leaned over the table, eager for an answer. "What words does this holy book contain?"

"That is not your concern," Jonathan replied, taken aback. "The book is written in an ancient language and can only be deciphered by the most learned of scholars. If this is the book we think it is, the knights will be walking in their last days on earth."

"If?" Umar leaned back in his chair. "If it is the right book? My master was led to believe that there was no if, only fact."

"We cannot be sure until we have the book in our hands," Jonathan said. He should not have mentioned the book might not be the one they sought. He needed these assassins. They were skilled in their craft, and he required outside assistance for his plans. It would not do for the Knights Hospitaller to be seen working directly against the Templar -- not until the unholy rites of their brother-knights were uncovered.

"Tell your master to rest assured," he said. "We have done everything in our power to be certain this is the correct book. *If* you bring us this book, the Templar's destruction will become reality."

"I will give him your assurance," Umar said, rising to his feet. "We will bring you this book." He cast his gaze on the men in front of him. "It will be best for all concerned if it does prove the downfall of the Templar. My master is not known for his patience in dealing with those who have deceived him." His gaze lingered a moment on each of the knights in turn. "We will send a message when the book has been located and the blooding is imminent."

"Inform your master we will be waiting," Jonathan said. He rang a bell to summon the squire back into the room.

"Sir?" the squire said, peeking his head in. His eyes betrayed the nervousness he felt in the assassin's presence.

"Show the messenger out, squire," Jonathan said.

They sat in silence for a while, and then Lothar turned to Jonathan. "Do you think they will be successful in locating the book?" he asked. "The Templar are as cunning as they are powerful. They will not be so easy to follow as that one suspects. "

"I don't think following them will be the problem," Jonathan answered. "The assassins are skilled in their craft, and even the Templar will have trouble shaking them from the trail. The Isma'ilites will find them, yes, but will they be able to defeat them?"

"That one looked capable enough," Lothar said. "He looked at me as though he would as soon slit my throat as shake my hand."

"Yes, they are ruthless." Jonathan nodded. "And they bear no love for us knights. The Old Man has driven into them that the death of a knight will win them rewards in paradise. But we aren't talking about just any group of men they are up against. We are talking about the Templar."

"There are ways to kill the blood-drinkers," Francisco said. "You remove the head from the body and any manner of being will find it hard to keep coming at you."

"The difficulty would be in getting that head removed from the body," Jonathan said. "The Templar are trained warriors, and the spirit of the beast gives them great speed and strength."

"The sun, also, is rumored to be a weakness they share," Francisco said.

"We've tried that," Jonathan said. A look of surprise passed over Francisco's face.

"You didn't know we've tried to destroy them in the past?" Jonathan asked. "Do you remember the battle of Akka three years ago?"

"When the Salah al-Din laid siege to the city?"

"Yes." Jonathan lowered his voice to a whisper and continued, "We were in contact with the Sultan. Salah al-Din knew he could not move his forces close enough to lay siege with our knights in the area. It was made known to him that, if he were to move on the city, our knights would receive orders to move away from the area to garrison a nearby town."

"To what purpose?" Francisco asked, frowning.

"There were many high ranking Templar in the city at that time," Jonathan replied. "We urged the Sultan to time his arrival for the hours just before dawn, trapping the Templar inside. It was our hope that the rising sun would prove the bane of the Templar, but when dawn arrived, a group of the knights emerged from the gates and fought their way through the Sultan's forces. It was a fierce battle, and the Templar sustained losses, but the bulk of their knights survived despite the sun rising against them."

"The sun had no effect, then?" Francisco asked.

"I do not know," Jonathan admitted. "They do seem to avoid the sunlight, but whatever effect it has on them, they are still a powerful force."

Lothar spoke up, "The ancient texts speak of holy symbols or water blessed by a priest. But they are knights of the church..."

"Yes," Jonathan said. "Much of the old lore has proven untrue, or at least inaccurate. These demons we face are not beasts of myth and legend; they are creatures of flesh and bone. Where the legends may say one thing, the reality might be very different."

"You don't think the Isma'ilites can do it, do you?" Lothar asked.

"Not alone." Jonathan shook his head. "It will take a great many men to take down the demons. As powerful as the assassins are, their strength is through stealth and cunning. They may know as much as we do of these demons, perhaps more. But it will take more than lore to take down the evil of the Templar. It will take force. The Isma'ilites will need our aid if they are to be successful."

"How many men do you think it will take?" Lothar asked. "If there are only a few of the Templar, it shouldn't be too difficult to overwhelm them."

Francisco laughed. "Shouldn't be too difficult? It shouldn't be too difficult with a score of men, perhaps. Bring less and you will just be lining up dead bodies for them. Don't underestimate them, my friend. The Templar's Inner Circle is a powerful lot.

It could take a half dozen men for each one of them to be successful."

"Francisco is right," Jonathan agreed. "We will need to outfit a score of men and make them ready for the call. That, along with the Isma'ilites, should be enough to ensure victory. Have them pack torches. The bodies will need to be burned."

Lothar frowned. "Tell me, Sir Jonathan, do you believe this book we seek will truly be the downfall of the Templar?"

"I certainly hope so," Jonathan said. "I know that many in the knighthood have their doubts. Already, there are those that openly question the logic of my plan. They are loath to trust a common born, like myself, with such a task."

He stood up and paced around to the other side of the table. "This book is the best hope we've had in a decade of searching. If it holds the writings I believe lie within its covers, and we can lay our hands on it, the power of the Templar will be crushed."

CHAPTER FIVE

The woman was dangerous. The Isma'ilites could be dealt with, but a stranger roaming the monastery halls during the daylight hours presented its own unique danger. Yet, after listening to her story, Gerard knew Geoffrey had been right to give her sanctuary. The Isma'ilites were up to something.

He knocked on the door and opened it without waiting for an answer. He wasn't surprised to find Geoffrey pacing in the middle of the room. The older knight often paced when he was lost in thought.

"Have the knights retired for the night?" Geoffrey asked.

"Yes," Gerard said. Three knights had arrived in the hours before the sun set. They were Templar, but not of the Inner Circle. They knew what must be hidden from most, else they would not have been sent to the Holy Lands, and if they survived long enough, they would soon ascend into the Inner Circle. "Micah has given them quarters near the girl."

"Good," Geoffrey said. The older knight smiled at him. "What are your thoughts on a little night-time activity?"

"I could use a diversion," Gerard replied. "Do you want me to check on those keeping such a close watch on the monastery?"

Geoffrey shook his head. "I'll have Edward do that. How long would it take you to reach the girl's house?"

"That's quite a spread of land," Gerard replied, calculating the distance in his mind. "Perhaps an hour at full sprint, maybe longer."

"Do you think you could make it there, search the house for information, and be back before the rising of the sun?" Geoffrey asked.

"Yes."

"Good. I'll see you out."

In an area nominally reserved for guest quarters, but in fact rarely used, was one of only two locked doors in the monastery. Behind the door was a simple room containing a bed, a small table, and a desk. The room was clean, the linens on the bed fresh. Micah was careful to keep the rooms tidy, just as he was careful to house guests in another wing of the monastery.

In the center of the room was a small rug. The old, faded pattern was barely visible, the brown and gray colors together. Gerard flipped the rug over and ran his fingers along the floor until they found the hidden catch. With a click, the trapdoor was open.

"I'll close it behind you," Geoffrey said. "And open it again an hour before dawn."

Gerard nodded. He gave the older knight a quick smile and then hopped into the hole, vanishing into its depths. He landed hard and took a step forward to keep his balance. Looking back up, he could see Geoffrey hovering over the edge of the hole above him. There was no rope or ladder that led back up to the trap door, but Gerard knew he could leap high enough to grasp the edge of the opening in his fingers. He also knew that no ordinary man could perform that same feat.

"An hour before dawn," came Geoffrey's voice floating down into the darkness. The words still hovered in the air when the door was shut, leaving Gerard to the darkness. But Gerard did not need the light, his vision cut through the dark as if the moon shined its light through the solid ground and lit the tunnel walls.

The tunnel was not long. This was no ordinary bolt hole that led far from the monastery grounds. The knights needed no elaborate escape plans. They trusted in their own powers to blend into the night should escape ever become necessary. The tunnel led only a short distance, ending just beneath the stables. The tunnel ended without rope or ladder, but far above Gerard's head was a metal hook.

Gerald gathered himself and made a powerful leap straight into the air until his hand grasped the hook. Swinging gently, he reached out and flipped a hidden catch above him. He shoved hard on the trap door, flipping it open, and then swung through the opening. Now in the farthest stall in the stables, he closed the door and carefully replaced the hay that concealed it.

The horse occupying the stall took several nervous steps, its ears twitching from the perceived danger. Gerald smiled at the beast, catching its eye in his gaze, and whispering soothing words. The horse calmed under his influence, and Gerard was able to leap over the gate to the stall without worry the horse would give in to fear.

He paused just inside the large wooden door of the stables and listened for any stray sounds in the night. It was quiet. He remained there for several minutes, listening. When he was sure there were no stray movements nearby, he slid the door open a crack and flowed out into the night. The stable was not part of the main structure. It was in back of the monastery, closer to the small wall that circled the grounds than to the monastery itself. Clinging to the shadows, he made his way across the courtyard and over the wall.

Gerard took his time making his way over the hill. He knew eyes watched the monastery, and he couldn't afford those eyes to spot him. Finally, assured that he was far enough away, he broke into a sprint. An ordinary man would have been unable to keep up the brisk pace all the way to the village. Even the girl's horse had almost given out covering the distance at full gallop. But Gerald could have kept going long after the village began taking shape in the night.

He did not know exactly where the merchant's house was located, but there was a faint scent of stale blood in the air. Following this scent, he approached a small house on the edge of the village and searched for any sign of the Isma'ilites.

Finding no sign of the assassins, he entered the house. The stench of blood was strong, and it ignited the embers of desire within him. The bodies of the family had been hauled away, but the stain of blood on the floors remained. Shards of shattered glass and shreds of destroyed books intermingled with the splinters of broken furniture that littered the house. In the chaos of the main room, only a pair of chairs and a single table remained intact.

He searched the back bedroom, and the desire inside him was doused by what he saw. The bloody mattresses had been sliced to pieces, and crimson feathers flowed out creating a ghoulish pattern on the floor, as if the mattresses bled from their wounds. A small chest in the corner had been smashed, and the clothes piled in a corner. In the center of the room was a small wooden duck, a child's toy. The duck had been smashed under the heel of a boot, the neck broken, and the body lying in a pool of its owner's blood.

In his mind, he saw the Isma'ilite enter the room and plunge a blade through a young girl. The girl screamed, waking her sisters, and the assassin cut down the next before she could rise from her bed. The last girl ran from the room, but the assassin didn't follow. Those in the other room would deal with her while he searched the room.

Gerald went to the master bedroom and found a similar scene. The floor was covered in feathers, though these were not stained with blood. The parents had still been awake when the assassins attacked. Against the far wall of the room, a strong box had been ripped open and its contents spread across the floor. There were several coins lying amidst the contents, evidence that this was no ordinary crime of theft and murder.

Sighing, Gerard returned to the main room. He gazed at the torn pages of books strewn across the room, counting the leather bindings. Eight. The books had been searched, and then destroyed, the assassins clearly frustrated at not finding what they sought.

Satisfied he had not missed anything, Gerald left the house and entered the village proper. He had been to the village in the past and knew the way to the local magistrate's house. He went there now and banged on the door to wake the man.

"Yes, who is it?" came an irritated voice. The door opened slightly and a small man with a balding head peeked through the crack.

"Sir Gerard de St. Amand, Knight Templar," Gerard said in a formal tone.

"What do you want?" the man asked, opening the door slightly wider and pushing his haggard face through the opening. "Do you realize it is the middle of the night?"

"I am aware of the time," Gerard said. "I have come to discuss the murder of the Mowbray family a few nights ago."

"Oh?" The man's face paled at the mention of the murders. The village was unused to such bloodshed, and the violence had, no doubt, sent a shock of fear through the villagers. "What do you know of it?"

"A young woman, Josephine Mowbray, came to our monastery a few nights ago seeking sanctuary from the foul murderers," he replied. "We are concerned our young visitor might remain in danger. I have come to get the details of the crime."

"I'll be here in the morning," the magistrate replied. "You can come speak to me then. We can break our fast together."

"I really need to speak to you now, sir," Gerard said. He stepped forward and placed the palm of his hand against the door to keep it from shutting in his face. "I plan to be back at the monastery by morning."

The door opened a crack more and the magistrate looked around behind Gerard. "You traveled by foot?" he asked, not seeing a horse.

"My horse is tied up near the Mowbray house," Gerard lied, noting that the magistrate was not quite as slow as he looked.

"Well, if you can't wait until morning, I suppose you'll have to come in then," he said. The man led him into a small kitchen. "Would you care for some tea?"

"No, thank you," Gerard replied. "You go ahead without me."

"Best not," he replied. "I'll be up all night if I do. You say you are investigating the Mowbray murders? How is the girl... what was her name again?"

"Josephine," Gerard responded, smiling. "But you know that well enough."

"Yes, I suppose I do," the man replied. "And how tall is she? What color might her hair be?"

"A hand shorter than me and brown," Gerard replied.

"Very well then," he said, satisfied. "The name's George and, as you are surely aware, I am the local magistrate of these parts. I can't be speaking to just anyone about these matters, but you sure have the look of a knight about you and you seem to know the girl, so what can I do for you?"

"Josephine's father was a merchant?"

"That he was," George nodded.

"What sort of items did he deal in?"

"He was interested in many things. Pots and books and small trinkets. He traveled around quite a bit buying from the locals. Anything he thought might turn a coin, but not anything to get murdered over, I wouldn't think."

"Do you know if he had any enemies?"

"Joseph? No, he was a good enough fellow. He kept mostly to his family, but he had several friends here in town."

Gerard nodded. "You've been to the house?"

"Yes." The man frowned. "It was the worst sight I've laid my eyes on in all these years as magistrate. I knew these Saracens could be savages, but the way they cut down that family, even the little girls, was beyond even what I thought they were capable."

"What makes you think it was Saracens?"

"I don't imagine a good Christian would do such a thing," George replied. "Oh sure, I've seen some kill another man, but to run a blade through a small child while she slept?"

"Did anyone see anything, or hear anything?"

"No, sad to say, they didn't," he said. "I questioned everyone in the village, and they all slept sound as a babe that night. A few of them mentioned having nightmares, but I suppose that is to be expected when such evil is afoot."

Gerard nodded, though he knew evil could be inches away and still a man would sleep soundly.

"Did you find any unusual tracks outside the house?"

"That was the strangest part of it," George replied. "We searched the dirt all around the house but couldn't find any footsteps, whether man or beast. We weren't even sure what had become of Josephine. A neighbor assured me that Joseph had three horses, and there were only two in the barn, but if she rode off, then the horse must have hovered above the ground, for we found no tracks."

"Very good, then," Gerard said, standing. "It seems you have things well in hand. Josephine will remain with us for a time until we can be certain she is no longer in threat of danger."

"You will tell her old George is sorry for her loss, won't you?" the magistrate said, showing Gerard to the door. "Her family was thought of well in these parts."

"I will," Gerard said.

His trip back to the monastery was uneventful. Geoffrey had opened the trapdoor and left a rope dangling. He shimmied up, retrieved the rope, and put the rug back over the trap door. Geoffrey would be impatient for his report, so he went straight to the wing reserved for their private use and slipped through the door.

"You're back," Geoffrey said. "What did you find?"

Geoffrey paced the center of the room, and Edward sat in the corner with his sword laid out on his thighs. The big knight was passing a whetstone over the blade, and it hissed at each pass.

"I found nothing of note in the house," Gerard said. "As we expected, it had been searched thoroughly by the assassins. The house was a wreck, most of the furniture had been smashed, with fragments of the destruction littering the floor. There were books, but they had been torn to shreds."

"Any secret hiding spots?" Geoffrey asked.

"Not that I could find," Gerard said. "Though I admit it would have been hard to spot one amidst the destruction."

Geoffrey nodded and stopped his pacing. "Did you question the local magistrate?"

"He had been there," Gerard replied. "The bodies had been removed. After making a search of the house, I paid him a visit, in the name of the Templar, of course. I informed him that we were giving sanctuary to a daughter of the house who had escaped the massacre.

"He took me into his house and told me what little he had found. The family was dead, and the house was in the shambles I described. There were no witnesses to the deed. The merchant lived on the far side of town, away from the other citizens, and no one had heard the screams coming from the house that night.

"He seemed to miss the one clue at the scene. The merchant's strongbox had been broken open, and several coins lay nearby, as if the contents were tossed out in a search. He neglected to mention that to me, which makes me think either he missed it or wasn't prepared to be forthcoming with all of the information."

"What did you tell him?" Geoffrey asked, resuming his pacing.

"Nothing." Gerard shrugged. "I simply asked about enemies the merchant may have had, what business he was in, if tracks had been found. The usual questions."

"He doesn't suspect the murderers were after something specific?"

"If he does, he didn't confess such suspicions to me. He seemed a capable man, very methodic. He also showed an obvious dislike for the Saracens. I suspect he'll only make a cursory attempt at solving it. In his mind, it is simply the work of evil men. That is enough motive for him."

"Good." Geoffrey nodded. "The fewer investigating this the better. At least, until we know more of what the Isma'ilites were after. Did you find any clues as to what this holy book the girl spoke of might have been?"

"No," Gerard said. "He seems to have dealt mainly in old artifacts. There were many different urns, crucifixes, clay pots, and other items dug out from the sands. The books had been gutted, with their pages torn out but, judging by the titles on their binders, they were not exceedingly rare."

"I had hoped for a clue to why they search for this book and what it may hold," Geoffrey said, sighing. "We know that the Isma'ilites have worked with the Knights Hospitaller in the past. Both groups want nothing more than to see the Templar destroyed. You spotted a Knight Hospitaller coming from the Isma'ilite's stronghold not a week ago.

Now we have a girl being chased by the assassins and this mysterious book."

"What do we do now?" he asked.

"Simple," Edward said in his gruff voice. "Without the girl, the assassins will have no one to lead them to a book. Sacrifice her and the game is over."

"So you would be willing to kill an innocent?" Geoffrey asked.

"The girl is nothing," Edward said, making a slashing motion with his hand. "And yet, while she lives, we are in danger."

"We are here to protect such as she," Geoffrey said.

"And how will we protect them if we are not here?" Edward asked. "If this book leads to our destruction, or the dismantling of our order at the hands of Rome, who will the people turn to? It is for the greater good. Sacrifice one and save many."

Frowning, Geoffrey turned to Gerard. "And what do you think?"

Gerard didn't reply immediately. He glanced at Edward. The blood rose within the body in different forms. In Edward, it had given power to his base savagery. The burly knight would think nothing of killing Josephine. He might even enjoy it.

"If we are to kill the girl because she is a danger," Gerard said, "Then we must keep on killing until a river of blood flows around us, for we have many enemies and all of them are a danger.

"No." Gerard shook his head, "That is not the route I would advise. It is an admission of defeat." He turned to look at Edward and a sly smile formed at the corner of his mouth. "We would be choosing the easy route for fear of facing the Isma'ilites directly, and I, for one, do not fear the assassins."

"I never said I was afraid," Edward said, his cheeks flushed with anger. He stood up and took a huge step toward Gerard. "I'll show you what fear is, little man."

"This is not the time," Geoffrey said, stepping between the two. "Sit down, Edward," he continued, turning to the big knight. "I said sit down."

Edward snarled and took a seat. "What shall we do, then?" he asked. "This search of the old man's house has led us to nothing."

"Perhaps we just didn't know what to look for," Geoffrey said. "We are searching for a clue, but we don't know if we would recognize a clue. We need someone who knows the merchant to help us search."

"It will be difficult on her to go back there," Gerard said.

"True," Geoffrey said. "But she must face those memories sometime. And, perhaps, she will find something you missed. Or she may remember something that will prove helpful. Either way, we must take her back there and find out more."

"So be it," Gerard said.

"When do we leave?" Edward asked, his face brightening at the prospect of action.

"Tomorrow, at dusk," Geoffrey said. "We'll need to arrange a distraction for our watchers. Nothing too harsh, we might need them later. Just something to run them off for a while."

"I will take care of it," Edward said.

Geoffrey stared at the rough English knight for a moment, and then nodded. "Meet us in the hills behind the monastery when you are finished. You know the tree that was hit by lightning two years ago?"

"Yes, the one that grows at an angle."

"We'll wait for you there. Be careful not to be seen. Distract our watchers and slip into the hills. Hopefully, it will take a day or two before they notice we have gone missing. We'll leave one of the newly arrived knights here to keep them confused."

"Shall I inform Micah?" Gerard asked.

"I'll take care of it," Geoffrey said. "Make your preparations."

CHAPTER SIX

Micah woke knowing someone else was in the room with him. He was a light sleeper, often coming awake several times each night to an owl's hoot or the distant howling of a wolf in the hills, but this was different. He had not heard a distinct sound; he simply felt a presence was close by.

"You are awake," a voice whispered from the darkness.

"Yes." He recognized Geoffrey's voice, but that knowledge did not warm the chill running through his veins.

"I do not mean to startle you, Micah," Geoffrey said. "You know you have nothing to fear from us."

"I know that, sir." Micah's breathing betrayed his lie.

"Calm, Micah, calm..." Geoffrey spoke in a low tone, and Micah stared into eyes that flowed from brown into red. "Calm..." Micah felt his heartbeat slow, and his breathing became lighter. The muscles in his shoulders relaxed, and his fingers no longer clutched the blanket.

"Good," Geoffrey said. "We will be leaving in the hour of dusk on the morrow. I need you to prepare the girl for travel."

"I will do so, sir," Micah said. "What will I tell her of the travels? Where will she be going?"

"We are taking her home," the old knight said. "We need her help in investigating the murder of her family. Our search of the house revealed no clues; we need her knowledge to help us."

"She will be upset at the idea. Is it so important that we discover the reasons for her family's massacre?"

"It is, Micah, else I would not be asking this of her. You know that I am not a cruel man -- not intentionally cruel, at least."

"I know, but it is early yet for her to be facing those memories. I would prefer to give her a few more days. But, if it is important, I will prepare her the best that I can."

"Prepare yourself as well, Micah, you will be traveling with us. I believe the girl will handle the situation much better with her newfound friend at her side."

"Very well, sir. I will be prepared. What shall I tell her of..." Micah paused a moment, always fearful of broaching this particular subject. "Of the peculiar travel arrangements, of traveling at night."

"Assassins work by night, Micah. It is better for us to travel by night, and thus be alert and prepared, than to be sleeping in beds waiting for them to strike. Tell her that we feel it is safest to travel in the darkest hours until we know more of what these assassins want."

"I will do so."

"Good," Geoffrey said. "You serve us well, Micah. You know, if there is something we could do to repay you I would not hesitate."

"No, sir, no!" Micah's eyes widened, his breath coming in short gasps. "Not that, sir, please not that."

"Easy, Micah." Geoffrey laid his hand on the young monk's chest. "You know, we would never do so without your permission."

"I'm sorry, sir." Micah calmed at the knight's touch. "I know. I am sorry I acted like that; I meant no disrespect."

"I realize that, Micah." Geoffrey smiled, though in the dark of the room Micah could not see his smile so much as feel it. "I did not mean to frighten you, I only wanted you to know that, if you wanted it, you could have it. Perhaps not now, not while we still need you in the way we do, but later, as a gift repaying your long service to us. You would not be the first loyal retainer rewarded in this way. If you should change your mind in the future..."

Geoffrey lowered his voice to a whisper. "There are some that view it as a gift, and others as a curse. To be honest with you, Micah, I am not sure what I believe. I think, perhaps, it is neither, or both. But, we will always respect your wishes. If there should come a time that you change your mind, you just have to let us know, but we would never act without your word."

He stood up and hovered over the monk for a moment longer before exiting the room. Micah still felt the calm of that voice long after his shadow had gone, but he could not find his way back to sleep. He wondered what it would be like to live forever, and prayed for the strength to never find out.

Dawn found him still clinging to the covers of his bed. He could not see the newly arrived sun rising on the horizon -- there were no windows in the monastery -- but he could feel it all the same. He jumped out of the bed and began his preparations.

Josephine, he knew, would wake soon. He rushed through his morning prayers and went to the kitchen, taking down the bread rolls and honey they both enjoyed in breaking their fast. He was on his way back from the well with a fresh pitcher of water when he spotted her walking down the hall.

"Good morning to you, my young lady," he said. She had a special way of putting a smile on his face.

"Micah," she said, returning his smile. "I had the most wonderful dream last night. I was a butterfly with beautiful wings of gold and silver. I lived in your garden and spent the day fluttering from flower to flower tasting the sweet nectar and enjoying the sun beating down against my wings."

"I must remember to clear out any spiders that may have taken up residence in my garden," he said, laughing. "I wouldn't want my butterfly to find any nasty surprises."

"Oh, don't do that," she said. "I know how to spot the spider's web, and you need them to keep your garden free of pests."

"Well, so long as you promise to stay far from their webs."

"Don't worry, you won't come out to find me hanging from a strand, my blood sucked dry."

Micah stopped, his cheeks turning white.

"What's the matter?" she asked.

"Nothing," he said, looking away. He continued walking, but picked up the pace, eager to arrive at the dining hall and begin their meal.

"I guess what I said really was ghastly, wasn't it?" she said, but she giggled. "I guess I'm just not afraid of spiders. I know I should be, all of my sisters were..." She fell silent for a moment. "I don't suppose they are now."

"Don't speak like that," he said. "Your sisters now exist within the very essence of happiness, their days spent under the clearest of suns. The blue waters of an ocean swims before them, existing only for the moment they might desire a quick dip in the water."

"Do you really think it's like that?" she asked, sitting down at the table. Picking up one of the rolls of bread, she dipped it into the sweet honey. "I know that is what they say in church, but I wonder what it is really like."

"It's like when you were a young child, playing on the kitchen floor with your sisters, happy and content because your father sat in a chair close by, watching over you and caring for you."

"It sounds wonderful," she said, looking far off and taking a bite of the bread.

"It is," he said. "And that is where your family is now. They miss you, but they bask in the comfort of the Lord, and wait patiently for the day they will see their sweet Josephine again."

She smiled at his words. "Thank you," she said. "Thank you for the kindness you have shown me these past few days."

Micah reached over and held her hand. He remembered watching her that first morning when she came out into the garden. Her great beauty struck him. Her deep brown hair flowed down to the middle of her back like a waterfall dancing down the side of a cliff. Her slender arms ended in petite hands that danced gracefully in the breeze. Her dress fit tightly around the shapely curves of her body and brought thoughts of temptation to his mind. He remembered saying a prayer against that temptation.

"You have brought me comfort, too, dear Josephine," he said.

"How?"

"It can be lonely, sometimes," he said. "I have my garden, and my choirs, but the knights spend much of the day away from the monastery, and I am often left here alone. We are too far away from any village to hold mass, and we rarely see travelers on the road these days.

"This time has been a blessing for me, too. I have enjoyed our talks. I have enjoyed our walks in the hills and the time we've spent together. I guess I didn't realize how much I missed companionship until you came here."

She glanced sharply at him and, for a moment, he thought she might misjudge his words for those of a different kind of passion. But then she smiled, silently telling him she understood his meaning. He smiled back at her and squeezed her hand.

"I have to ask something of you," he said. He paused and gazed into her eyes for a moment. "Something you will not like."

She remained silent, and he got the sense that she knew what he was going to ask. "Sir Geoffrey wants to travel to your home to investigate," he said, turning his head to stare at a wall while he

69

spoke. "He requests your presence at the house as well. He hopes that you will provide some clues to what the assassins might have sought."

"Me?" she asked, "Travel with them?"

"Yes," he said, and turned to look at her again. "But I will be with you."

"You are coming too?"

"Yes," Micah said. "Sir Geoffrey realizes that the investigation will be difficult for you. If he did not deem it important, he would not ask this of you. He has asked me to come along as well in hopes that I might provide you some comfort in this task."

"Why do you think it is so important to him?" Josephine asked. "The..." she swallowed, "The men did not find what they wanted, but surely they will be gone by now."

"He believes you may still be in danger."

She gasped. "Do you think...?"

"I'm not sure," Micah admitted. "Sir Geoffrey is wise; he knows about these things. I'm just a monk. He believes it important to find out what the assassins sought, to determine if you remain in danger."

"I..." She breathed deeply. "I guess I thought it was over."

"I hope so," Micah said. "But it is important to know the truth. You will not be alone. I will be with you."

"I will go," she said, but her voice wavered. She shook her head, and repeated in a voice firm with resolve, "I will go."

"Good," he replied. "We will leave in the hour of dusk."

"Tonight?" She asked. "Wouldn't it be better to travel during the day?"

"Sir Geoffrey thinks it best to travel under the light of the moon," Micah said. He glanced away from her, unwilling to stare into her eyes while telling the lie. "He mentioned that the assassins work at night, and it would be safer to be awake and, uh, alert should they attack."

Hearing the lie fall clumsily from his lips, he knew she would hear the untruth in his voice. He waited for her to ask him more, to quiz him on this strange reason and to slice her way to the truth, but the questions didn't come.

"I guess he would know better than us," she said.

"Yes," he agreed. "I suppose he would." The lie was necessary, but it was still a sin and he felt uncomfortable with the deception. He opened his mouth to add more, but was interrupted by the dining room door bursting open. A young knight with hair still tangled from a sound night's sleep stepped into the room.

"Breakfast?" the young knight croaked.

"I will fix you a plate, Sir William," Micah said, standing.

Sir William was one of the three knights that had arrived late last evening. Micah knew that Sir Geoffrey had called for the knights soon after Josephine's arrival. Sir William had stayed at the monastery before, and Micah knew he was a good man at heart. The other two knights were strangers to Micah, but he was somewhat relieved the three of them had arrived while the sun still made its descent across the horizon.

Micah spent the majority of the day running errands for the knights and helping pack the supplies needed for the trip. Josephine had only the dress she had been wearing the night she had arrived and would need a bedroll and a canteen. The knights would also need bedrolls, canteens, weapons, bolts for the small crossbows they carried, grain for the horses, whetstones to keep their weapons sharp, a small hammer to bang out any dents in their armor, and the list went on.

It was tiring work, and a few hours before the sunset, he was finally able to retreat to his room to rest before the journey. He knew they would want to ride to the house and search it that night. He also knew, without needing to be told, that they might not be coming straight back. Whatever the case, it would be a long night, and he needed what sleep he could get now.

He was unsure if he would be able to sleep with the sun still present in the sky, but soon he was dozing. He was, thus, surprised when he came awake with the same feeling he had experienced earlier that morning that someone was in the room with him.

"You sleep lightly," Geoffrey said, and Micah heard approval in his voice.

"Are we ready to leave?"

"Yes, everyone is gathering out back. Even the girl is ready. If it wasn't for the look of sadness deep in her eyes, I would almost think she was eager for this trip."

72

"It's the action she is eager for," Micah said. He hopped out of bed and picked up the sack containing his spare robes and bedroll. "The act of traveling may seem simple, but the action of it takes her mind away from the memories. If it weren't for the destination, I'd say it was almost good for her."

"It will be rough on her," Geoffrey agreed. "But it is something that needs doing. She has to confront those memories sometime."

Micah nodded at him. "I have two sacks of food supplies in the kitchen that I must fetch."

"Two sacks?" Geoffrey asked.

"I thought the trip might last longer than expected," Micah said.

"It may very well." Geoffrey nodded. "You've done well, Micah. Let me help you with the supplies."

Sacks in hand, they met the others at the stables. Two of the newly arrived knights, Sir Christoffe and Sir William, were accompanying them on the journey. The third, Sir Michael, was staying behind with orders to be seen by the watchers during the day and give the appearance that the knights were still at the monastery.

"It won't fool them for long," Geoffrey told the knight. "The Isma'ilites are not so naïve as to buy into the charade for more than a day or two, but it will cause them some delay, I hope."

"I will do my best," the knight said. "I will change clothes at midday and be seen again in the afternoon in the new attire. Hopefully this will give the appearance of more than a single knight. I may even don the robes of the monk."

"Very good," Geoffrey said. "Just don't trample on his flowers too much. You wouldn't want to catch his ire when we return."

They all laughed at the jest, Micah joining in louder than the others. The mere thought of him displaying ire to one of the knights was almost enough to unseat him from his horse. Sir Michael promised to stay far from the garden to keep it safe. The final preparations were made, and the group was soon off into the hills. An unmounted horse trailed behind them, and Micah realized one knight was not present in the party. Sir Edward was absent.

They reached a tree that grew at an odd angle, and Geoffrey called for a halt. In the distance, the sound of wolves howling reached their ears. Josephine shivered at the sound, prompting Gerard to edge his horse close to hers and grant her a comforting smile.

Soon, a shadowy figure emerged from the night, holding his hand up in greeting. Micah recognized Edward when he stepped into the moon's light, but noticed the distant, almost alien, look in his eyes.

"Is it done?" Geoffrey asked.

"Yes," Edward replied.

"Then let us be off."

CHAPTER SEVEN

"Has there been any change, Aziz?"

Aziz jerked, and Zain knew he had surprised the man. Zain had not meant to sneak up on him, but stealth was a habit.

"Nothing since early morning," Aziz said, his face red. "The monk tended to his gardens in the morning, and the newly arrived knights held weapon practice in the courtyard at midday. Just before sunset, one of the knights drew some water from the well but then retreated back inside."

"The girl did not come out with the monk?"

"No. The monk was not long in his tending."

"That is strange," Zain said, his voice pitched low.

In the distance, a wolf howled. Zain turned his head to stare in the direction of the sound, but he could see nothing moving under the light of the full moon.

"Strange?" Aziz asked.

"It might be nothing," Zain said. "The monk and the girl have spent time in the garden every day since her arrival."

Aziz shrugged. "I haven't seen the girl all day."

Another wolf took up the night's cry, this one closer than the first. "Well, one break in the routine means little. We'll see what happens during tomorrow's sun."

A third howl, this one distant, but Zain's hands went to the scimitars hanging at his belt. His entire body shrank into itself, becoming a tense ball ready to act at any sound or movement.

"The wolves seem very active tonight," Zain whispered. His eyes searched the land stretching out in front of them. "There!" He pointed. A dark form moved through the tall grass, barely a whisper as it wove its way toward them.

Zain's hand moved from the hilt of his sword to his left forearm, where a set of knives were attached to the leather bracer. The wolf was almost upon them when Zain's arm flashed forward and the knife shot toward the wolf.

A howl of pain and anguish erupted in the night. The wolf twisted in the weeds, a full four inches of iron lodged in its throat. Movement sprang up all around them as more of the beasts were now launching their attacks.

Another knife flew from Zain's hand, this one finding its mark in the left eye of one of the animals. Zain unsheathed his swords and prepared himself for an attack. A wolf launched at Aziz, striking him in the chest, and they both went down. The fidais managed to ram his sword through the beast's stomach, but the dying wolf continued thrashing trying to get its fangs around Aziz's throat.

Zain lashed out with his boot, kicking the animal off Aziz. Twisting, he stabbed at another of the wolves with his scimitar. A streak of blood splashed against his cheek and the beast bounded away howling in pain. There was a growl behind him. He spun, and lunged into the wolf's leaping attack with his short sword.

Aziz rose from the ground and struck down the last of the beasts surrounding them. The two turned their eyes to a distant tree where another watcher battled against more of the animals. They watched helplessly while their brother went down against the onslaught, the wolves tearing into his body with a ferocity dreadful to behold.

"We must help him!" Aziz said.

"No," Zain replied. "He is already lost. We must be away from this place before they leave him to death and come after us."

Zain ul-Baqir did not wait for an answer. He turned and sprinted up the hill, trusting his follower to obey the command. Their campsite was not too far from the watching posts, but he knew the paw of the wolf could travel much faster than the feet of a man. He urged his legs onward, keenly aware of the howls getting closer.

They arrived with the wolves close behind, but the Isma'ilites in the camp were not taken by surprise. The air filled with the hiss of arrows repelling the attacking beasts. Zain turned and was surprised at the sheer number of the animals. He counted over a dozen beasts attacking the campsite, but they were soon cut down by the fidais.

When the last of the wolves had fallen, Zain walked to the edge of the camp and stared off in the direction of the monastery. The sky was overcast, but the light of the moon shined through the clouds and, in the distance, he could see movement within the shadows. A distant howl came from the darkness, and then another answering howl, but then the night went eerily silent.

"I've never seen anything like that," Aziz said. "The wolves seemed to come out of nowhere and attack, as if they were following orders."

"Who knows with those beasts," one of the men replied. "They were probably rabid."

"No," Aziz said. "Rabid wolves do not attack in packs, and normal wolves would shy away from our campfires."

"It has been dry for some time," another man added. "The wildlife has been scarce. Perhaps the wolves were driven by their hunger."

"Wolves don't eat men." Aziz shook his head. "They would have to be starved to the point of death before they would be so bold, and those wolves certainly did not look weak."

"Aziz is right," Zain said. "The wolves acted as if they had orders to attack us. And they may have."

"What do you mean?" one of them questioned.

He turned to them, looking each up and down with appraising eyes. "You know what manner of men we watch. They are not of this world. We cannot dismiss anything that happens around such men. If the wolves seemed to be following orders, then perhaps they were."

His statement was met with a hissing intake of breath, each man coming to terms with the words he spoke. "Devils," one whispered, and spit on the ground.

"Devils is right," Zain said. "They have made pact with the dark powers of the night. We must be careful in our deeds, but we must not shy away from them. Allah knows the good work we do in seeking the destruction of these demons that walk the earth, and he will grant unto paradise any follower who aids him in this cause."

The fear disappeared from their eyes, replaced by reverence. Several mumbled prayers, and more than a few spoke of their desire that the demon-knights come themselves so that they might do battle with their enemy directly. Zain swelled with pride at their faith.

"We must set up watch again. We cannot afford to let this attack distract us from our cause."

"I'll go," one of the men said.

"I'll return to post," Aziz added.

"No, Aziz," Zain said. "You have watched throughout the day. As brave as you are, you cannot fight exhaustion with a blade, only sleep."

He chose several of the men to return to the watch, this time doubling them up at their posts in case any further attacks came during the night. "Report any strange finding, no matter how minor it may seem," he said. "And may Allah go with you."

Despite his advice to Aziz, and despite having been up since dawn himself, Zain found it difficult to sleep. His thoughts shifted from the girl's curious absence to the attack of the wolves. The two seemed connected. It was part of his job to notice the patterns within life, to know when to strike, and to know when those patterns had shifted. He knew the pattern had shifted.

Finally, he was able to drift into sleep. Even then, his thoughts tainted his sleep. He saw them in his dreams -- vicious knights with glowing red eyes riding large wolves. In his dream, he battled them throughout the night and watched as first one and then another of his brother fidais fell until he was the last still standing. The beasts held back then, taunting him until he finally woke feeling less rested than before he lay down to sleep.

Zain spent the day overseeing the camp of men. They had no word of strange activity from the monastery. The sun set and, eager for any news, he made the trip over the hill to the watchers. Aziz and Nizam were standing watch behind one of the trees. He crept toward them, his body one with the shadows and his footsteps silent in the night.

"Greetings, my lord Zain," Nizam said without turning his head.

"One day, I will reach up from behind and place a rock on your shoulder, and you will jump out of your boots in surprise," Zain said, smiling.

"That day, you will have grown the wings of a raven." Nizam had unusually sharp senses and was rarely surprised. It was one of many reasons he had risen so high in Zain's favor.

"Any news?"

"Nothing." Nizam turned back to look at the monastery. "Several times during the day someone went out into the courtyard on an errand, but it was mostly quiet."

"The monk?"

"He was out there, he drew water from the well just after midday."

"Did he go to his garden?"

"No." Nizam turned to Zain. "He simply drew some water from the well and retreated back inside."

"That is odd," Zain murmured. "Was the girl with him?"

Nizam shook his head.

"Very odd. Did anything seem strange about him?"

"Not that I noticed," Nizam said. He returned his gaze to the monastery, but his eyes became glazed. Zain remained quiet knowing his friend was reliving the memory in his head and going over every detail. "Now that you mention it, there was something odd."

"What was it?"

"His walk," Nizam replied. "He walked differently."

"Differently? How? As if from some injury?"

"No." He continued staring at the monastery for several moments. "It wasn't the same monk," he said. "I didn't notice it before, but the walk was completely different, it had a sliding gait, instead of a hopping one."

"There's only one monk there," Zain said, turning his own eyes on the monastery. "Unless..."

"Someone wanted us to think it was the monk," Nizam finished the thought. He closed his eyes and bowed his head. "I've failed," he said. "I should have recognized it immediately."

Zain put his hand on his old friend's shoulder. "You succeeded because you recognized it. No matter that it was late."

"I should have done better."

"You will, in the future." Zain said, staring at the monastery. "We need more information. Wait here."

Before Nizam could ask where he was going, Zain set off in the direction of the monastery. His progress was slow, his steps chosen with deliberate care. He sent his awareness out about him, hearing the light brush of a bird cleaning feathers in a distant tree, aware of a rabbit waking from a fitful dream, but disturbing nothing as he passed silently through the fields to the monastery.

He avoided the door, knowing that answers could come from the outside as well as inside. Instead, he snuck around back and peeked inside the stables. There were six knights, a monk, and a girl staying in the monastery, but he counted only three horses in the stables, one of them more of a pony than a horse.

His suspicions confirmed, he was tempted to skip entering the building, but knew that more information could be vital to the success of his mission. He knew that some of the knights had left, probably during the attack of the wolves, but how many?

Slipping inside the building, he passed through its halls with no more sound than the dust settling on the stone floors. He weaved his way to the back of the compound and into the dining room, where he paused. There, on the table, sat one mug and one plate with the leftover crumbs of a recent meal feeding the ants.

A half hour later, he was back with the watchers, telling Aziz to abandon any attempt at stealth and return to camp with orders to prepare for departure.

"What did you find?" Nizam asked.

"There is only one within the monastery walls," Zain replied. "The others, five knights, the monk, and the girl, are gone."

"Where to?"

"That is what we are about to find out, but my instinct tells me it is the merchant's home." Zain grimaced. "We should have posted someone there. But it's too late for that now. Arrange the best tracker to meet me in the hills behind the monastery. They would have avoided the main road to keep from being seen, and it is my guess they traveled overland to the village.

"And Nizam, I need you to return to the Old Man and give him word of what has transpired here. We need to be ready to contact the Hospitaller as soon as their destination is known."

"Surely someone else can carry word to the Old Man." Nizam said.

"No, I need you to do this," Zain replied. "And I need you to do one more thing."

"Yes?"

Zain lowered his voice to a whisper. "That time of reckoning that we spoke of? It draws near. I need you to be near the Old Man and make preparations."

"Yes, Zain." Nizam frowned. "He's going to be furious that we lost a day."

"He's a fool," Zain replied. "The knights allowed us to watch them. He may delude himself on that point, but we should not believe those delusions. Had we gotten too close, they would have been forced to deal with us, but they need us just as we need them."

"How so?" Nizam asked.

"We expect the girl to lead them, and us, to the book. They keep us around in case she doesn't. Then, we will be their only clue to the book's whereabouts."

"At some point, there will be bloodshed," Nizam said.

"There will be much bloodshed, my friend," Zain said. "And this will only be the beginning."

CHAPTER EIGHT

"Would you like me to go over that night?" Josephine's voice broke, and she swallowed hard. "I can point out..." she raised her arm in the direction of the master bedroom. Her arm shook, but she managed to point a finger at a spot on the floor where traces of blood were still visible.

"No, child," Geoffrey said, shaking his head. He silently cursed that it was necessary to put her through this so soon after it had happened.

"Maybe she'll remember something new," Edward said.

Gerard gave the knight a scathing look. "The answers we seek are further back than that night," he said.

They had spent the better part of an hour scouring through the chaos of items on the floor. Geoffrey felt an urge to put a stop to the questions and let the girl have some peace, but he ignored it. Gerard, for all of his cold logic, had a compassionate side. If anyone here could guide the girl through her memories, it was him. He glanced at the French knight and nodded.

"Josephine," Gerard said, cupping her hand in his. "Think back to a week ago, before the darkness of that night," he said. "Remember the peaceful nights you spent in the room with your family. Picture the room as it was then and tell us if anything is missing."

"I don't know," she said. "I just don't know..."

"It's alright, Josephine" Gerard said, his voice gentle and soothing. "Is there any special place your father might have stored things he felt were dear to him?"

"Behind the painting." She nodded her head in the direction of a painting that lay torn into pieces on the floor. The sight of it caused new tears to well in her eyes.

Gerard glanced at Geoffrey and raised his eyebrows. Geoffrey understood the look. They were getting nowhere with this.

"Is there any other place?" Gerard asked. "Perhaps a secret spot he may have hidden something valuable?"

"Well, there is one hiding place," she said. "In the corner, there is a loose board. I saw him putting something there once."

Edward went to the corner and used the toe of his boot to tap each of the boards until the sound of a hollow echo greeted their ears. Stooping down, he ripped the board out of the wall, reached in, and retrieved a small bag hidden behind the wood. He rummaged through the bag, and they could all hear the clinking of metal while his fingers moved through the contents.

"It's just filled with coins," he said, scowling as he rose to his feet.

Josephine shrunk a little from that scowl. "I didn't know what he kept there; I never checked. It was father's secret."

Edward shrugged and tossed the bag to Geoffrey who, after a cursory examination, handed it over to Micah. "Count it and add the total to the one from the strongbox," he said.

"I'm sorry." Josephine's shoulders slumped. "I haven't been of much help."

"Nonsense," Gerard replied. "You cannot give us information you do not have." He smiled at her. "I think you have done wonderfully."

Geoffrey remained quiet. He stared at the young woman, his eyes curious, appraising, until finally, he asked, "Where will you go when this is all through?"

Her eyes widened. "Go?"

"Not now, child," Geoffrey quickly amended. "You will stay with us until we are satisfied that you are in no danger. But after that, where will you go?"

"I hadn't really thought of it," she replied. "To my uncle's, I suppose. He lives in a village not too far from here."

Gerard and Geoffrey exchanged looks. "Your uncle?" Geoffrey asked. "Is that your father's brother?"

"My mother's," she replied.

"Your mother's," Geoffrey repeated, absent-mindedly scratching the old scar on the side of his chin. There was a chance the Isma'ilites had dismissed the merchant's wife completely and, perhaps, they did not know about her brother. "When was the last time you saw your uncle?"

"Months ago. Much of Father's time was occupied with his business. Uncle was always busy as well."

"What sort of work does your uncle do?"

"Similar to Father's, but different somehow. I'm not sure how. I think he collects different things than Father did."

87

"And you haven't seen him in months?" Geoffrey glanced Gerard and knew they were both thinking the same thing. If the book was not here, it very well could be with the uncle.

"No, it's too far for a girl to travel on her own," she said, shifting in her seat under the newfound intensity of their stares. "Father saw him more often, of course."

"Oh?" Geoffrey said. "When was the last time your father saw your uncle?"

"A few days before..." A tear came to her eye, and her lower lip began to tremble.

"Are you sure it was just a few days before?" Geoffrey asked.

"Yes." She sniffed. "Father stayed away all night, which was rare."

"I see," Geoffrey said. He turned to the monk. "Micah, have you finished making out the receipt?"

"Yes," he replied. "I have it here."

"Good. Give it to Josephine."

"Receipt?" she asked.

"Micah has counted the money found in the house. He will give you a receipt for it. When you are ready for some or all of it, just let him know."

"Money? I don't understand."

"The money is now yours, child. It's not much, but it will get you to where you are going," Geoffrey said. "Don't worry of it now, though. One of the many tasks of the Templar is to handle money."

"I thought you were knights?" she asked.

He laughed. "That we are, but we also deal in the transfer of money. A wealthy nobleman traveling to the Holy Land does not want to carry around a large amount of coin with him. That would be very dangerous. Instead, he leaves the money with us before he begins his travel and then takes what he needs when he arrives."

He smiled at her confused look. "Don't worry on it, child. Just keep the receipt safe until such time as you need it." He turned to the monk. "Micah, could you help Josephine pack up some spare clothing? We can't have her traveling about with just the one dress."

"Certainly," he replied and led Josephine into the back room.

The door closed, and a strange silence filled the room. Geoffrey glanced at the other two knights. Edward still wore a snarl, his impatience evident on his face. It was clear he considered the trip a total waste of time. Gerard was lost in thought, his eyes staring unseeing at the closed door. Geoffrey knew he contemplated the girl. Here, in this house where her family had died, she seemed childlike, but she had a core of strength deep within her that was only now emerging.

"The uncle?" Gerard finally asked, breaking the silence.

"It sounds like it," Geoffrey said. "He is the mother's brother, which means he does not share the same name. The Isma'ilites may have missed that little detail."

"Do you think he will have the book?"

"We won't know until we are there."

"Straight away?" Gerard glanced over at the closed door.

"I think so," Geoffrey replied. "We will need her with us, and it is better done in one trip instead of two."

"Very well, I will prepare the horses."

Micah and Josephine returned just as Gerard and Edward were exiting. "Are we leaving now?" Josephine asked.

"Yes," Geoffrey said, "but not for the monastery. You said your uncle does not live far from here? Do you know the way?"

"He lives just over half a day's journey by horseback," she replied. "I have been there several times. I know the way."

"I think it would be best if we paid him a visit," Geoffrey said. "He should be informed of what has happened."

She nodded and followed them out of the house. The other two knights had stayed outdoors, feeding and watering the horses as they waited. The group mounted, but just before they were to leave, a man came hobbling up to them.

"Oh, it is you," he said as he came into the light of the torches and recognized the knights gathered about the house.

"Sir Magistrate," Gerard greeted him.

"I was woken by the news that there was some commotion here, but I see it is just you. And is that Josephine you have with you?"

"Yes, George," Josephine replied, smiling slightly and wiping away stale tears from her eyes.

"I'm sorry it has come to all of this, dear Josephine," he said. "Your parents were good people. Is there anything I can do for you?"

"No, sir," Josephine said.

"We just came to investigate, Magistrate," Geoffrey said. "But, alas, we have found no more clues than you had and are back off to the monastery." The Isma'ilites would be back this way soon, and it was better if the magistrate knew as little of their plans as possible.

"Very good, sirs," he said. He turned and started to walk away, but then he stopped. "Josephine is going with you, then?"

"Yes," Geoffrey replied. "She has nowhere else to turn."

"I thought she would be staying with family," he replied. "Didn't your mother have a brother somewhere east of here, child?"

"She did," Josephine replied. "But he went back to Mother England some months ago, George. I'm sure I will be returning there shortly as well."

Geoffrey smiled. He knew he was right about the girl.

"Very good, then," the magistrate said. "Again, I am sorry for all that has happened, child. I wish you the best of journeys."

"Thank you, George."

They watched him hobble back down the street, and when he had disappeared into the dark of the night, they turned their horses to the east and rode off. It was a calm night with a gentle wind, and they were able to cover much ground in the few hours before dawn.

When the hour of dawn approached, Geoffrey began searching for a suitable spot to set up camp for the day. The countryside was level, but in the distance he spotted the shadows of a rock formation jutting up from the ground. He led them off the road toward this formation, hoping the boulders would provide some protection from prying eyes during the day.

"The sun will be up within the hour," he told them. "We'd better get some sleep. We can continue at dusk and hopefully reach our destination at a reasonable time tomorrow night."

"It's not too far from here," Josephine said. "Perhaps another two hours of riding. Maybe we could press on?"

"No, child," Geoffrey replied. "It's better if we stay here for the day and continue on tomorrow night."

"But I'm not too tired, I could make it," she said.

"I know you could." Geoffrey smiled and beckoned to her. "Come to me, Josephine, I have something to tell you."

She stepped forward, her face curious, and looked up into his eyes.

"You are tired, Josephine," he said, his voice pitched low and even. "You are much more tired than you know." It was important to repeat the same words several times, always keeping the tone of the voice mellow and soothing. "You will sleep now. And when you awake tomorrow evening you will feel very rested. You will remember nothing except curling up and falling into this deep sleep."

Her head slumped, and he had to catch her before she fell. He laid her gently to the ground.

With Micah's help, he covered her in a blanket and used the sack with her clothes as a pillow.

Edward tensed. "Who goes there?" he called.

"What is it?" Geoffrey asked.

"Something's out there," Edward whispered.

Geoffrey peered in the direction Edward was staring. At first, he did not see anything, but then the night parted, and a shadow appeared before them. Edward tried to draw his blade, but the figure slammed into him, knocking him to the ground. There was a strange pop, and Edward lay still.

Gerard already had a blade in each hand and was bolting toward the strange figure, swords whirling. The figure stepped into the light, and Geoffrey could see that it was a man. Flowing like water toward them, the stranger easily slipped between Gerard's blades and sent a booted foot to the side of his temple. Again came the loud pop, and Gerard dropped to the ground.

Geoffrey stood protectively over Josephine. He expected Edward and Gerard to spring back to their feet at any moment. No ordinary blow from a boot could keep them down, but they did not rise.

Clutching his sword, he watched Sir Christoffe and Sir William approach the mysterious figure. This time, the stranger did not strike back. Instead, he waved his hand, and the knights suddenly slumped over. Geoffrey heard the thud coming from behind him and knew without looking that Micah had fallen as well.

He took a step forward and prepared himself for a fight he knew he could not win. But the stranger stopped and regarded him with a strange look for several long moments. Finally, he spoke.

"Put away your weapon, Geoffrey Furnivall. Surely by now you realize it will do you no good."

"Who are you?" Geoffrey asked.

His question was met with silence. The stranger pulled back the hood of his cloak and took another step into the light. Geoffrey studied the face that stared back at him. It was the face of a very, very old man. Wrinkles danced across the cheeks and forehead, and stringy gray hair fell in patches from his head. He looked frail, as if he barely had the strength to keep standing. Yet Geoffrey, who had the speed of five men and the strength of ten, felt helpless as a newborn babe. It was a feeling he was not used to, and one he did not like. Slowly, under the gaze of those eyes, he lowered his weapon.

"What did you do to them?"

"You, who are versed in the art, ask that of me?" the old man asked.

"The power," Geoffrey said. "I have never seen it work against..."

"Against one of you?" the old man finished. "Yes, it works against us."

Geoffrey glanced to where Edward and Gerard still lay unconscious on the ground. He had once seen three inches of blade sticking out of Edward's stomach in the aftermath of a battle and watched it heal within a day, but he could not be confident in those same healing powers working against wounds this mysterious stranger inflicted.

"Worry not about them, Geoffrey Furnivall," the old man said. "They will wake before the sun rises overhead. The wounds they received will heal."

"Who are you?" he asked again.

"The answer to that matters little. You may call me Damon if you wish. A better question would be why am I here?"

"Why are you here?" Geoffrey said, feeling silly at repeating the question.

"I am a messenger, Geoffrey Furnivall. You seek a book, a very holy book. I can see you are surprised? Oh yes, I know of your mission and I am here to impress upon you the importance of finding this book. You suspect it is a danger to the knights, but I am here to tell you it is a danger to us all."

He had no need of explaining who 'us all' was. Geoffrey knew the answer. He had never known whether there were others like them that walked the earth. The Knights Templar of the Inner Circle believed they alone possessed the power of the blood, but Geoffrey had never been quite so sure himself. Now that he had met another like them, he wished he never had.

"Forces are aligning against you. More than you know. When the sun retreats back from the sky, go straight away to the uncle's house and retrieve the book, and then beat a path as quickly as you can back to the monastery. Do not delay. I will do what I can to trim down the forces of those who oppose you, but you would do well to expect a fight before your journey is through."

"Will you..."

"Accompany you? No. I have other work that must be done, but you will see more of me in the

95

near future if you are successful in retrieving the book."

"But..."

"Never mind your questions for now. The sun makes its way into the sky. Make your preparations, and come dusk, be straight away with your task. Save your questions until there is more time for answers."

And with those ominous words, the stranger departed. He retreated into the night and the darkness seemed to swallow him.

CHAPTER NINE

"Your time grows short, Sir Jonathan, as does the Grandmaster's patience. You have been given free rein to deal with the Templar as you see fit, but you must realize that, publicly, the Grandmaster must deny all knowledge of your activities."

Jonathan sat quietly, his face not betraying the rage of emotions inside him. He was close to victory, and these fools were debating his tactics. He was not exactly on trial, but the very fact that his chair had been placed well in front of the table where all five of the men could see him made it seem so.

"Have you nothing to say in your defense?" asked Sir Edgar Berard, Knight-Captain of the Shield of St. John. "With the fall of the Holy City, the Mother Church in Rome takes increased interest in our activities. If they should find out that you, that we have had dealings with the enemy, how would that look?"

"There is a greater evil that we face," Jonathan said. "The heathens recognize that evil, which is why we have been able to gain their aid in our endeavors. The Mother Church must come to realize this as well."

"The Mother Church will do no such thing," Edgar said. "She will see only that we have allied with the enemy while the Templar have fought them, and what shall she think of that? You have no proof backing your accusations of the Templar and their corruption. You may not need proof with us. We have fought alongside those demons and know them for what they are, but you will need more than words when you confront the Mother Church.

"The Templar have allies in high places. The Kings of France and England bend their ear to the Templar, and don't think the church is blind to this. Secretly, they may wish for the downfall of those demons as much as we, but openly they will do nothing so long as such powerful allies back the Templar. We need proof that will turn the ears of England and France away from the Templar and bolster the church's claim."

"And proof you will have in good time," Jonathan said. "Soon, we will have what we need. Once the Templar are no more, our own numbers will be bolstered. We will present a united front to the heathens, and the Lord will ride once again at our side. The Holy City will be ours, but first we must root out the evil within ourselves.

"Do not forget, noble sirs," he continued. "The corruption of the Knights Templar goes beyond their own ranks. The Lord in Heaven can hardly back an army with such evil riding among them."

"You'd better stop him before he begins quoting from the mandate," Sir Velos said, and several of the knights chuckled.

Jonathan balled his hand into a fist. It was this very attitude that turned the eyes of God from them. There were many in the knighthood that were repentant of past sins, Jonathan among them. There were more than a few, though, that chose the life of a knight more to save their family honor than to save their soul. He gathered himself to continue, but a soft knock on the door interrupted him.

"Sirs," a page peeked his head into the room. "There is a messenger outside for Sir Jonathan."

Jonathan spun toward the man. "Can you not see that we are busy in here?"

"Yes, sir," the page said. "But..."

"Very well." Jonathan impatiently lifted himself from his chair. Stalking to the door, he brushed past the page as if the man were no longer there.

"I'm sorry, sir," the page said, trailing after him. "I had thought..."

Jonathan paused. "You did fine," he said. "My show was for them, not you. An impatient man is a busy man and a busy man is an important man."

"Yes, sir." The page bowed his head.

"Never let them see you idling about," Jonathan said, resuming his long strides down the hallway. "You must always look busy even when you are not, and always be short with those beneath you when others are about. This is the mark of a man with much on his mind, and others will note that about you."

"Yes, sir."

"Now, be off with you," he said, smiling. "I can find my own way."

Reaching the end of the hall, he stepped outside and spotted the darkly clad man clinging to the wall of the keep. He gave the man an appraising look. He had expected to find Umar, the previous messenger, but this man was a stranger.

"I am Sir Jonathan Alderson," he said.

"My master greets you and sends message," the man replied, his accent thick. "The destination of the demon-knights has been confirmed. They head for a relative of the merchant, and we ride after them."

"A relative?" Jonathan frowned. "I thought the merchant had no kin in these parts?"

"His wife's brother," the messenger explained.

"Damnation," Jonathan said. "Very well, I will have the knights out here promptly. You will be able to lead them to the uncle's place?"

"I can lead," the messenger said.

"Wait here," Jonathan said. "They will be ready within the hour."

Rushing back inside, he made his way to the back of the keep. In the past two years, he had done little more than study the Templar, searching for a weakness. He was close now; he could feel it. And yet, there was a seed of doubt. What if the old Traveler had been wrong about the book?

He shook this doubt from his mind. It wasn't just the Traveler's words he was trusting; it was his own intuition. Something told him the book was important, far more important than he knew. And now, it was coming within his grasp.

He stopped at a door and knocked. "Sir Francisco?" he called.

"Yes?" the knight replied, opening the door.

"The time has come," Jonathan said in a rush. "Gather your men and meet outside."

"Very well," Francisco replied. "The men are prepared. They have been instructed to remove all insignia of the Hospitaller from their armor and their packing."

"Good," Jonathan said. "Any witnesses will be led to believe it the work of mercenaries. The Templar have made many enemies in their time here."

"It will be done," Francisco said, nodding.

Minutes later, Sir Jonathan Alderson returned to the meeting room. There was new color in his cheeks and new confidence in his step. He smiled at the gathering of knights and announced, "It has begun."

***

Outside, the knights gathered. Gone were the red surcoats emblazed with the white cross. They did not wear their customary chain vests, nor could the insignia of their knighthood be seen on their shields. Instead, they wore plain leather tunics and simple broadswords at their sides. This day, they did not ride out as knights. They did not ride out against the heathens of the land.

They rode out against the devil himself come to this land in the form of the Knights Templar. And, to all the world, they would look like simple mercenaries. It would not do for word to get out that the two knightly orders battled each other. Fighting the devil required stealth, not pride. It required secrecy, not pomp.

Sir Francisco Narvaez mounted his horse. He turned the steed to face his men, flashing a smile of assured victory before bowing his head in momentary prayer. When he finished asking for the Lord's blessing, he raised his sword high in a silent cheer. The knights raised their own swords in response.

He remained silent, looking over the twenty knights gathered before him. They were well trained, each man a veteran of many battles. His confidence grew while he took stock of the men. He knew better than any what they faced. But he also knew the value of his men. They would succeed. There was no hope that a handful of the Templar, as powerful as they may be, would overcome such odds.

He turned to the messenger and nodded. The Isma'ilite, his black cloak wrapped tightly about his body, had watched the ceremony without word. He stared back at Sir Francisco, eyes glittering in the depths of that hood, and finally gave a return nod. With that simple gesture, he wheeled his horse around and sent it galloping down the road. At Sir Francisco's signal, the knights followed.

Throughout the morning they rode in silence. They were hardened knights, and the thought of a long ride with battle at the other end did not bother them. There had been harder rides, and harder battles, fought in the past few years. Each knight rode with the knowledge that death might be what he found at journey's end.

They stopped at midday to rest. Francisco walked among the men, catching snippets of conversation borne to him on the wind. The men boasted about feats of bravery in past battles and proclaimed their courage for the fighting to come. However, Francisco sensed uncertainty in some of the knights and realized the bravado was as much for the speaker as for those who listened.

Their meals finished, they mounted their horses again. Throughout the remainder of the day, they rode hard. The sun vanished over the horizon, and the night stole upon the land, but still they rode. Francisco knew there was still a great distance to be covered before their journey's end.

The night had just fallen when they came upon the stranger. He was difficult to see, dressed in dark clothes and hugging the shadows. At first, the knights did not realize why their horses went from full gallop to a moderate trot, refusing to obey the heels that dug into their sides to urge them on.

The horses slowed to a walk and then stopped completely with the stranger right in front of them. He had his back turned to the knights and was staring up into the sky, seemingly unaware the troop of knights was right behind him. A slight whisper carried on the night air as if the stranger spoke to the darkness, and the darkness spoke back.

Sir Francisco tried to steer his mount past the mysterious figure and down the road, but his horse refused. He cursed. Looking at the other knights, he realized they were having the same problem. He turned to the Isma'ilite and was startled by the strange look in the assassin's eyes. He recognized the look. It was the same one he had seen on many a Saracen's face during the heat of battle.

"Who goes there?" he called out, his voice cracking.

The stranger turned and, for an instant, it seemed they were caught within that moment of time. The wind died, the very air receding into the dark of the night. The sound slipped away, the insects silent, the breathing of the men coming in quiet gasps. And, when the stranger finally faced them, there was a hiss.

Time exploded forward again. The horses reared back and began bucking back and forth, trying with all their might to unseat their riders. The horses screamed in fear while the knights bellowed in confusion. Everywhere around Francisco was chaos.

His own horse reared back on its hind legs and then came down on the ground, nearly unseating him. He dug his hands into the mane of the horse and squeezed his thighs together, fighting to stay mounted.

Beside him, a man fell to the ground, and the stranger was on him. A sword flashed in the night, and the smell of blood arose. Another man went down, and the stranger was there. And then another knight fell, the shadow embracing him the instant he hit the ground.

Francisco battled his horse and his fear. The horses had gone mad. Those succeeding in throwing their riders did not stop there. They rose up on their back legs and kicked out at other riders with their forelegs, trying to dislodge them. All about him, knights were being thrown to the ground, the screams of the dying rang out, and the smell of blood and death filled the air.

The assassin's mount, a black stallion, sprang at him, bashing into his shoulder with a crack. Losing his balance, he was flung from his steed. The ground rushed to him, and an intense pain racked his body. He tried to scramble to his feet, but his legs refused to respond. Managing to roll over and off the road, he looked down at his legs. His right leg lay at an odd angle from his body, and he realized it was broken.

Huddled at the side of the road, he watched the dark shadow pounce on first one, and then another knight, until all of them lay still. The stranger turned toward the assassin that stood in the center of the road. The assassin had not waited to be thrown from his horse. Instead, he hopped off as soon as the chaos had erupted. He stood now within the center of that chaos, his long scimitar held out before him.

Francisco wondered, briefly, why the Isma'ilite had stood there during the carnage, not attacking the stranger, and also not fleeing the scene. He thought, for a moment, that the assassin had betrayed them. He was in league with this dark sorcerer and had led them all into a trap. But that was not true.

The stranger turned to the assassin and regarded him for a moment. The assassin responded by drawing a dagger in his left hand. Francisco could tell by the white knuckles tightly gripping the dagger the assassin knew death approached and was willing to meet it with courage.

It was over so quickly he thought his eyes had betrayed him. One moment, they were staring at each other preparing for battle. The next moment, the stranger stood right next to the messenger, his fingers clawed around the assassin's throat. He released his grip, and the assassin's body thudded to the ground.

Francisco hoped the stranger would not notice him lying beside the road. He willed the shadows cast by the moon to pass over his body and hide him from the dark stranger's sight. He shut his eyes and forced his breath to cease, but he felt a strange chill pass through him and knew the stranger knelt beside him.

He opened his eyes and stared up into the pale face of the stranger, the words to a prayer tumbling through his mind, but not able to pass his lips before death's embrace overtook him.

CHAPTER TEN

"I think it is best if you let me break the news to him," Geoffrey said.

It was an hour after dusk. Micah was tending to the horses, and the other knights were helping him. None of them remembered the stranger that had visited their camp just before dawn. Gerard and Edward awoke soon after he departed. They were groggy, but any injury to their heads had already healed. William and Christoffe might have slept through the night if Geoffrey had not woken them for guard duty.

"He's my uncle," Josephine said. "Don't you think I should be the one to tell him?"

She was strong. Some might have taken any opportunity to avoid delivering such news, but she felt it was her responsibility and would not shrink from it. "No," he said. "It is best delivered by me. Such news should be delivered quick and to the point to allow the mind time to absorb it. And you are still healing from those wounds."

Josephine nodded.

"William, Christoffe." The knights broke away from the horses and approached. "I need you to stay outside and keep a look out. I don't think we were followed, but the Isma'ilites are exceedingly clever."

"Yes sir."

"If you see or hear anything out of place, you are to alert us," Geoffrey said. "I don't care if it is just a cricket chirping in the night, I don't want you to leave this yard to investigate. You are to let us know immediately if you sense something amiss."

He turned to look at the house. There was a glimmer of light escaping between the curtains of the window, and Geoffrey knew the man was still awake. He might have heard their horses approach and be peering out at them at that moment. It was no matter; he would soon have the answers he sought.

"Are you ready?"

"Yes," Josephine said. She lowered her head, and Geoffrey knew she was afraid. This was her mother's brother, and Josephine knew the pain he was about to experience.

"Micah?"

"The horses have been fed and watered," Micah said. "I tied them to the fence."

"Good," Geoffrey said. "Let's go."

Geoffrey had faced the enemy in battle countless times. More than a few times, he had been outnumbered. He had grown so accustomed to it that he could use a break in the battle to catch a few minutes of sleep should the need exist. But he would never become accustomed to what he was about to do. There was nothing worse than telling someone they had lost a loved one.

He knocked on the door.

"Yes?" Robert Williamson was a short, rotund man with graying hair that circled a bald spot on top of his round head. His clear, blue eyes seemed out of place amid the wrinkles and pox scars that marred his face. They were innocent eyes; the eyes of one whose greatest joy was finding a clay pot dug from the sand. But the eyes peering through the crack in the door were wide with fear. He was not used to armor-clad men calling on him at night.

"Robert Williamson," Geoffrey said. "I need to speak to you."

"Who are you?" Robert asked.

Geoffrey stepped to the side and let him see Josephine.

"Josie?" he said, letting the door open wider.

"May we come in?" Geoffrey asked.

The man glanced at Josephine, his eyes questioning, and she gave him a weak smile. "Certainly." He moved to the side and let them enter. "Is something the matter?

Geoffrey entered the living area and waited for the man to follow. "Have you had word from your sister or her husband in the last few days?"

"No." Robert stared at the insignia on Geoffrey's armor. "You are a knight, aren't you? One of the Templar? Why do you ask of my sister and her husband?" He turned to Josephine. "What has happened, Josie?"

"Easy, sir," Micah said. "Have a seat."

"Are these knights holding you against your will?" Robert asked.

"Of course not," Micah said. "The Knights Templar are here to protect, not abuse. Please, have a seat."

"I'll have a seat when I damn well want to," Robert said. "After all, it is my home you have invaded."

The man was scared. He knew something had happened to his sister and her family, but he wasn't quite ready for that knowledge. Geoffrey was about to intercede, but Micah had things well in hand.

"Please, sir," the monk said, putting his hand on Robert's shoulder. "I think it would be best if you just took a seat." Micah moved his hand from Robert's shoulder to his elbow and gently guided him to a chair. "You can see Josephine willingly accompanies," he said. "She is upset. It would do us all good to sit down and remain calm."

The man's shoulders slumped, and he took a seat. Josephine buried her head in her hands, unable to contain her tears any longer. She wept in silence, but Geoffrey could see the tears escaping between her fingers.

"When was the last time you spoke to your sister, or her husband?" Geoffrey asked.

"What has happened?"

It was best done quickly. "Your sister is dead, sir."

"Dead?"

"I am afraid so. Her husband and two of her daughters were also killed. Only Josephine escaped. It happened several nights ago."

"Dead?" Robert's eyes were lost, his face pale. "All of them?"

"I am sorry for your loss," Geoffrey said.

"Who could have done such a think?"

"Assassins," Geoffrey said. "Isma'ilites."

"Isma'ilites?"

"Yes. Do you know of them?"

"Only from tavern gossip. I didn't even know they were real. And they've killed my Annie, and her two little ones, and Joseph too."

"The Isma'ilites are real, sir," Geoffrey said. "They appear to have been after something. Josephine was able to get away during the chaos and fled to our monastery where she has been given sanctuary."

Geoffrey fell silent and let the man come to terms with the news. Robert's head was bowed down and shaking in disbelief. Several minutes passed, and then the merchant lifted his head. And there was a new look in his eyes. Anger.

"Who are these Isma'ilites, and what did they want?"

"They are assassins, sir," Geoffrey replied. "Saracen assassins. They work for someone called the Old Man of the Mountain. We believe Joseph came into possession of an item that they wanted. Josephine recalls hearing one of the assassins mention something about a book."

"A book?" Robert asked. "A book you say?"

Geoffrey knew at that moment the man had the book. "Yes, a book. Have you seen Joseph recently?"

The man looked to Josephine, questioning, and she nodded at him. "It's alright, Uncle. These men have been very kind to me." She raised a hand to her face and wiped the tears from her eyes. "They believe the assassins will continue to be a danger so long as the book remains out of their grasp."

"So long as they think you can lead them to the book," Geoffrey corrected.

"I..." He buried his head in his hand. "It is in the bookcase." He stood up and walked over to the corner of the room. There was an old wooden bookcase filled mostly with clay pots and other small items, but it also held three books on the top shelf.

Robert grabbed one of the books and stared at it. He shook his head and then tossed the book to Geoffrey who snagged it deftly out of the air. "Take it," he said. "Take the damned book and get it far from here. If it has brought death to the ones I love, it is not worth any amount of money it could bring. A king could pay a handsome bounty for it and still it would not be worth the blood it has cost."

Geoffrey stared at the book. The leather binding was wrinkled with age, and he couldn't place the strange script on the cover. He delicately flipped through several pages. The writing was clear and precise, unblemished by time. Like the words on the cover, the language was unknown to him. This was the book that had cost so much blood, and it had been sitting on the bookshelf for all to see.

But of course it was. The merchants would not know the danger the book represented. Geoffrey didn't even know the danger; he only knew the Isma'ilites were desperate to get their hands on this book. Robert and his brother would figure it to be just another curiosity, a book that might fetch a fair price from a nobleman or from the church.

He closed the book and smiled, but it was not a smile borne out of pleasure. Finding the book was just the beginning of a long journey, and he felt uneasy about where that journey might lead.

Micah broke the silence. "What do we do now?"

"Return to the monastery," Geoffrey said. "We'll need time to think about what to do next."

Gerard looked at Josephine. "All of us?"

"I think it best if Josephine accompanies us," Geoffrey said. "But the decision is up to her."

"Do you think I am still in danger?" she asked.

When he had first laid eyes on Josephine, she was broken. Her family had just been murdered. She had ridden for several hours with an enemy close behind, and she had fainted at first sight of him.

In the past few days, he had watched as she mended. She had performed bravely at her father's house, trying her best to recall every detail no matter how painful. She had shown her quick wit with the magistrate, picking up on Geoffrey's deception and pushing it forward. At the mention of continued danger, he saw both fear and the courage to overcome it in her eyes. She was mending, and in the process, she was growing stronger.

"Yes," he said. "I believe you are still in danger. The assassins will not know that we have found the book. They will still look to you as being a link to their prize and, so long as they view you in connection with the book, you will be in danger."

She nodded. "Then I should return with you to the monastery until the assassins are no longer a threat." She looked at him, and he could see the strength rising up to meet the challenge. But there was also concern. "What about my uncle?"

It was dangerous enough for them to have Josephine at the monastery. The knights had secrets, and they could ill-afford those secrets to be revealed. But, they were also duty-bound to protect those in need. "Sir," Geoffrey said, turning to the man. "I cannot guess the Isma'ilites intent. They seem intent on Josephine, and they may not even know about you. But, should they trace us to this house, you might be in danger. I can offer you the sanctuary of the knights if you should so desire."

"But what of my business?" He looked around the room at the knights. "I cannot just leave..."

"You might be in danger," Geoffrey said. "If you don't come with us, I suggest you stay somewhere else for the next few nights."

"I have a friend I can stay with," Robert said. "But I wouldn't want to put him in any danger."

"I don't think you will," Geoffrey replied. "They will be more intent on us than you. It should be safe to return within a few days."

The merchant glanced at Josephine. "I will stay with my friend. I do have my business to think about, after all. I have an important buyer coming into town within the week and would like to be here to meet with him."

"Very well." Geoffrey rose to his feet. "With your leave, sir, I think we had best be off. The sooner we get back, the safer we will all be."

Nodding, Robert rose from his chair and walked to Josephine. He put his hand over hers. "I'm sorry," he said. "Your mother was a good woman."

"I know, Uncle." Josephine rose to her feet. She put her arms around him and whispered in his ear, "She was a good sister too."

114

"You take care of yourself," he said. "As soon as this dark business is over with, you get back here."

She gave him a peck on the cheek. "I will."

***

Edward grunted. They should go. Something didn't feel right, and he felt exposed standing in front of the open door while William and Christoffe prepared the horses. The merchant and the girl were standing together, holding hands and saying their goodbyes. But this wasn't the time to be sentimental. Edward nudged Geoffrey and the other knight nodded. He sensed it too.

Edward peered into the night, trying to make out what caused his alarm. There was something out there; he knew it. But he couldn't see it. Whoever, or whatever it was, they were doing a good job remaining unseen.

And then a shadow moved in the night. There was a flash of moonlight on metal and Edward's eyes followed it across the lawn until it ricocheted of Geoffrey's plated gauntlet. The knight had blocked a dagger aimed for Josephine.

Edward burst into action. He grabbed the merchant and pulled him around the side of the house. There was a stab of pain in his shoulder from a dagger thrown with enough force to penetrate his armor, but he ignored it. "Get to the hills," he whispered.

One of the assassins came at him from the side, and he lashed out with a booted foot sending the

115

man sprawling to the ground. Two more assassins approached, but Gerard was there. The knight had a blade in each hand, and he launched himself at the attackers. Gerard deflected their blows and the sound of metal on metal echoed in the night. With a graceful move, the knight knelt low the ground, sliding his blade through the assassin's defenses and impaling him.

Edward turned back to the merchant. "I said, get to the hills." He pushed the man towards safety. "And don't come back until it is safe."

The man needed no other urging; he ran. Gerard had finished the second assassin and was fighting a third. Another tried to sprint past Edward toward the merchant. Launching himself in the air, he drew his long sword from its scabbard and slashed through the man's face.

He looked around. Gerard was still battling the third assassin, this one giving him a better fight than the other two. Geoffrey was standing protectively over Josephine. He was bleeding from a small cut on his cheek and, as Edward watched, he deflected another knife thrown at the young woman. William and Christoffe were engaged in a fierce melee with several assassins. And, in the midst of it all, Micah was calmly walking from the house to the horses.

Edward shook his head. The monk was bound by his faith not to draw a weapon, even in his own defense. A lesser man might have cowered in fear or ran for the hills, but the monk showed the courage of a warrior. He might not be able to fight, but he wasn't going to run.

Edward surged forward to help William and Christoffe, but two of the assassins descended upon him. They tried to trap him between them, but he eluded their strikes. Batting a blade to the side, he lunged. His sword slid through the man's chest and, with a smile, Edward twisted the blade before turning on the second assassin. This one attacked with a savage ferocity. Edward bided his time, easily parrying the blows while Gerard snuck up from behind and ended the assassin's life with a quick thrust of his sword.

"Go to the others," Edward said. William and Christoffe did not have the strength of the blood and could not survive for long under the onslaught. "I will hold them off from here."

Gerard nodded and sprinted toward the horses. Geoffrey was helping Josephine on to a horse while the two younger knights were trying to hold back several more of the assassins. Gerard charged in, downing one of the assassins, but Christoffe went down, a dagger sticking out from his neck.

Edward looked around for the unseen foe launching the knives. He spotted the assassin at the edge of the torchlight. Yelling, he launched himself in that direction. He did not need stealth to kill his enemy; he had the strength of many men running through his veins. Better the assassin focus on him than continue launching daggers into the fray.

Edward expected the assassin to meet his onslaught with the same zealous fury of the other assassins, but this one was different. Unsheathing his blades, the assassin held a scimitar in one hand and a short sword in the other.

Edward ignored the short sword. Wielding two weapons at once was difficult, almost impossible. Most used the second weapon for defense, to parry incoming strikes. Gerard was the only man Edward had ever seen wield two blades with enough precision to make both blades a threat.

He rushed forward, utilizing his great strength to overcome his enemy, but the assassin deftly parried. Twisting around, the assassin lunged with his short sword, the blade slipping under his shoulder where two metal plates came together. Howling, Edward stumbled back and barely managed to parry the next blow. The assassin launched into an attack with almost supernatural speed, his blades becoming a whirlwind of iron, and Edward was beaten back again.

He had underestimated the assassin. Brute strength alone would not be enough. He focused on parrying the blows and waited for the assassin to commit with his scimitar. When the attack came, Edward parried it, and then turned to the side to avoid the lunging short sword. He launched forward, his shoulder crashing into the man's chest and knocking him to the ground, but the assassin rolled back to his feet before Edward could press his advantage.

***

Geoffrey lifted Josephine into the saddle of the horse beside Micah, and began mounting his own steed when he heard Edward's yell. He twisted his head, words for the knight to quickly dispatch his

118

foe hovering on his lips. The words caught in his throat when he saw the fight raging in front of the house.

Edward was the strongest man Geoffrey had ever known. He combined this strength with the incredible speed the blood gave him. Geoffrey had seen Edward single-handedly dispatch four enemies at once during the siege of Akka. But as fast as he was, the assassin was faster. And what the assassin didn't have in strength, he made up for in skill. Edward rained down powerful blows of his sword, but each swing was countered by the assassin's blade. The assassin returned with quick ripostes, scoring several hits against the knight.

A cry of pain brought Geoffrey's attention to the battle raging around him. Two of the assassins had overtaken William. Gerard was just finishing up with another, but was too slow to save his fellow knight. William went down with the blade of a sword sticking from his gut.

Gerard howled and leapt on the assassins, finishing both of them and then looking around with rage in his eyes. Geoffrey could feel the bloodlust in his mind. Gerard had seen two of his fellow knights cut down in just as many minutes, and he wanted the enemy's blood in payment. Three more assassins were nearby, gathering themselves for a charge. The knight leapt, his sword arcing through the air and impaling one the moment his feet hit the ground. Spinning, his other blade whipped out and a second assassin fell. The third backed away, courage giving way to fear, but Gerard surged forward and drove his blade through the man's chest.

Two more assassins jumped to either side of Gerard, and Geoffrey cursed under his breath. "Finish him, Edward," he yelled, not looking at the knight. He pulled the reins and edged his horse to the battle raging between Gerard and the assassins. Gerard spun between them, his swords a blur in the night, and then one sword slashed through an assassin's throat. Geoffrey kicked out with his boot, connecting with the other assassin's head.

"Get mounted," he said. "We must ride out of here before more arrive."

Geoffrey turned to look back at Edward. The knight had just reached out a mailed fist and batted one of the assassin's blades to the side. Lunging, he aimed his sword for the body of his foe, but his enemy was too quick.

The assassin spun around and deflected the lunge with the blade of his short sword. Still spinning, he whipped his scimitar around with such speed it whistled in the air before connecting with the flesh of Edward's neck. The knight's body fell to the ground, his head following an instant later.

Shocked, Geoffrey could do no more than stare for a moment. The assassin turned to him. There was no smile on the man's lips, no look of victory in his eyes. His face held no emotion, but his eyes bore the cold, hard stare of death. "Quickly, man, mount up," he yelled at Gerard, his eyes still on the dangerous assassin.

Gerard's eyes followed his stare and went wide when they saw Edward's headless body lying still on the ground. More attackers poured from the darkness of the night surging around the assassin that stood over Edward's body. Geoffrey could see the hesitation in Gerard's form, the lust for vengeance in his eyes. For a moment, Geoffrey feared the knight might lose control and rush out to meet the assassins. But, to his relief, Gerard shook his head and mounted his horse. The French knight raised one of his blades into the air as a silent salute, squeezed the horse with his knees and sped off into the night.

Geoffrey reached over and tapped Josephine's horse with the flat of the blade. The beast surged forward, following Gerard's horse. Micah whispered a quick prayer and followed after them. Geoffrey spared one final glance at the fallen knights, made the sign of the cross, and then sent his own horse into motion.

CHAPTER ELEVEN

Zain ul-Baqir stood amidst the lifeless bodies and cursed. Victory had been within sight, but the demon knights managed to deflect the ambush. He wanted to race after them, to follow, to kill, but he knew that was the voice of battle lust and dismissed it. He counted the dead bodies. They had attacked with over two dozen men against a quarter as many knights. Now, a dozen of his men lay dead, and a half dozen more lay wounded. He had underestimated the power of the knights.

"Do we follow after them?" Umar asked.

Zain did not answer immediately. He stared in the direction the knights had fled as if, even now, he could see them riding further and further away. Sighing, he turned back to his companion.

"Look around, Umar, and tell me what you see?"

Umar surveyed the yard for a moment, silent and intent. "The bodies of our brothers, the bodies of three knights," he said. "A few injured," he added, "and several more just arriving from their posts behind the house."

"And tell me, Umar, what does it mean? How does it answer your question?"

Umar sighed. "We don't have enough."

"Exactly," Zain said. "It would be obvious if your mind was not riding the waves of the battle. You still have the feeling of invincibility that comes with battle. But we cannot allow these feelings to affect our judgment, else we make that fatal mistake."

Umar frowned, but nodded.

"I know, you still wish to ride onward and avenge our fallen brothers," Zain said. "As do I, brother Umar. There is nothing I would like more than to send those demon-knights to the hells they deserve, but we take aim on the whole, not just the few we fought here. We must keep our sight on that goal."

Zain turned and stared into the night. "If only those damned Hospitallers had arrived on time, we would have been victorious. Are you sure the knights knew the importance of acting swiftly?"

"The knight told me he would have a squad ready to ride at our request. Hadi was sent to inform him. He is a skilled guide and rode the fastest of our horses. He had more than enough time to reach the knights and guide them back here in time for the battle."

"Then something delayed them," Zain said. "Either that, or the knights were not as prepared as they had promised they would be." He spat on the ground. "This is what we get for putting our trust in those infidels."

"Zain!" He turned to see two of the men dragging the limp body of the merchant behind them. "We caught him trying to slip off into the hills at the edge of the village."

"Is he dead?"

"There weren't orders to kill him." They released their grasp on the merchant and let the body fall to the ground. One of the men tapped on the hilt of his scimitar and raised an eyebrow.

Zain pursed his lips. "No, let him live. He does us no good dead. I assume you searched him?"

"Of course. No weapons, and no sign of the book."

"Search the house for the book, though I doubt you will find it."

The fidais nodded. "And the merchant?"

"Drag him into the house. We will leave him here. We might have need of him later."

As the fidais dragged the unconscious body of the merchant into the house, Zain turned to Umar, "How many uninjured men do we have?"

"Seven," Umar replied, "and two more whose injuries are only light. Including myself."

"Damnation," Zain said. "Have one of our men watch the house and follow the merchant should he leave. I would prefer if we could leave two, but we cannot spare the extra man."

"You think the book might still be within the merchant's reach?"

"No," Zain replied. "But I want to be sure. Have the merchant watched for two days. If he does nothing of the ordinary in that time, have our man return to al- Kahf."

"And the bodies of the knights?"

"Burn them and spread their ashes across the hills."

Umar nodded and turned to leave, but Zain reached out and grabbed his elbow. "On second thought, leave four men and have them wait two weeks before returning."

Umar turned to look at Zain, his eyes questioning.

Zain smiled. "And choose men that are uncomfortably loyal to the Old Man."

Umar returned his smile. "Soon?" he asked.

"Very soon, I think. Tell the rest of the men we ride out within the hour. We will trail the knights from a comfortable distance. Perhaps, if we are lucky, we can track them to their day camp when their strength will be lost under the glare of the sun."

CHAPTER TWELVE

They galloped down the trail, not speaking, each dealing with what had happened in silence. The night echoed their mood with dark clouds covering the moon's light, threatening rain, and casting the land in a deep darkness.

Geoffrey was barely aware of the others. His mind was intent on what was behind them, not what lay ahead. He spared no glances behind him, knowing he would not spot the enemy with his eyes. Instead, he focused on the sounds of the night. He concentrated, eliminating all sounds he could account for from his hearing. No longer hearing the creak of the cricket's legs rubbing against their bodies, the whispering wings of a bird flying overhead, or the tapping of their horses' feet clattering against the ground, he listened for the sound of a hoof winding its way over the hills.

Slowly, Geoffrey became confident that the assassins did not trail close behind them and began to relax. But, with his mind no longer concentrating on the present danger, it slipped into the past.

Again, he saw Edward fall. This was the same knight that had defeated four men at the siege of Akka. Edward, the veteran of countless battles these past dozen years. Geoffrey had once witnessed Edward lift a dead horse in his arms and pitch it off the road as if it were no more than a sack of grain. And, now, he lay still in the front yard of a merchant, his head no longer attached to his body.

Geoffrey could not claim to have liked Edward. He was a rough man, a savage man, whose transformation had released that savagery. Geoffrey had to constantly keep the knight under control, else he run wild with the supernatural power invested in him. But, he was a Knight Templar, part of the Inner Circle. He was always there when needed, followed orders when given, and could be counted on in the heat of battle.

Edward was not the first of the Inner Circle to fall. Battle could be cruel, and despite their strengths, they were not invincible. However, Geoffrey had never seen an Inner Circle knight fall to a lone enemy in armed combat.

He again saw the assassin. Geoffrey recognized the man; he recognized that face, that confident poise, and that dangerous stare. His memory slipped back to the day Josephine arrived at their doorstep. The Isma'ilites had entered the courtyard when Geoffrey had opened the door. He had searched their eyes then and seen their confidence crack into fear at the sight of him.

All except that one. That one had stared back at him with eyes that betrayed no fear, only danger. At the time, he thought the assassin was foolish, ignorant of the power wielded by the knights. Now, he knew the assassin was simply confident in his own ability.

Geoffrey knew his enemy now. They had played cat and mouse with each other for the past several days, each judging what the other would do, how much they would allow, how they would react, and making decisions based on that knowledge. Geoffrey had been surprised by the attack at the uncle's house. He assumed the assassins would bide their time, waiting until confirmation the prize was in sight before launching their attack. He had guessed wrong. His enemy, like any great tactician, was a gambler. He had taken the chance that the prize was within grasp and seized the opportunity to attack with surprise. And he had almost been victorious.

Geoffrey sighed. His miscalculation had cost the life of Edward and the two young knights that had faithfully accompanied them on this journey. Perhaps, had he been more suspicious of an attack, they would have been better prepared. He should have left Edward outside with the others. There was little chance the younger knights could have spotted the Isma'ilites setting up their ambush, but Edward, whose eyes could cut through the shadows of the night, might have spotted them. They might all be riding away from the house, instead of just four of them.

Geoffrey put the thought out of his mind. There was no going back, no changing the past. He could only learn from the mistake and try his hardest not to repeat it in the future. He knew his enemy better now. The man would take risks to get what he wanted, and would not stop while breath was left in his body. And Geoffrey knew that, of all of their enemies, he was the danger. He was the threat.

Shaking these dire thoughts from his mind, Geoffrey glanced at Josephine and Micah riding side by side. Micah had done well. The young monk had calmed the uncle when he was on the verge of panic. When the chaos of battle sprayed forth, he had kept his wits about him, acting with a clear head and getting out of the way of the commencing battle. Geoffrey wondered if Micah had thought of picking up one of the swords of the fallen and joining in the battle.

He smiled. No, not Micah. His faith was strong. The priests and monks of the church were forbidden from drawing blood. It was a special mandate that allowed the knightly orders, the Templar and the Hospitaller, to bring death in the name of the Lord. For Micah to do so would have meant excommunication from the church and eternal damnation. Geoffrey thought about the conversation they had a few nights before. No, Micah would have let one of the assassins run him through before he would have picked up a blade to defend himself or anyone else.

Geoffrey leaned back in his saddle and let the night air pass over him. The muscles in his back, bunched into knots, finally began to relax. He let his mind wander for a time and then gathered his awareness to the present, putting his focus on their current situation.

Dawn was approaching. He could always sense when the sun began clawing its way over the horizon to reach up into the sky. He dug his knees into the side of his horse, winding his way around Micah and up beside Gerard, signaling for a halt.

They brought their horses to a stop and dismounted. The others remained silent, waiting for direction from Geoffrey. "Dawn approaches," he said.

Gerard nodded back at him. "Should we camp here, or should we ride further and look for a more suitable location?"

"I don't like staying so close to the road. The Isma'ilites may not be following close behind, but we can be sure that they will follow. We need to put some distance between our camp and the road and be sure to cover our tracks well."

"Backtrack?" Gerard asked.

"I think so," Geoffrey replied, nodding. "They were able to track us to the village. We can assume they will be able to track us this far and will take note of where the trail ends."

"Shouldn't we just continue riding?" Josephine asked. "If you are worried about me, you needn't be. I am not tired, I can ride for the rest of the day if the need exists."

"Geoffrey knows best," Micah said. "Help me with the horses. They are exhausted and need to be lathered before we make camp."

She looked at the horses. "They could continue on," she said. "We might need to slow our pace, but we need not stop completely."

Gerard exchanged a look with Geoffrey, and the older knight sighed. "You are tired, Josephine," he said. "The excitement and the ride have you all wound up, but soon your exhaustion will become too much for you."

"I can hold up," she said, but her words betrayed a sudden exhaustion coming over her.

"You are tired," he repeated. He moved his hand out slowly in front of him and her eyes trailed it. "You are more tired than you know. Even now,

130

you can feel the weight of your eyelids pressing down with a force you cannot resist."

"I can hold up," she said, but her eyelids fluttered, struggling to stay open.

Gerard caught her before she hit the ground and gently laid her down. Geoffrey turned to Micah to ask for his help, but the distant crack of a stick caught his attention. He tensed, his eyes searching the darkness. Beside him, Gerard drew his blades and moved protectively between the unconscious form of Josephine and the sound.

"Put your weapons away, Gerard de St. Amand." A dark figure flowed out of the darkness. Micah, startled, stumbled backward in fear.

Gerard ignored the command.

"Put your weapons away, Gerard. I do not think he is here to do us harm," Geoffrey said and, under his breath, added, "Nor do I think we could do anything if he did mean us harm."

Gerard glanced sharply at him. The words were uttered so lightly that the very wind would have obscured them, but Gerard's sharp ears had caught them. He hovered there a moment, swords still in hand, eyes on Geoffrey, a questioning look on his face. At Geoffrey's nod, he sheathed the swords.

The older knight stared at the stranger and recognized a smile of amusement pass across his face. The stranger approached, and then cast an odd look at Micah.

"He knows," Geoffrey said.

"I think I will gather some wood for a fire," Micah said.

"No fires tonight, we don't want to warn the enemy," Geoffrey said. He then glanced back at Micah and realized the monk was not interested in a fire. "But you can look for a stream. Perhaps we can refill our water supplies."

Micah nodded and sprinted off into the night. They both knew there was enough water to reach the monastery.

"What are you here for, old one?" Geoffrey asked.

Damon did not immediately respond. He tilted his head back and stared up into the night sky, breathing in deeply. "Dawn approaches," he said.

"Yes," Geoffrey replied. "We are gathering for camp."

The stranger sniffed the air. "Your enemies also approach."

Gerard's hands went back to the hilts of his swords but stopped there when the stranger laughed.

"They are still more than a league away," Damon said. "But they approach, nonetheless. It will be dangerous to camp here."

Geoffrey nodded. It would be dangerous to camp anywhere. They did not have the younger knights to guard them during the day. If the Isma'ilites happened upon their camp, they would not hesitate to attack.

"It would be better for the book to continue on to your monastery where it will be safe."

"I don't see how that is possible," Geoffrey said. "As you said, dawn approaches, and you know we cannot travel with the sun in the sky."

"I can," Damon said.

132

"What?" Geoffrey said. His voice was louder than he meant, and the word echoed back to him from the night air. He winced at the sound. "I assumed..."

"That I was one of you," Damon said. "That I am. And I am more."

"You speak in riddles, old man," Geoffrey said.

The stranger sighed. "When you have walked this earth for as long as I have, Geoffrey Furnivall, you will learn to walk in the shadow of the night even on the clearest of days. Until that time, you would do well to respect those that can."

An aura of power converged around the stranger. It wasn't something that could be seen, but it could be felt, and it was so powerful Geoffrey had to turn from the stranger. A few moments passed, and the aura faded. He could, again, look at the stranger, but this time he stared with a mixture of awe and fear.

"I see that you are beginning to understand, Geoffrey Furnivall," Damon said.

"Such power," Geoffrey gasped. He thought back to the battle earlier that night and realized that this stranger could have stood in the midst of that chaos without fear of danger or injury. "We could have used you earlier."

"I was busy," Damon said. "I don't think you would have fared as well as you did had the squadron of Hospitallers been allowed to arrive."

Gerard, silent until this moment, cast the stranger a sharp look. "So it is true they are aligned with the Isma'ilites?" He looked over to Geoffrey. "It is as we suspected."

133

"Yes," Damon said. "The Hospitaller conspire with the enemy to bring down the Templar." He smiled, and added, "But the time for that has not yet come, and you will find the Hospitaller not so eager to stand against you after this night."

Geoffrey sighed. "You want to take the girl," he said. "And Micah?"

"With the monk's help, you can go underground. You will be safe during the daylight hours, and I doubt any will concern themselves much with a solitary monk."

"And the book?" Geoffrey asked.

"It goes with the girl."

Somewhere deep inside of Geoffrey there was a voice, the voice of logic, the voice of reason, a voice still of this world that questioned handing the book and the girl over to this strange being. But Geoffrey was no longer of this world. He hadn't been for the past forty years, and that part of him that was no longer of the world assured him he was doing the right thing.

"So be it," he said. A surprised look passed over Gerard's face, but his fellow knight did not question his decision. "So be it," he repeated.

CHAPTER THIRTEEN

Sir Lothar Malle shifted in the chair, unable to get comfortable. It wasn't the chair; it was the environment. He tried to keep his eyes off Rashid-al-din Sinan. The leader of the Isma'ilites was taking a long puff on his hash pipe, a habit Lothar found both sinful and disgusting. He speared a piece of unrecognizable food and moved it around his plate, but was unwilling to eat the spicy food that caused his stomach problems.

Rashid-al-din exhaled a stream of smoke and smiled pleasantly. "I would offer you a taste," he said, "but I hear you Knights do not taste of the pleasures of the hashish."

"The body is the temple of God," Lothar said. "It goes against our beliefs."

The chief assassin smiled even wider. "I believe Allah created the hashish as an example of the pleasures awaiting them in the land beyond if they remain true in their faith. But, I have heard that you followers of Christ have different beliefs, and I respect them."

Lothar nodded. Several high-ranking knights in the Hospitaller hoped to convert the Old Man to Christianity. Rashid-al-din often invited the knights into his stronghold to speak of such matters, claiming the exchange of knowledge would help both of their people come to a better understanding of each other, but confiding in private he was intrigued and moved by the words of Christ.

Sir Jonathan Alderson, Lothar's superior, didn't believe any such thing, no matter how sincere his

135

fellow knights claimed the Old Man to be. He believed Rashid-al-din was simply playing a game with the knights, holding out hopes of conversion to buy the time needed to repel them. Lothar tended to agree with Jonathan. Seeing the Old Man in person, he felt assured that, although Rashid-al-din might turn his back on his religion, he would never turn his back on the hashish.

"You eat lightly, sir knight," Rashid-al-din said.

"I always eat light after a hard ride," Lothar lied. "I will break my fast in the morning with more heart."

"Well, then, if dinner is over, we can get down to business. What brings you to my abode? Do the knights have more news for me?"

Lothar hid a cough behind his hand. The assassins made him uncomfortable. He had hoped to speak his message upon arrival and ride out as quickly as possible. The old assassin had other plans. He insisted Lothar join him for dinner and not discuss business until they had eaten. Lothar knew this was not a matter of custom. The Old Man was stalling for time, but for what ends, he could not fathom.

"A squadron of our knights fell in battle several days ago," Lothar said. "They were riding out to assist your men in acquiring the prize and were ambushed in the night. The entire squadron was lost, including the Isma'ilite guide."

"This is dire news indeed," Rashid-al-din said.

Lothar knew it was not news to the chief assassin. Little escapes the eyes of the Old Man, especially the loss of one of his men. "There are some in the knights that suspect your followers were involved and that our knights were purposely led into an ambush."

Rashid-al-din Sinan's dull eyes flashed in anger.

"My lord, Sir Jonathon Alderson, dismisses these rumors, of course," Lothar added. They could ill afford to alienate the assassins at this point. "However, the loss has caused him to lose favor with some in our order, making it difficult for him to continue offering his full support on these matters. Sir Jonathon wishes to be reassured on the progress of the mission. Have you been able to obtain the book we seek?"

"I received word earlier this day that our agents were unable to retrieve the book." His eyes burned with an inner light, and Lothar knew this was a sore point. "We are certain that the Knights now hold the book."

"This is unacceptable," Lothar said. He choked back his words. It would not do to show anger in these halls.

An Isma'ilite approached the old assassin and whispered in his ear. Rashid-al-din nodded and turned his attention back to Lothar. "I understand your displeasure at our failure to obtain the book," Rashid-al-din said. "I assure you, the Isma'ilites do not tolerate such failure. I have word that one comes who can better explain the events of the last few nights. I believe you will find this to be very informative."

Lothar followed the chief assassin's gaze to a dark figure approaching the table. "Zain, you return from your mission," Rashid-al-din said. "Please, give us the details. Have you brought the book?"

Zain looked at Lothar and his eyes smoldered. Rashid-al-din knew his assassin had failed and was forcing him to explain that failure in front of an outsider. And Lothar knew the Old Man's show was meant for him as much as for his followers.

"The book still eludes our grasp," Zain said, his voice cool and crisp. "But, I suspect, you already knew that."

"Tell us how this comes to pass," Rashid-al-din said.

"We watched the monastery for days, spotting no unusual activity. Finally, on the fifth day, three knights arrived at the setting of the sun. The following night, our watchers were set upon by a pack of wolves that savagely attacked the men, forcing them to retreat to our camp. The next day seemed to go by without incident, but because of a break in their normal patterns, I felt it important to investigate further."

"You should have investigated sooner," Rashid-al-din interrupted.

"We were well aware the knights may have used the wolves as a distraction." The assassin's eyes burned at the rebuff. "It was, after all, our intention to let them lead us. I investigated and found horses missing in the stables. I searched the inside of the monastery and found evidence that only one man was still within the walls. The knights are restricted to traveling only at night, and we knew we could easily track them to their destination."

"Yes, yes," Rashid-al-din said, "Your messenger informed me of all this."

"We tracked the knights to the village of the merchant," Zain said. "While the knights searched the house, one of our assassins, using the guise of a lowly native, woke the magistrate. He informed the man that there was unusual activity at the house and learned the girl had kin in a nearby village."

"This was information we did not have," he said. "Guessing the knights' destination, we dispatched a messenger to the Hospitaller. We planned to ambush the Templar after they had finished their business in the next village. The infidel's stay at the house was short, only a matter of an hour. This confirmed our belief that they had found the book. Even though the Hospitaller had not arrived, we carried through with our attack."

"And failed," Rashid-al-din said.

"We cut down three of their knights, but the rest eluded us," Zain said.

Lothar gave the man credit; he did not offer an excuse for his failure. He stood ready to take whatever punishment for failure his master deemed appropriate, but another assassin approached the high table before Rashid-al-din could reply. This one Lothar recognized. It was the messenger, Umar.

"Our brother speaks humbly," Umar said. "In truth, three of those we faced were demon-spawn. And when the knights retreated, one of those demons lay dead at the hands of our brother."

"You slew one of the Inner Circle?" Lothar asked. He had witnessed the Templar in action during several battles over the years. They were fierce warriors, and those of the Inner Circle possessed supernatural strength and speed. "How did you manage this? And what did you do with the body?"

"The bodies of the knights were burned, their ashes spread." Zain turned to face Lothar, and the knight could see hatred in his eyes. "How did I manage it?" He tapped the hilts of his two swords. "With these, knight. And we would have slain the rest had your brothers arrived at the battle."

"A full squadron of knights were sent to your aid," Lothar said. "They were set upon by enemies before they could arrive."

"Enemies?" Zain asked. "The Templar dispatched no messengers while we watched them. What enemies set upon your knights?"

"Whoever they battled hauled away their dead from the field," Lothar said. "We found no sign of the enemy, only our own dead, and the dead body of your messenger. The knights we sent were handpicked, veterans of many battles. It must have been a sizable force to have defeated them."

"So," Rashid-al-din said, his voice humming. "You see the full extent of your failure, brother Zain. You failed us once at the house of the merchant, letting the girl run to the demons and thus enlightening them to our mission. You failed us again in letting the Templar out of your sights. And you failed us a third time, letting yourself be maneuvered into an ambush fated for defeat.

"We do not accept failure lightly, brother Zain. You seem to have become distracted as of late. This distraction has led you to failure, and we cannot accept that. For your failure you will be taken to the dungeon where you may pray for Allah's forgiveness while I meditate on your judgment."

Rashid-al-din Sinan stood up and leaned over the table to look his follower in the eyes. "I do not think your prayers will be heard, brother Zain," he said. "But you are still welcome to pray even if it will not do your soul much good." He turned to Zain's companion. "I trust you are still loyal to us, Umar?"

Umar bowed his head. "Yes, master."

"Then take him to the dungeons," Rashid-al-din said. He sat back down and watched Umar lead Zain from the hall. Smiling, he turned to Lothar. "So you see how we deal with failure."

***

Umar stopped walking and turned to Zain. "What do we do?" he whispered.

"Keep walking, brother," Zain said. "For now, do as you have been told and escort me to the dungeon."

They continued to walk down the many twisting halls of the fortress, and came to the stairs that led down to the dungeons. When they had passed down a dozen steps, Zain slowed his pace and turned to his friend.

"When you have left me at the dungeon, get word to Nizam al-Qadmus."

"He already knows," Umar replied. "He was within the hall, taking a post as one of the guards."

Zain smiled. "How many of ours were posted as guards?"

"Not as many as we would have liked," Umar said. "But enough, I think. We did not know what would happen, but feared the worst and made our preparations in case you were forced into action."

"Our leader is a fool," Zain hissed. "The hashish has dulled his mind. He hopes to show his power by imprisoning me before my execution. He means to send a message to all those that have disloyal thoughts, but he has succeeded only in strengthening our plan. He has given us the time to work out all of the details."

"How long?"

"Soon, I think," Zain said. "Very soon."

CHAPTER FOURTEEN

The monastery came into view, and Geoffrey sighed in relief. He had hardly drawn a breath during their ride, his body tense for what awaited him. But the monastery looked the same as they had left it a few days ago. There was no blood in the air. And, even from this distance, he would have caught the scent had even the barest drop been shed.

"We're home." He let his horse slow into a soft trot.

Micah smiled, and Geoffrey was glad to see a light brighten his eyes. Micah had stayed awake throughout the day guarding them from any danger. The monk had not complained during their ride, but Geoffrey knew he was ready to collapse during the last leg of their journey.

They led their horses to the stables, and only after they were well-brushed and fed did they approach the monastery. Geoffrey knew the instant he stepped foot into the building that something was wrong. There was a strange feeling in the building and a touch of fear in the air.

Was it Josephine? He should have never let that strange man take her from them. And yet, what could he have done? He had stood before the man and tasted his power, and it was unlike anything he had ever witnessed on this Earth. Damon would have killed him as easily as squashing a spider beneath his boot.

He glanced at Gerard. The French knight frowned, and his eyes smoldered. He felt it too.

Geoffrey nodded and led them through the dark halls to the back of the monastery.

Sir Michael was slumped at the table. His hair was greasy and matted to his head, his eyes red from a night spent without sleep. Geoffrey gripped the hilt of his broadsword and scanned the room for any hint of danger. "The girl?"

"She's here," the knight replied. He smiled, but the smile was not reflected in his eyes. "She's around somewhere."

Geoffrey approached and put his hand on the man's shoulder. "You've heard about Christoffe, William and Edward?"

The knight nodded.

"They died defending us from an ambush. Without their brave acts, I believe all of us would have fallen. They fought well, taking many heathens down before they finally fell."

Geoffrey stared at the younger knight. Perhaps his appearance was borne simply out of grief? But the distant sound of a footstep brought a look of fear to the young knight's face, and Geoffrey knew grief was only part of it. A tingling sensation caressed the back of his neck. He sensed approaching danger. He heard Gerard slipping his blades out of their scabbards and knew he felt it as well.

A moment later, the door burst open and Josephine appeared. Had Geoffrey not ridden with her these past few days, he might not have recognized the woman that walked into the room. Gone was the girl that walked with her head bent slightly to the ground and stared out at the world with sad, serious eyes. That girl had been replaced by a woman who walked with head held high, moving with a seductive grace that accentuated the curve of her hips.

"You are back." She smiled.

Geoffrey exchanged a sharp glance with Gerard. They both recognized the change. He turned to the young knight slumped at the table. "Michael, you are tired. Get some rest."

"Yes, sir." The knight bowed and left the room.

Geoffrey was about to say the same to Micah, but the sad look in the young monk's eyes stopped his words. Micah knew his limits and would excuse himself if he thought it best to leave. He could tell the monk knew what had happened, and Geoffrey would not begrudge the monk his wishes if he wanted to stay.

He turned back to Josephine. "You've changed."

Her eyes sparkled with mirth and she laughed. "That I have, Sir Knight." She danced between them, brushing a hand against Geoffrey's shoulder, and took a seat in one of the chairs. "I didn't know you knights kept such wonderful secrets."

Geoffrey frowned, but he did not begrudge her joy. Well he remembered the time of his own changing when his veins seemed filled with raw power instead of mere blood. The first days of the changing were spent in a deep euphoria, the mind trying to adapt to its newfound abilities while the body exulted in it.

"Tell us how it happened," he said.

"I'm sure you know. I drank the blood of life, and the life was reborn within me."

Geoffrey took a seat opposite her. "Tell us."

Micah and Gerard took seats at the table. Josephine remained silent, staring at each of them in turn. When she came to Micah an odd expression came over her face. "You are not like us."

"No." His eyes widened, and his hand made the sign of the cross.

Josephine shrank back as if he had struck her a physical blow. Geoffrey knew the two of them had grown close in the past week, very close, and the monk's reaction took her by surprise. Perhaps for the first time since it happened she realized the enormity of the change.

"How did this happen?" Geoffrey asked.

"I..." She looked confused, apprehensive. Doubt entered her eyes. "I awoke in the afternoon in my room. I was scared at first. I had no memory of how I came to be at the monastery. I had a wild thought that we had been attacked again and I had been injured, but I was not in pain nor could I see any wounds.

"Getting dressed, I walked about the monastery searching for you. I still felt tired, like I had not slept much the night before, and wasn't even sure what day it was. The halls were empty, and the fear I had woken with grew. And then, I saw him. Damon. At first, I thought he was a priest. I'm not sure why, though, for he did not dress like one, or even talk like one.

"I was worried when I first spotted him, but he assured me that the three of you were all right. You had sent me on ahead while you remained behind to ensure that we were not followed. He said I had fallen asleep on the way here, but I didn't remember any of it.

"He assured me that this was understandable, given what I had been through, and we fell to talking. He urged me to talk of my parents and my sisters, much like the discussions I had with Micah.

"We talked for several hours. He was easy to talk to, and the words seemed to flow out of me at his beckoning. I spoke of my mother and my father and my dear little sisters and of their cruel deaths at the hands of those heathens. He..."

She stopped and looked down.

"It's alright." Gerard laid his hand on hers. "We understand, but we need to hear what happened."

She took a deep breath. "He asked me if the memories brought fear of my own death. I hadn't thought about it like that, but after he asked, I realized it did. I don't know, I guess I'd never really thought about death until it happened. And, though I grieved for my family, somewhere deep inside of me I also feared for myself.

"He asked me, if there was something I could do to evade death, would I choose to do it, knowing that it would delay being reunited with my family in Heaven." Her lower lip trembled. "I said I would choose life."

Geoffrey clenched his hand in anger, but he hid it under the table. Had he known last night what Damon had planned... but there was nothing he could have done about it. "Did he tell you of the price you must pay?"

"The price. Yes, he was quite clear on that. He insisted I be fully aware of the price before I agreed to it. He said that, to walk among the living for so long a time I must drink the blood from those about me." She glanced at Micah and then averted her eyes. "But he said they need not die from it. He said only a taste of the blood would do. That's true, isn't it? I don't have to kill anyone, do I?"

"No," Geoffrey said. "You don't have to kill anyone."

She sighed. "I don't think I could do that," she said. "I know I couldn't do that. But he said it was not necessary to drink so deeply. He also said that I must walk in the darkness of shadow, else I will grow weak. Is that why we only traveled at night?"

Gerard nodded.

"I don't understand," she said. "I saw him in the full of daylight, but he said that I would wither under it. He said it would be ages before I was able to look up into the sky and peer at the sun without feeling the pain within my soul."

"He spoke the truth," Geoffrey said. "He is the only one of us I have met that wasn't burdened by that curse. Perhaps, in time, we all overcome that weakness, but these many decades have not given me the power to walk under the sun as if it were night, and I suspect it would be decades, even centuries, before I could dream to do so."

She nodded. "I agreed to the price." She bowed her head. "He said that, in exchange, I would never grow old, never grow sick, and would heal quickly from any wounds I should suffer. He said I would gain strength and speed and, though death would remain a possibility, it could be evaded for centuries if I was careful."

148

She stopped talking and looked at Micah, searching his eyes. "It seemed a small price to pay for what was gained."

Micah didn't immediately respond. He glanced away, staring off into a corner of the room. And when he did finally speak, the words dripped from his lips as if he feared what he was saying, but knew it must be spoken.

"I have lived for many years with this knowledge. I do not condemn you, dear Josephine, but I do not envy you either. Long ago, man was cast out of paradise for his weakness. We pay for that in many ways, one of which is our mortality. I fear any breach of that payment is an affront to God.

"I watch over these knights, knowing full well what they are, and I do my best to protect them and keep them safe. Funny how that sounds, a mere monk keeping armed men safe, but it is true.

"Last night, I helped dig two pits into the earth. I watched as Sir Geoffrey and Sir Gerard descended into them, and then used my hands to pour the earth back into the holes, covering them completely. I packed the earth tightly back into the ground, and then I spread out my blankets over the freshly dug earth to conceal them. I sat upon those two graves, and I guarded over them the best I could through the long hours of the day.

"But the one weakness I can never protect them from are the sins of the soul. I do not pretend to know the mind of our Lord. The gift you now bear may be his blessing, or it may be the enticement of the serpent that led to our expulsion from that

149

paradise. But I do fear the answer, and it is that fear you see in my eyes when you look at me."

"You must despise me." She slumped onto the table. "I am a pitiful thing who would drink the blood of the living to sustain her own life."

Micah reached across the table and placed his hand on the back of her neck. "I told you I did not know the mind of our Lord. I would not pay this price because I fear it could be the lure of the serpent, but I must also remember the teachings of our Savior, who bade his followers to drink his blood and eat of his flesh to salvage their own immortality.

"Don't think I have not been so tempted myself." He glanced at Geoffrey. "I have given thought to the gift you now bear. I have thought of life unending, and I have thought of the sun and the flowers and my garden. It's much too harsh a price to pay for immortality that I would have to live my life in darkness. I have thought of the gift and I have declined it. I did so under my own terms. You have accepted it under your own terms, and now you must bear the gift, and the curse that accompanies it."

"Thank you," she whispered.

Geoffrey knew Micah's forgiveness was a greater gift to her than what Damon had given her. "Could you tell us what happened afterward?" he asked.

"Yes," she said. "After I drank of his blood I felt... wonderful. How do I describe it? I felt on fire with passion, as if there was nothing I could not accomplish were I to set my path to it.

150

"He seemed amused by this. I admit, I said some silly things. I talked of tracking down the murderers of my family and bringing justice to them, and I talked of traveling the world and doing what I could to see that murder did not come to the innocent, and I talked of many other things, some serious, some not.

"Finally, my mind turned to the book. The book had been bought with the blood of my family, and I asked him if he knew of it. He said he did. He said he knew much about the book. He said it contained many secrets of the world, secrets that would prove very dangerous if uncovered right now."

"Did he tell you of these secrets?" Geoffrey asked.

She shook her head. "He said it contained the secrets about us, but seemed to speak in riddles when he spoke about the book."

Geoffrey laughed. "Yes, that he did."

"He said something, right before he left, that I found very strange at the time. He said the book was still not safe, that it still had not found its destination and would continue to travel on its path, and that I would have to accompany it on this part of the journey.

She frowned. "He said I was chosen for this, but I don't know if he meant the book had chosen me, or someone else."

"Most likely, he chose you," Geoffrey said.

"He said the book was not yet safe in the Holy Land. Soon, he said, it would be safe here and it could return, but for now it must continue its journey."

CHAPTER FIFTEEN

The horse trotted the path, and Father David gaped at the landscape. With each rock they passed, he asked himself, "Did our Lord once sit upon that rock?" And each tree gave rise to the thought, "Was it even a sapling when our Gospel was just spreading out from this place?"

An uncomfortable grunt from Cardinal Vick told him his companion was not having the same thoughts. The Cardinal stared idly at the landscape, a permanent scowl on his face. For the past decade, the Cardinal had petitioned his superiors for a mission that would take him to the Holy Land. He was not amused by the irony that his mission had been granted two years after the Holy City had fallen.

Father David had heard the Cardinal's complaints nightly during their long travels across the sea. He knew his companion stared around him through eyes bitter from years of refusal and did not see the inner beauty that sprung from each blade of grass and hid behind each grain of sand.

Cardinal Vick swung his scowling face in Father David's direction. "What did that knight, that Hospitaller, say about this place?"

Father David was not paying attention. "Who?"

"The knight." Cardinal Vick's tone held a note of irritation. "What did he say about those within the monastery?"

"He said they have a woman staying with them." David made the sign of the cross at having to utter such words after his holy thoughts.

"A woman with them." Cardinal Vick nodded. "And he mentioned they might have been involved in the disappearance of a score Knights Hospitaller."

"I was unclear on why he thought these knights were connected with that," David said. "The woman we will see with our own eyes, but even the knight admitted that there was no evidence to connect the Templar with the attack on the Hospitaller. No bodies of the enemy were found at the site of the battle."

"The Hospitaller will take any opportunity to spread rumor about the Templar," Cardinal Vick said. "It is obvious that whoever attacked their knights wanted their identity to remain a secret. That is far from linking it directly to the Templar, but enough for the Hospitaller to whisper gossip into the church's ears."

"Why is that?" David asked. "The Templar and the Hospitaller are both here with the same mission. Why would the Hospitaller go out of their way to spread these rumors?"

"Money," Cardinal Vick said. "Power. Both of which the Templar have in far greater amounts than the Hospitaller. The Knights Templar are the military arm of the church and the advisors of kings, and with that position comes jealousy from their rivals."

"If these rumors are born out of jealousy, why is the church so interested in investigating them?"

The Cardinal turned and regarded the priest before responding. "The church does not take lightly to words of heresy and corruption," he said.

"It takes these matters very seriously, and an investigation is warranted. Very often, truth is revealed within the words of jealousy. We will investigate these rumors and seek out that truth, if it exists."

Father David nodded. But he knew the church was as wary of the Templar's growing power as were their brother-knights. The Knights Templar had made many enemies in their rise to power. The most powerful enemy might be the bishops of the very church they served. The bishops felt the Templar abused their papal privilege, were jealous of the exemption of the Templar from tithe payment and outraged by the breaking of ecclesiastical interdicts. Feeling their own power being undermined by the Templar, the bishops had marked them as an enemy.

David was new to his priesthood, barely in his third year of serving the Lord. The thought of politics within the church churned his stomach. He had made his vows with the idea of being a guide to those who wished to pass through the gates of Heaven, not to squabble with fellow priests. Politics was for cardinals, not priests, who concerned themselves more with the saving of the faithful. Yet he couldn't help but be a little glad that the current politics allowed him the opportunity to journey to the Holy Land.

"Look." The Cardinal pointed off in the distance where the top of the monastery could be seen peeking over a hill. "We should arrive soon, just in time for dinner I think."

The two of them stared at the monastery as they approached. Like many of the Templar buildings, it was formed in the shape of a circle and ringed with a small wall. In the back of the monastery was a small stable and, in the front, the great double doors led into the building. They approached these doors and dismounted, the priest holding the reins of the horses while the Cardinal knocked on those great doors.

"Hello?" The doors opened a crack, and neither the Cardinal nor the priest were able to penetrate the shadow of the building. "Oh." There was a note of surprise in the voice. The doors sprung open and a monk stepped into view. "Come in, Cardinal. Come in, Father."

Cardinal Vick raised an eyebrow and glanced at the horses.

"Oh yes, the horses," the monk said. "I will take them around back and get them settled. The two of you must have journeyed hard to make it here. Step out of the sun and rest. I will be back momentarily."

The Cardinal exchanged a look with the priest, and they stepped into the shadow of the building. The sunlight from outside barely penetrated into the interior of the building, and, though still daylight outside, the room needed to be lit by torches.

"Strange," Cardinal Vick said.

"What?" David asked. His voice echoed through the empty hall.

Cardinal Vick frowned at him. "The building has no windows."

David looked around. "So it doesn't." He felt a sudden discomfort. He had been in many different churches throughout the land, but this one felt different somehow. There was no feeling of holiness here, only an ominous sense of foreboding.

***

Micah took the reins of both horses and led them around to the stables. He remained calm, though the unexpected visit by the Cardinal and the priest had taken him by surprise. It was not unheard of for the church to pay a visit to their monastery, but for them to have sent a cardinal did not bode well. Micah knew that the Hospitaller and the Templar were political enemies in the church, and it would not surprise him if a rumor started by the Hospitaller spawned this visit.

He led the horses into two of the empty stalls in the very front of the stables and poured out a generous helping of grain for each of them. Knowing he should not leave the guests unattended for long, Micah still took the time to scratch between the ears of one horse and pat the other horse lightly on the nose. He liked horses. There were no secrets between them. If a horse didn't like you he let you know by biting at your hand while you fed him, trying to buck you off when you rode, or generally being irritable toward you. There were no secrets and, thus, no reason to lie to them.

Micah sighed. He knew his work here with the knights was God's work, but he disliked the sin necessary in dispensing his duties. "Thou shalt not bear false witness against thy neighbor," he whispered, exiting the stable. He looked up at the sky. It was still early evening, and the clouds that had gathered earlier in the day had all but disappeared, leaving the sun to shine with great brilliance in the western sky. He took in a breath and let the glory of the declining day fill him before returning to the monastery.

"I'm sorry about the odd greeting," he said. "We've been having some problems with the Saracens lately. A few weeks back, some of the knights clashed with the heathens. Three of the knights were lost in the battle, and we've been wary since."

"Understandable." The Cardinal exchanged a sharp glance with the priest, and Micah understood the underlying thoughts. They had not given much thought to the dangers of the land in their travels to the monastery.

"I am Brother Micah." He bowed in introduction.

"I am Cardinal Vick, and this is Father David."

"Let me show you to our dining hall and prepare a meal for you. I am sure you are famished after your journey."

"That would be excellent," Cardinal Vick responded, following him through the empty halls to the back of the monastery. Micah showed them to the dining table and left them momentarily to prepare a quick meal. He brought back two plates filled with sweet meats and cheeses.

"Is there no one else here?" Cardinal Vick asked.

"There are several knights," Micah said. "I am afraid you have come at a frantic time, however. The knights were up late in council."

The words had barely left his lips when the door opened and Sir Michael walked into the room. The knight was not wearing the chain mail or tabard of his position, but he had a broad sword fastened to his belt. The scabbard clinked against the leather leggings and Micah winced. Their guests must think them barbarous to wear weapons within the house of the Lord.

"Cardinal Vick and Father David, may I present Sir Michael," he said.

Michael nodded to the pair. "God bless you, Cardinal, and Father. It is good to see fellow Christians in these times of trouble."

"We've heard that you recently clashed with the heathens?"

"Yes. I am sorry to say that we lost three of our own to them." Michael frowned. "I was not at the battle, but I hear the fighting was fierce. Our knights were ambushed outside the house of a merchant, the uncle of a young woman to whom we have given sanctuary."

"A woman?" Cardinal Vick asked.

"Yes, Cardinal," Micah said. "The woman's family was foully murdered during the night. She was able to escape and found her way here where the knights have offered their protection to her, fearing she is still in danger. It is believed these same men were those who attacked the knights."

"Why all the interest in this woman?" Cardinal Vick asked.

"We are not sure," Micah said. "The knights were investigating that very thing when they were attacked. Sir Geoffrey could answer your questions better than I. He has been ill for the past two days, but perhaps he is recovered enough to speak with you."

"I don't want to put a strain on him if he is ill," Cardinal Vick said.

"He should be strong enough," Micah said. "He was feeling better early this morning, but decided to retire early to build his strength. I will check to see if he is still awake."

Micah left the pair in Michael's care and hastened to the area of the monastery he usually avoided. He came to a room at the far end of one of the halls, reached into the pockets of his robe, and took out a key. He stepped inside and carefully locked the door again. He would not leave it unlocked for any longer than needed. The room was empty, the bed not slept in, but Micah's attention was not on the bed, it was on the corner of the room opposite the door.

He took cautious steps to the corner and then bent down, feeling on the ground until his hand discovered the small latch concealed in the wood. He lifted the trapdoor, careful not to make the slightest noise when he rested it against the wall.

His heart pounding, he climbed down the stairs. The hidden basement was covered in the darkest of shadows, but Micah did not bear a torch. His hand rested on the wall beside him, and he used his hand to guide his way into those shadows. He had just turned the corner of the dark hallway when he felt a sudden chill embrace him.

"Micah." The voice sounded hollow within the shadows.

"Geoffrey?"

"It is I, Micah," Geoffrey said. "What trouble brings you here?"

"A cardinal and a priest have paid us a visit," Micah said. He had only once before stepped foot into these halls, and the fear he felt had not receded in the repetition. "They are asking questions. I thought it best that you make an appearance."

The shadows were silent, and then, "I will be up momentarily."

Micah wanted to bolt out of that place, but he held strong against his fear. "I have informed them that you are not feeling well. If you should feel too weak..."

"Very good, Micah," Geoffrey said. "The fear of disease should make their stay a short one." Micah hadn't thought of this, but realized it was true. Those newly arrived from Europe were often cautious not to catch a strange disease. "I will inform Gerard and will be there soon. The sun does not touch the halls of the monastery, and there is only an hour left before it dips below the horizon. I will be weak, but I should be able to overcome it."

"I will let them know," Micah said. Turning, he rushed up the stairs and out into the monastery proper, eager to be rid of the chill and the fear of the basement.

He returned to the dining area. "Sir Geoffrey should be with us momentarily."

"I hope he is feeling well?" Cardinal Vick asked.

"He is better," Micah said, "but the sickness has left him tired."

"What manner of disease is this he suffers from?" Father David asked.

"We have been unable to determine the nature of the sickness," Micah said. "It brought weakness and loss of appetite, but few other symptoms. It is not uncommon for the knights to become afflicted with a strange disease for a few days. They are so often in the presence of blood and death that disease seems to be just one of their many enemies."

Father David nodded and was about to ask another question when Geoffrey entered the room. The knight looked pale and walked with slow steps but smiled at the visiting priests. "I apologize that I was not able to greet you sooner, good sirs. I fear you have come at a bad time and found our house in disorder."

"Think nothing of it." Cardinal Vick rose from the table to help the knight into one of the many chairs.

"Do you think you are up to eating something, Sir Geoffrey?" Micah asked. He had a hopeful look in his eyes, but Geoffrey shook his head.

"I hope we have not gotten you out of your bed needlessly," Cardinal Vick said, returning to his own place at the table. "We were curious as to why a young woman is stalked by the heretics, and Micah mentioned you might be able to shed more light on this puzzle."

"I am afraid I will give you more questions than answers, Cardinal," Sir Geoffrey said. His voice wavered from the effort of speaking. "You know of the Isma'ilites?"

"I have heard of them," Cardinal Vick said. "They are led by someone called the Old Man?"

"The Old Man of the Mountain," Sir Geoffrey said. "They are skilled assassins and have often been a thorn in our side during these many years in the Holy Lands. We believe they were involved in the murder of the young woman's family, though for what reason we have been unable to find."

He coughed, and it was a few moments before he was able to continue. "We hoped to find out more from her uncle, but were savagely attacked when we approached the house. I do not know what they seek from the girl, but it is apparent that she remains in danger from them. We had hoped she would be able to take shelter with her uncle, her only kin in these parts, but we now fear she will not be safe in these lands and must soon return to England."

"The road back to England is dangerous for a woman," Sir Michael said.

"Yes, and we knights are few," Geoffrey said. "The Peace of Ramla will not last long with the death of Salah al-Din this fall. And the assassination of Conrad of Montferrat has us on edge. The Isma'ilites are clearly becoming more active."

Micah watched the Cardinal grow alarmed and suppressed an urge to smile. Geoffrey was making it seem as though he wanted to give Josephine into the care of the priests. The thought of a strange woman, hunted by assassins, traveling with them alarmed the Cardinal. They were not knights. They were men of the cloth and could hardly protect the woman.

"We are, unfortunately, not due back to Europe for many weeks, perhaps months." The words rushed from Cardinal Vick's lips. "We would be happy to accompany her at that time."

"I fear she would be in too much danger staying here that much longer," Geoffrey said. "I am sure one of the knights can be spared to pay escort to her."

"If she be a good Christian woman, she deserves no less," Cardinal Vick said.

"Where is this woman?" Father David asked. "Has she, also, retired early?"

"She began feeling ill early this morning and has been in bed most of the day," Geoffrey said. He turned to the monk. "Micah, have you had time to check on Lady Josephine?"

"I looked in on her an hour ago and she slept," Micah said. "I can check on her again, if you need to speak with her?"

Geoffrey turned a questioning gaze on the Cardinal, who frowned and shook his head. "No, that will not be needed. I would not wish to wake her, and I am sure you are doing everything you can."

The room fell silent for a moment, and Geoffrey took the opportunity to turn the conversation to matters of the church. He asked about several high-ranking cardinals, inquiring to their health, and gathering information of recent rulings made by the church. It was obvious the Cardinal wanted to turn the discussion back around to the recent happenings with the Templar, but Geoffrey adeptly managed the conversation for another hour before allowing the priest to continue his questions.

"We came upon a Knight Hospitaller with a strange story earlier this week," Cardinal Vick said, when he finally got the chance. He was about to add more when the door opened and Gerard entered the room.

"Sir Gerard." Geoffrey coughed lightly and rose to his feet. "What news do you bring us?"

"Sir." Gerard bowed. He glanced at the two priests, appearing surprised at their presence, and nodded gravely to them. "I am sorry to disturb you."

"Think nothing of it," Geoffrey said. "We are eager to hear what news you have gathered."

"As you asked, I spent the day searching the hills," Gerard said. "I spotted two men watching the monastery closely. I was unable to get close enough to tell, but I believe they were Isma'ilites."

"Did they spot you?" Geoffrey asked.

"I don't believe so," Gerard said.

"This is dire news indeed," Geoffrey said. "The assassins continue to have an interest in the woman, it seems. We must get her to safety as soon as possible."

Geoffrey sat down, his gaze staring through the walls, lost in his own thoughts. Gerard bowed to the priests and left, while an uncomfortable silence descended upon the room. Finally, Geoffrey turned back to the Cardinal. "I am sorry, Cardinal Vick, you were saying?"

"I, uh," the Cardinal stammered. He pursed his lips and then began again. "We heard a tale of a troop of Knights Hospitaller that were lost in battle several days ago. They were out on patrol, apparently, and were ambushed by an unknown enemy. There were no survivors."

"What night was this?" Geoffrey asked.

"The knight said, uh, a week ago?"

Geoffrey frowned, his entire face going dark except for a strange light glittering in his eyes. The intensity of his thoughts left the others in the room momentarily taken aback until he broke out into a long coughing fit that left him gasping for air. He turned back to the Cardinal when he finally found his voice. "We were attacked a week ago as well," he said. "I had assumed it was connected to the woman, but if our brother-knights were also attacked on the same night, perhaps there is more trouble brewing than I first suspected."

The Cardinal frowned at Father David. Micah could imagine their thoughts. Neither expected to become embroiled in the troubles of the land, and both must have assumed the roads to be relatively safe. This talk of fighting was putting them on edge.

"It is getting late," Cardinal Vick said. "Father David and I have been traveling all day, and I fear I am tiring earlier than normal."

"Of course." Geoffrey rose from his chair, but staggered with his first step. He put a hand on the table to steady himself. "Brother Micah, would you show them to their rooms?"

"Right this way, sirs," Micah said.

They were at the door when Geoffrey's voice stopped them. "Cardinal?"

"Yes, Sir Knight?"

"I fear it is dangerous for you to travel alone on these roads. With your permission, I would like to send Sir Michael, here, with you as escort, at least until you reach your next destination."

The Cardinal smiled, relieved. "That would be most appreciated, Sir Geoffrey."

Micah showed them to their rooms. Neither spoke a single word during the walk, but Micah noticed several silent looks between the two. He would not be surprised to see them up early in the morning and ready to be off on their travels.

After being assured that they needed nothing else from him, Micah returned to the same locked door he had gone through earlier. He had a key in the pocket of his robe, but he did not use it. Instead, he knocked lightly.

"Come in," Geoffrey said.

Micah scurried into the room and went to join Josephine who was perched at the end of the bed. Geoffrey was pacing the center of the room, and Gerard was watching him. "You played the part perfectly," Gerard said. "Their suspicions should be turned aside."

"At least for now," Geoffrey replied. "You performed excellently as well, Gerard. Your timing was perfect."

Gerard bowed as if he were an actor on the stage. "Thank you, good sir."

166

"You did well too, Micah," Geoffrey said. "You were right to fetch me. It seems that Rome grows suspicious."

"What are we to do?" Josephine asked.

"You are going to France," Geoffrey replied. "We must keep the book safe, and I fear it is no longer safe in these lands. I will accompany you on your trip. Gerard, you will stay here and do what you can to create confusion among the Hospitaller and the Isma'ilites."

He turned to the young knight. "Michael, you will accompany the priests. Keep your ears open to what they discuss, but be careful not to pry. Try and play escort to them as long as you can, but if you are dismissed, do not argue with them. We cannot have them regain any of their former suspicion. When you are done, report your findings to the Inner Circle."

"Yes, sir," Sir Michael said.

"Micah." Geoffrey turned to the monk. "You will need to return to one of the nearby monasteries. It is becoming too dangerous here."

Micah frowned. "Gerard is staying here?"

"Yes."

"I would like to stay here as well," Micah replied. "I know I am just a monk, but I think I am useful."

"I fear for your safety, Micah," Geoffrey said. "If you wish to stay, you will certainly be of great use. But we are facing a powerful enemy, and it will be dangerous for you to stay."

"I know," Micah said. Geoffrey was just being kind in saying he was of great use, but he also knew

167

that there were things he could do which Gerard could not. The gift of the Inner Circle was not without its drawbacks. Micah prided himself on being a good caretaker and, while it might not be as important as the work of the knights, it was the task the Lord had given to him. "I would like to stay. It is my duty."

Geoffrey nodded at him. "Very well," he said. "But if Gerard advises you to leave, then you must leave at once."

"I will," Micah promised.

Geoffrey dismissed them, and Micah was making his way to the back altar to say his evening prayers when Josephine caught up with him in the hallway. "Micah," she said, taking his hand within hers. "I'm going to miss you. I know I cannot walk in your gardens any longer, but I hope that we are still friends."

"Of course." He squeezed her hand. "Whatever would make you think differently?"

"The change," she said. "I know it troubles you. I can see it in your eyes."

"It is something that is beyond my understanding," he replied. "And, I must admit, I have worried that it severed the friendship I cherished in you."

"Never." She touched his cheek. "I have had few friends in my life. There weren't many others my age in the village besides my sisters. I hope you will always be my friend."

He smiled at her. "I confess, I have missed your company in my garden. I will miss it more when you have gone to France."

"Me too."

CHAPTER SIXTEEN

Zain ignored the curious stare of the guards and kept up his exercise. He marched the length of his cell, from one corner to the next, and kept his muscles clenching and unclenching. He marched until he felt the first signs of exhaustion, and then he stopped and sat cross-legged on the floor. It would be a mistake to get too tired. There was no telling when he would need his strength.

The door to the room outside his cell opened, and two guards entered. Zain remained sitting while the new guards exchanged brief words of greeting to those going off-duty. He examined the guards, and his gaze was returned with gruff looks. The plain faces betrayed no sense of fear, loyalty, or sympathy.

Twenty-four. The guards had changed twenty-four times since he had first come to the cell, which meant four days and nights had passed since he had first been locked up. He wanted to smile, but didn't. He recognized one of the guards, though neither he nor the guard had shown any hint of it. He had recognized at least one of his guards for every shift in these past four days. Nizam did his job well. He was ensuring that Zain was never truly alone. Should the order for his death come, the guard would be there to slip the hilt of a dagger into his hand.

He imagined what might unfold should that order come before they were ready. The guards would demand he turn his back to them. With hands bound behind him, he would be turned and led from the cell. He would keep his hands out behind him, palms up, waiting for the hilt of that knife and ready to slip it up into the sleeve of his shirt.

He would cut the cords binding him. Not immediately -- he would need to be cautious -- but long before he reached the destination. Once his hands were free, the one whose loyalty was unsure to him would die.

There would be another guard somewhere on their path waiting to take the dead guard's place. Nizam would see to that. Zain would be taken before Rashid-al-din Sinan. The Old Man of the Mountain would want to gloat over him before the end. He could picture the elder man now, his eyes glassy from the hashish. Zain would need to be patient, waiting until he was as close as possible to Rashid-al-din before he acted. When he did act, it would be quick, his dagger leaving his hand on its way to Rashid-al-din before the Old Man knew what was happening.

Zain saw all of this in his mind's eye as clearly as if it were actually happening. And once he saw Rashid-al-din dead, he repeated the vision, over and over again. Each time he played out the scene differently to account for any variations to the event. He must cover all possibilities. Each step must be executed as if choreographed. He planned all of this even though he hoped it would never come to pass. If it did, they had already made a mistake. They had waited too long to act.

Soon, he thought, very soon indeed. Nizam was patient. He would wait for the best time, but he knew not to wait too long. Those that waited for the perfect time, instead of the best time, often found themselves failing in the end, their actions never materializing before events swept them away.

Zain rolled onto his stomach and began pushing himself off the ground. He continued this exercise for well over an hour. He had kept up this rigorous routine of exercise since the first day of his imprisonment. He ate regularly, and well, far better than Rashid-al-din expected him to eat. The orders were to serve him only bread and water, the barest amount to keep him alive, but the rolls of bread were secretly stuffed with meat. The food, and the exercise, kept him fit and ready for what was to come.

The outside door opened again, and a man entered carrying a plate of bread and a small glass of water. The guard Zain was unsure about approached the cell. Zain stood to his feet and put his back against the wall furthest from the cell door. The guard looked at him a moment, not giving the slightest hint of emotion, and then placed the key in the lock.

Zain heard the click of the lock and saw the guard's eyes widen in surprise at the same time. The man opened his mouth to say something, but all that emerged was a blood-filled bubble. The other guard had cut his throat, and blood was streaming to the ground with each heartbeat.

Zain approached and stared at the man with neither sympathy nor damnation. "Go to Allah." He reached out his hand to touch the man's forehead, careful not to get any blood on his clothes. "You have been a loyal servant. Allah does not punish the loyal, and paradise will await you."

The man slumped to the ground, and Zain said a quick prayer over his body. True to his words, he did not begrudge the man's loyalty to Rashid-al-din, though that very same loyalty had just cost the man his life. Zain held no anger, nor hatred, for those fidais still loyal to their leader. His grudge was for Rashid-al-din Sinan, and him alone.

He stepped out of the cell at the same time that Nizam entered the room. His friend smiled and tossed him a wad of clothes. "Get changed," he said. "I will present you as a messenger from the monastery."

Zain nodded, stripping out of his clothes and into the new ones. It was a good plan, allowing Zain to walk armed within the Old Man's presence. He suspected their leader would be deep within his hashish. His mind would be too dulled to recognize the man who stood before him until it was too late.

"How many do we have inside the hall?" Zain asked.

"Not many," Nizam said. "But enough. I had not planned this for tonight, but our leader is in a very beneficial state."

Zain smiled, his suspicions confirmed. The Old Man would be in a stupor and slow to react. He would be dead before he realized what had happened.

"I will announce you to Rashid-al-din," Nizam said. "Umar will escort you in." He glanced at Umar, who was using the discarded clothes to wipe the blood from his knife. "Umar will stay to your right, one step ahead. Bend your head in his direction, and, hopefully, none of the guards whose loyalty remains a question will recognize you until it is too late."

"You have done well, Nizam," Zain said.

Nizam nodded. "Just remember to let the sounds of your feet echo in the halls when you walk. There are not many with your grace of step and, should your feet fall silently on the hall, some of the more astute may realize who you are regardless of your covered face."

Zain nodded, surprised. He had not thought of that in the many times he had played out this scenario in his head. Nizam had. He had planned out every detail, as Zain knew his friend would.

"Come, let us go," Nizam said.

"The sign?" Zain asked.

Nizam made a strange sign with his hand, holding it up to the light for them all to see. Zain stared at the fingers intently, memorizing their positions, and then nodded.

The walk down the halls was almost serene. Only once did they pass another in the halls, and that person bowed to them. Nizam nodded at the man as they passed, and Zain knew their brother was off on some special duty. Perhaps he was keeping watch over the sleeping quarters, or taking the place of the guards in the prison.

They paused outside the great hall, and Nizam went ahead. Several minutes passed while Nizam approached the head table and waited to be heard by the Old Man of the Mountain. Umar stood at the edge of the great hall watching Nizam intently, and

174

Zain remained in the shadows until Umar touched him on the elbow silently telling him it was time.

Zain entered the hall and walked one step behind Umar. He walked with his heels first, listening as each one tapped against the stone floor. The sound seemed unusually loud to Zain, who was accustomed to brushing past the floor with no more sound than a soft wind. He wanted to peer out around the hood of his cloak for any flash of movement that would signal one of the guards had seen through their ruse, but he dispelled the urge. A messenger wouldn't be peering at those he passed. He would be staring straight ahead.

They reached the halfway point in the hall, and Zain's confidence surged. He tipped his head up and kept his vision focused on Nizam. His friend was standing to the side of Rashid-al-din with his head turned toward the pair walking down the hall. Nizam appeared to be paying little attention to his surroundings, in fact he looked rather bored, but Zain knew his friend was watching the entire hall for any sign he had been recognized.

They were within a dozen footsteps of the Old Man. Nizam's stared forward, the bored expression on his face, but his fingers twisted into the sign. They had been found out. Zain did not hesitate. He removed the dagger hidden in the sleeve of his robe, stepped out from behind Umar, and threw the blade in one fluid motion.

Rashid-al-din Sinan, as fate would have it, held the hashish pipe to his lips and had just taken a deep breath of the drug when the blade of the dagger impaled his throat. The point of the blade sunk into

175

the back of his chair with a loud thunk at the same time that the guard who recognized them yelled, "It's Zain!" The hash pipe fell from Rashid-al-din Sinan's hand and clattered on the table while a stream of smoke snaked out of lips that had taken their last breath.

The hall erupted. Zain drew his sword and spun around. Everywhere he looked, fidais loyal to him were drawing swords and holding them against those loyal to Rashid-al-din. Umar stood over the guard who had yelled the warning, a large welt already appearing on the side of his head where Umar had slammed the hilt of his sword.

Nizam had drawn his sword and was staring across the table where several of the Isma'ilites and a stranger sat at the table, each seeming at a loss for what had just happened, and none reaching for the weapons worn at their sides. Zain surveyed all of this, and when it became apparent that none of those loyal to Rashid-al-din would raise their blades against his killers, he approached the table.

He spared the stranger only a glance, recognizing him as the same knight that had shared the table with Rashid-al-din when Zain had been imprisoned. He met the gaze of each Isma'ilite at the table. Those wordless exchanges were all he needed to assure himself they would cause him no problems.

He turned to face the gathered Isma'ilites.

"This is a sad day, and this is a great day," he said. "Our leader has fallen, and this brings cause for sadness, for in his time he was a great man. But that time has long since passed. Through the

176

temptation of the hashish, he had turned us from our true cause."

He turned and pointed to the knight. "This is where he has led us. Infidels, sent here to take our land from us, now sit peacefully at our tables, breaking bread with us. And is this in the name of Allah? Is this in the name of Muhammad? Or is this in the name of that man they called Jesus Christ?"

There was a rumbling in the hall. Many of the guards, loyal to Rashid-al-din until the end, shook their heads in agreement at Zain's words. The knight shifted in his chair under the focus of their attention. But Zain was impressed that the knight did not show any fear or confusion on his face. Those emotions must be running through his mind, his fate uncertain, but the knight remained still, his emotionless eyes staring out into the crowd.

"No more!" Zain turned away from the knight. He faced the great hall and raised his hand to the crowd. "No more deals with the infidels, no more deals with the Christian knights who promise us one thing but deliver to us another. No more shall we stain our bodies and souls with this drug meant to lead us away from the paradise land, not toward it. And no more shall we stand meek in our own homeland while the infidels fight against us!"

"No more!" the gathered fidais shouted back at him.

"There are some of you that remained loyal to Rashid-al-din Sinan. No, don't hold your heads down in shame. Instead, lift them high in pride. You have done nothing to shame yourselves or to shame Allah. It was Rashid-al-din that has brought shame

177

to our names, and that time is no more. There is no shame in your loyalty. It is the greatest of deeds to be loyal. But remember from this day forward that our loyalty is first to Allah and then to Muhammad and only third to our fellow man.

"And let neither me nor any other man tempt you from that loyalty, be he a great man or a poor man, one of us or one of the Christian infidels that walk in our lands."

"We will not, Zain," Nizam said, turning to the crowd. "We will not fail Zain, will we?"

"No," came the unanimous reply from the crowd.

"We will not fail the new Old Man of the Mountain, will we?"

"No."

"We will not fail Muhammad, will we?"

"No!"

"We will not fail Allah, will we?"

"NO!"

"All hail Allah and Muhammad and Zain!"

"All hail!" the crowd cried, and erupted into cheers.

Zain smiled, taking a moment to bask in the center of their cheers, and then bowed humbly before them. "You will not serve me as your new leader," he said. "Instead, I will serve you."

He then turned back to the knight still sitting at the table. The knight shifted again in his chair, knowing that his fate was about to be revealed. This time, there was a crack of fear in those crystal blue eyes. Zain did not begrudge him this weakness. It would be a very strong man indeed that could face this moment without any of the surging emotions showing on his face.

"No, knight," he said, and approached the table. "You will not die this day. Instead you will ride out of here and bring a message to your masters. You will tell them what you have seen here today, and you will tell them that we no longer do their bidding."

The knight nodded.

"Nizam?" Zain asked, turning to his friend. "Pick out two of the most loyal and trusted among us and bid them escort this knight safely outside and see him on his way. No harm is to come to him in these halls. Make that understood."

"Yes, Zain."

Zain turned back to the knight.

"Remember what you have seen here today."

CHAPTER SEVENTEEN

Josephine impaled a hunk of meat with her fork and placed it in her mouth, relishing the rich spices that tantalized her tongue. She marveled at this new world she was living in, one where colors shined with new intensity, smells were as vivid as an image, and tastes sent tingles down her spine.

"It's interesting," she said. "After the change, I thought back to what I remembered of you and Gerard and Edward. I realized I had never seen any of you eat. I thought, perhaps, our only sustenance was..."

"We eat." Geoffrey gave her a penetrating stare, a warning they were not alone. "All living things must have food. And, though we must satisfy our peculiar craving from time to time, we sustain ourselves on a daily basis much like anyone else. We can do without food for weeks if needed, but without it we will begin to weaken, much like anyone."

"Then why?" she asked. She glanced down at his plate, mostly untouched.

He smiled at her. "Do you recall falling to sleep on our trip to your father's house?"

"Of course," she said.

"I don't mean waking up and knowing that you must have fallen asleep. Do you recall us preparing camp, getting out the bedding, laying down. Do you remember trying to make yourself comfortable before slipping off into sleep?"

She frowned. "I remember stopping for camp, but not much after that."

"Do you remember my eyes?"

She stared at him, peering into his deep brown eyes. "I remember dreaming. I think it was that night, it could have been on the next night, riding from Uncle's. I dreamed that your eyes flashed from brown to red and you said something, I don't recall what. But the words seemed to come from far away, though you stood very near."

"Our eyes hold a mystical ability," he said. "They hold the minds of men within them. Those skilled in the knowledge can issue commands to be obeyed by the one trapped within our stare. We can command them to sleep, to dream, and to forget.

"There are others that practice this craft, normal men branded heretics and warlocks because of the strange power their voice has over others. They use trinkets and lights to distract the mind of their subject while whispering gentle commands into his ears. We have no use for trinkets, though, because men are naturally drawn to the power they see within our eyes."

He stared at her. "Feel with your tongue the sharpness of your teeth, especially the two upper teeth on each side of your mouth."

"They are sharp," she said. "And extended. I noticed this change after that night. I assume it is for our special needs." She shuddered. It had been over a week since that night, and she had yet to feed on blood. She knew she would have to soon, and she dreaded that time.

Geoffrey nodded. "There are better methods," he whispered, "but yes, that is what they are for."

"What do they have to do with our eyes?"

"You asked why we did not seem to eat," he said. "When we speak to someone their sight is naturally drawn to our eyes, to that power they see there, but when we eat, their sight is drawn to our mouth. Here, in the dark corner of a tavern, it does little harm to eat, but you must learn to avoid food and drink in public, lest someone spot your unusual new feature."

"They are just teeth," she said, confused.

"I have seen a young girl, much younger than you, burned alive because of a brown patch of skin no larger than a fingernail," he said. "The local priest found hairs growing out of it and proclaimed it a witch's sign. I've seen babes born with an extra finger that were slain outright for fear of being possessed by a demon. And I've seen much worse. Men fear what is strange and unknown to them, and we can little afford to catch their fancy, for under the intensity of their stares, we will become the strange and unknown."

"What are we?" she asked. "Are we men and women, or are we something else?"

"We are called many things." He spoke in a whisper. "The Isma'ilites named us the demon knights. We are known by other names, some call us strigoi, and others name us bhuta. We are known as mullo, and uber, and vampir. I have heard us called many names by many different people, but the words do little to define who and what we are. Those of us of the Inner Circle refer to ourselves simply as the chosen."

"The chosen?"

Geoffrey did not answer right away. His gaze roamed across the tavern, falling first on one person and then another. Josephine knew he searched for any sign someone might be overly interested in the pair sitting in the dark corner.

"We travel to Ville Neuvu du Temple just outside of Paris." His voice was pitched in a whisper so mild that, had Josephine's hearing not been enhanced with the blood, she would have thought he only sighed. He barely looked at her while he spoke, his eyes continuing to roam across the tavern searching for anything out of place.

"It is our greatest seat of power in all of Europe. There sits the high council that governs all Knights Templar. And there, far below the temple, far below what the eyes of most men will ever behold, is a circular room. On an altar in the center of this room sits what appears to be a bottle of wine, but no wine does it hold.

"When a knight is chosen to become one of the Inner Circle, he travels to the Temple and is taken to this room where the rite is performed. He takes the sacred vows and drinks of the blood contained within the bottle, and from that day forth, he lives with the knowledge that he was chosen.

"It is believed by many in our order that the blood contained within that bottle is the very same blood that Our Lord, Jesus Christ, gave unto his disciples at the last supper. They believe God granted the knights the blood of our savior to bless them as his champions in the fight to win back the Holy Land."

Josephine digested these words in silence. She stared down at her plate and wondered, not for the first time since her change, about the world and her new life. There were so many secrets, so much that she did not know, and the thought of that knowledge both scared and thrilled her.

She looked back up at him. "You said *they* believe?" she asked. "Is this not what *you* believe?"

"I don't know what to believe." He smiled, but it was an empty smile that reflected a soul torn by searching. "When I was first chosen, I believed, but in the years since..." He stared through her as if he were looking into the past at distant memories. "The years, the decades, they trail past us and most live their lives like any other man, from one day to the next, believing in what they are told without question. But I have seen too much in this life, and I have begun to question.

"There was a time when I thought that we alone, the Knights Templar, were the only like us in the world. And yet, just a week past, I met one who was here long before the Knights Templar gained their mandate from the church. There are tales of creatures like us that existed long before we came to this land. It would be blindness not to speculate that we were not the first, that we are not the champions of God that we are led to believe, but that we are something else entirely."

She sucked in a breath, and he smiled, laying a comforting hand on hers. "That is not to say that we are damned, my dear. Only that we are different."

184

"There is so much to learn," she said. She glanced out the window and then at him. "The night. I suppose I must get used to it, though it still brings out a certain fear in me. You smile, but it's the truth. I think of days spent playing out in the sun, and I realize I may never again feel the warm rays bouncing off my skin and find comfort in them.

"What happens when the light of the sun hits our bodies?" she asked. "Damon told me to avoid the sun, but I saw him walk within its light."

"The sun is death," he said. "I do not know by what trick the stranger was able to withstand it, but I do know that its touch is poison to us. Oh, we do not wilt and die immediately, but we weaken and become pained until, finally, the poison of the sun touches our soul and we die."

"You look uncomfortable," she said. "You've felt this pain?"

"Yes." He frowned and gazed down at the uneaten food on his plate. "We were at the city of Akka. We had planned to ride out of the city that night, but in the hours before dawn, a great fire broke out on the docks." He shook his head. "We should have known something was amiss. The fire spread too quickly to have been natural."

He looked up at her, his voice still low and hushed. "There are only two ways out of Akka: the sea gate, and the land gate. To effectively lay siege to the city would take either a great many ships to run a blockade, or a skilled set of men to sneak into the city under the cover of night and set fire to the docks."

"The Isma'ilites?"

"Yes," he nodded. "The dark ones took care of the sea gate and, while we were distracted with the fire, the army of Salah al-Din marched toward the land gate. We thought the Sultan would launch an immediate attack. We were trapped in the city, and every minute he delayed was a minute we could use putting out the fires on the docks. But he did not launch his attack immediately. He waited.

"The men of the city thought it was a siege, but we knights knew the truth. He was there for us. Knowing our weakness to daylight, he planned to wait until the dawn before taking the city. He had taken care of our only way of escape. We urged the men to strike then before they were ready, but they refused. Nor can I blame them, they were safer holding the city from the inside rather than charging out into the plains to meet the Sultan's forces.

"We knights, however, could not wait. We were not afforded that luxury, and with the light of dawn cresting the horizon, we rode out to break through the lines of the enemy and win our way past. We were victorious, though many of our knights fell in that battle. Breaking through the lines, we rode through the morning sun to a nearby fortress, more than a few of us dying on that journey."

"What happened to the city?" Josephine asked, eyes wide.

He frowned. "It fell. The Sultan pressed the attack after we left and the army inside was outnumbered. They fought hard but, in the end, were defeated." He sighed. "We urged them to come with us, to break the siege. Together, we

186

would flee to the stronghold, but they stayed behind and they died."

There was a strange look in his eyes, and she could tell he felt responsible for their deaths. "What did it feel like?" she asked. "With the sun beating down on you, I mean, what did it do to you?"

"At first, I simply felt weak," he said. "My sword felt heavy in my hand, the armor that protected me seemed to drag me down. We fought through, many of us feeling this same weakness, and by the time we won through the lines, the weakness had spread to the mind. I remember feeling dizzy and, at first, was unsure if we even rode in the correct direction.

"We pressed on, riding with all speed toward the fortress. I felt a burning deep within, under the skin, and began to itch all over. Soon, I felt the turning of my stomach as if I had eaten meat that had lain out in the sun for hours growing rotten and diseased. Others felt the same. A few of the men fell from their horses on that journey, so weak had they become. We were forced to tie them to their saddles to complete the journey.

"More than a few didn't make it to the fortress. They died on the ride, strapped to the horses like animals, the poison of the sun finally reaching their hearts and stopping them for all time."

He fell silent, his mind on the events of that day, and she let the silence persist, eating the rest of her dinner without a word. She thought of the horror he must have borne witness to that day, the pain, the fear of that mad dash to safety, and she shuddered. She speared the last portion of meat and chewed it, barely aware of the flavors lavishing her tongue, and stared down at the now empty plate.

Strangely, she still felt hungry. She looked up, glancing around for the tavern wench. She was just about to hail her when Geoffrey's hand snaked out and clenched about her wrist. She turned back to him, surprised.

"You are still hungry?"

She nodded. She could tell he knew the answer.

"It's not food that you crave," he whispered, and the words sent a chill through her. "Tonight," he said, "you must learn to drink."

"No," she whispered. She could see her own fear reflected in his eyes. "I'm not that hungry. I was just wanting a little bit more, but I can wait."

"No." He stared at her intently. "You must do this now while the feeling is fresh in your body. If you wait, the hunger will grow, and the more it grows the less control you will have over it. If left to persist, it will dominate your every thought, reducing you to your basic savagery until you finally give in to the hunger.

"And then, it will be too late to control it." He took his hand off her wrist and leaned back in his chair. "You will not like what the hunger forces you to become."

She knew he spoke the truth. Deep within her, she could feel the hunger taking shape. That hunger would continue to grow until it consumed her. And with that knowledge came fear. "Help me," she whispered, her eyes pleading.

He nodded. "I will show you how. Death need not accompany us on this trip, but you will need to be strong."

"I will be strong," she said.

She stood from the table and followed him out of the tavern. They were in a city on the coast of the sea. She had forgotten the name, but knew they were due to take ship for Europe the following evening. It was late, but people still walked the streets of the city. Sailors, new in the port, walked in singles or pairs or groups, sometimes bursting out into laughter or song, most of them so inebriated, their staggering steps had to be supported by their shipmates.

There were others on the streets. There were women plying their trade and merchants hoping to sell a naïve traveler an overpriced trinket. There were stiff-necked guards trying to bring a semblance of order to the chaos and thieves looking for an easy mark.

She followed Geoffrey as he weaved through the various streets of the port city until he came to a small, shadowy path between two large buildings. The alley led to a street less popular than those they had come from, but Josephine could see a few people walking to some destination or another.

"Here," Geoffrey whispered. He stood in the shadow of the alley. "I will wait for you here. Go to the edge of the alley, just far enough into the street to be seen, and wait until you see a sailor walking alone. Smile at him and entice him over."

She turned to leave, but he grabbed her arm and pulled her closer. "Whatever you do," he whispered,

"Do not make a sound above a whisper. You will be frightened, but you must remain strong."

She nodded.

Walking to the edge of the street, she stood just inside the shadows and peered out at those that passed. She waited there for some time, patient, until at last spotting a lone sailor walking down the side of the street. She took a step into the street and let the light of the moon wash over her.

At first, he didn't look her way. His step was a little uneven, as if he were having trouble keeping his feet on the ground, and she could hear the hum of some song on his lips. He came closer and finally glanced her way. She smiled and pushed out her breasts like she had seen the other women on the streets do. It worked; he walked toward her as if pulled by an invisible line, his steps faltering but his eyes never leaving hers.

"How much?" he slurred.

She put a finger to her lips and took a step back into the shadows. He didn't follow. His eyes darted back and forth. He might be drunk, but he wasn't so inebriated as to have lost all common sense. She reached out from the shadows and touched his forearm with the tip of her fingers. Taking another step back, she caressed his arm until her fingers met his hand, and then she took hold of him. She pulled, but gently, beckoning, and he followed with a drunken grin on his face.

And then Geoffrey pounced. He clenched the sailor's throat and pressed him up against the wall of the building. Geoffrey peered into his victim's eyes, and whispered words that Josephine could not quite make out over the pounding of her own heart. But, she recognized their meaning, and she watched the fear leave the man's eyes. His muscles relaxed until his entire body went soft and would have fallen to the ground had Geoffrey not pinned him to the wall.

Slowly, Geoffrey laid the man on the ground and then, grabbing one of the man's hands, he bared the wrist. He drew the small dagger at his belt, held the blade out over the wrist and, with a quick motion, cut to the life's blood pumping beneath.

Blood squirted out in a solid stream and pooled on the ground until Geoffrey gripped the wrist tight, stopping the flow. He did not look up at her. Instead, he leaned down and put his lips around the cut on the man's wrist and loosened his hold, allowing the blood to flow into him.

It was horrifying, but strangely fascinating. The scent of blood filled the air, and she hungered for it. When Geoffrey finally lifted his head and beckoned to her, she was ready. Her hands shook, but she knelt down beside the man and put her lips around the slash across his wrist. She could smell the stench of sweat and alcohol covering the man, and the flesh beneath her lips seemed both warm and cold at the same time. But these sensations abandoned her when Geoffrey let up his pressure on the man's wrist.

A warm splash hit the back of her throat, and a salty taste circled her tongue. She gagged, almost spitting it out, but her body demanded of her, and she swallowed. The liquid flowed down her throat and into her chest, bringing her a warmth the rays of the sun could never provide. Her mouth tingled, suddenly delighting in the liquid, her throat beckoning for more. She swallowed again and felt a passionate euphoria lifting her up and away. She was no longer kneeling in an alley drinking the blood of a stranger, but flying high atop the clouds exulting in her power.

Geoffrey's words brought her back to the alley. "Stop," he whispered. But she didn't want to stop. He had tightened his hold on the wrist, slowing the blood flow to a trickle, so she sucked and was rewarded with more of the warm liquid.

"Stop." This time his voice was not a whisper; it was a command. She became aware of what she was doing and the liquid sliding down her throat was no longer the sweet nectar that had borne her through the skies, but the measurement of life in the man lying before her.

She stopped, gasping as she pulled away. She looked at the man lying in the alley, his skin pale and feverish, and cast a fearful glance at Geoffrey.

"He will live," Geoffrey said. "He will be weak for several days, but he will think it just the aftereffects of the drink. Watch..."

Geoffrey still gripped the man's wrist to stem the flow of blood. Reaching for his knife, he made a small cut on his own thumb and was rewarded with a few drops of blood. He rubbed the thumb back and forth against the cut on the man's wrist, making several passes before finally releasing his grip.

"Our blood mixes with his," he said. "Not enough for the change, but it will help the cut to heal. By morning, there won't even be a scar to mark what has happened."

Geoffrey stood up, and Josephine tried to stand beside him but found her balance difficult to catch. Her mind was still trapped in that strange euphoria. She took a struggling step forward, gripping the wall to her left until she finally found the leverage to stand.

"It will pass," he whispered. "It is strange the first time, a mixture of pleasure and pain, but you will get used to it, and in time, it will seem much the same as eating dinner in a tavern."

She looked down at the sleeping sailor, her wounded prey. His skin was white, and the sweat glistened on his forehead. No, she thought, it would never be the same as eating dinner in a tavern. But she *would* get used to it, that she knew.

CHAPTER EIGHTEEN

Krak des Chevaliers grew out of a massive outcrop overlooking the plains. The castle had a double wall surrounding it and thirteen towers sprouting over the walls, and the village below sprawled halfway up the hillside as if reaching up to touch the castle.

Gerard stood at the edge of the village and stared at the impressive fortress. The castle had been built around the remains of Hosn al-Akrad, which had been taken over by the Count of Toulouse a century ago. After the Hospitaller had taken control of the fortress, they strengthened and enlarged it until the castle became the monstrosity Gerard now observed.

Gerard wasn't there to storm the castle or even invade it through stealth. He was there to observe. He watched the main doors and inspected each person coming to or from the fortress. He watched, and he waited.

In the past fortnight, he had scoured the lands to the north. Each night, he would travel to a different fortress held by the Isma'ilites. He would sometimes kill, but oftentimes simply spread confusion. On one occasion, he had slipped right up to the entrance and mesmerized the guards, convincing them to leave their posts for the night. He knew, when questioned, they would not remember what happened. On another occasion, he shot a single arrow from out of the darkness and grazed a guard. The fortress emptied, and assassins searched the darkness for the attacker, but he was not to be found.

He soon found the guards doubled at the entrances and more watchers spread out near the fortresses. They had become more alert, expecting the attacks to be a distraction from a real assault yet to come. He stopped his play for several days straight and then hit three different fortresses on successive nights, stirring up more of his particular brand of chaos. And then, he stopped completely.

He smiled thinking about it. They would be on high alert for several weeks, wondering if another attack would come. Gerard had learned of Rashid-al-din Sinan's death, and he knew that a struggle for power commenced among the Isma'ilites. The chaos he brought might not distract them from the book -- that was too important for the assassins to forget -- but he hoped it would draw out the confusion left in the wake of their leader's death.

There, just exiting the Hospitaller fortress was a knight escorting a priest and a cardinal. Gerard dipped further into the shadows and turned his head to the side, listening. There was a light buzz of conversation coming from the village, but he was able to sift through the voices until he could focus on those of the priest and the cardinal.

"How long will it take us to reach Margat?" Father David asked.

"I don't know," Cardinal Vick replied. "Sir Michael, do you know how long it will take?"

"A week," Michael said. "Perhaps ten days. It depends on how fast we travel. If we keep the horses at a brisk pace we should get there within the week."

"That is good," Cardinal Vick said. "Jonathan promised us passage back to the motherland."

"Sir Jonathan Alderson?" Michael asked.

"Yes, do you know him?"

"No," Michael replied. "I heard mention of him during our brief stay here. He seems to be quite an important man."

"Yes," Cardinal Vick said. "He is investigating the mysterious disappearance of the knights."

"Have they found the cause?" Michael asked.

"No," Cardinal Vick said. "They have suspicions, but little proof."

"I wouldn't be surprised if it was the work of the Isma'ilites," Michael said. "They can be very treacherous."

"Do you think they are capable of dispatching a squadron of knights and not leaving a trace of themselves at the scene?" Cardinal Vick asked.

"They are capable," Michael responded. "I wonder their intent, though."

Michael was good. He knew how to get them to talk and how to slip in misinformation. The young knight knew enough not to state anything with certainty. Plant the seed and leave a doubt. It would leave them wondering.

"Where is this inn of which you spoke?" Cardinal Vick asked.

"It is just down the hill," Michael said. "The Lion's Den, it is called, in tribute to King Richard."

"It will be good to get a nice meal and a hot bath," Cardinal Vick said. "The knights have been gracious, but their food is very plain."

The trio approached, and Gerard retreated deeper within the village. He couldn't afford to be recognized, and he knew their destination now. Satisfied, he made his way to the market in the center of the town. It was a busy market, larger than one would expect from so small a village. The overlooking castle brought its own flow of business to the village, and Gerard knew the market would remain busy for a few more hours.

There were several taverns on the edge of the market where knights, squires and laymen from Krak des Chevaliers often spent their evenings. The drink would flow and, Gerard knew, their tongues would loosen. Dressed in a simple leather tunic and brown leggings with holes in the knees neatly sewn shut, he could walk among them and be dismissed as simply another villager.

The knights had little to talk about, though. There was no mention of the strange disappearance of a squadron of their fellows. There was some discussion concerning the death of the Old Man of the Mountain. Many of the knights wondered who would take his place and if his death, along with the death of Salah al-Din months earlier, would see a resurgence of fighting between the two groups.

Rashid-al-din Sinan and Salah al-Din had fought for many long years before signing a truce. The death of the two leaders might very well see that fighting begin anew, as well as a dissolution of the Peace of Ramla which would mean an insurgence of fighting between the Christian and Muslim forces. Perhaps, some of the knights wondered, they would be able to take back the Holy City.

With nothing of interest catching his ear in the tavern, Gerard left and browsed the marketplace. When he had spent enough time looking over the wares and eavesdropping on conversations, he headed over to the Lion's Den on the far side of the village. Once there, he suggested to the innkeeper that he was Sir Michael's brother and obtained directions to his fellow knight's room.

Gerard slipped into the dark room and approached the bed. Sir Michael appeared asleep, but his breathing was a little too quick in coming to his lips. Gerard smiled. "You are awake," he whispered.

"Sir Gerard." Michael breathed in relief. He shed the covers and placed a long dagger he was holding back under his pillow. "I thought it might be you."

"I can see," Gerard said, chuckling.

"Can't be too safe."

"Do you have any news for me?" Gerard asked.

"Not much," Michael said. "The priests arrived at the fortress just after noon. For much of the day they were sequestered with the knights, and I was left to idle around the courtyard. What knights I found to speak with were generally close-lipped, but I was able to obtain a little information from squires eager to impress a visiting knight with their knowledge."

"What did you find out?"

198

"The priests spoke with a Sir Jonathan Alderson. From what I gathered, he holds a very special rank among the Hospitaller. None of the squires I spoke with knew exactly what he did or what that rank was, but they knew it was considered important. Other knights frequently deferred to Jonathan's wishes when asked. The squires were quite in awe of him.

"I found it odd that none of them knew what he was tasked with. I spoke with several laymen about the castle as well, and each of them knew who Jonathan was and yet none of them knew exactly what he did. One worker did mention he had seen the knight speaking with a strange Saracen on several occasions."

"You did well," Gerard said. "I know Jonathan mostly through reputation, but I have met him on two occasions, both times at parties thrown for the minor nobility in their tours of the Holy Lands. I remember he seemed to take a special interest in the Templar, spending more of his time speaking with us than with the nobles or his own brother knights."

"Do you think he is the one setting the Hospitaller against us?"

"Yes," Gerard said. "I would wager that we are the special task he has been assigned. Yet, the split between us and the Hospitaller runs deeper than just one man. I suspect there are many higher up in the order that would like nothing more than to see us fall and not just because of the blood running through our veins. Did you catch any other names of those he might be working with?"

"No." Michael shook his head. "I feared it would look too suspicious were I to ask too many questions."

"You did well," Gerard reassured him. "Did you learn anything else in your travels with the priests?"

"Only that Cardinal Vick does not like to ride horses, nor does he like spicy foods, and he is quite convinced that he was sent here out of spite. He also complains that the Saracens smell bad, that the scenery is a bore, and that it is entirely too hot."

Gerard smiled. "It's been quite a harrowing mission for you, hasn't it?"

"It hasn't been that bad." He returned Gerard's smile. "Sometimes the Cardinal doesn't talk at all and it becomes quite peaceful. What shall I do once we reach Margat?"

Gerard thought about it. "Return with them," he said. "Escort them to the Mother Church and see what you can find out there. After a few days, travel to Ville Neuvu du Temple and report your finding to the Grandmaster. Robert de Sable must be informed of what transpires with the Hospitaller."

"I will do so."

CHAPTER NINETEEN

Josephine was tired of waiting. The ship had docked in Pont Audemer hours ago, but they had to wait for the sun to set. A week spent in a cramped cabin huddled under blankets to keep the light of day away from her skin had drained the strength, and patience, from her.

Geoffrey sat in the bed next to her, a blanket clinging to his shoulders while sweat rolled down his forehead. It was hot, a moist, thick heat made worse by the need to cover their skin. Josephine could feel her own sweat clinging to her body under the blanket. She looked at Geoffrey and raised an eyebrow.

"Almost." A weak smiled played across his lips. "A few more minutes."

She frowned, but accepted his answer. Sinking back under her covers, she closed her eyes and tried to imagine herself far away. She thought of Micah's garden and the brightly colored flowers the monk loved so much. She tried to remember their names, but couldn't. The vision blurred, a hunger deep within her rising up and disrupting her imagining. She shifted under the covers and grunted.

"Okay, it's time," Geoffrey whispered. His words were a godsend. "Get your things packed and ready. We need to be off the ship as soon as possible." He ran his hands through his wet hair, slicking it back. "Wear a hat," he added. "And keep your head down. We don't want anyone noticing how unkempt we appear."

She packed her bags in silence and followed him up to the deck. Geoffrey paused to exchange a few words with the captain, and then they disembarked. Once on land, she took a deep breath. She could smell the salt of the sea mixed with the pungent scent of human waste, but it was fresh air, not the stale air of the cabin, and it also carried the sweet flavor of bread being cooked, meats being smoked, and pies being baked. Josephine delighted in the smell and barely noticed the city they passed through.

"This one will do," Geoffrey said. The inn appeared drab to Josephine, but she knew Geoffrey preferred to stay near the gates of the city.

"We could leave tonight if you deem it necessary," Josephine said, though she hoped he would decline. Her limbs were stiff and her hunger was strong.

"No," Geoffrey said. "There are things I must do before we continue our journey."

With a silent prayer of thanks, she followed him into the inn. He asked for two rooms for the night and, to her pleasure, made arrangements for a tub and hot water to be delivered to the rooms immediately. The innkeeper was uncertain if he could arrange for both of the baths, but when Geoffrey slipped him a few coins, the uncertainty disappeared.

The rooms were plain, but they were much better than the ship. And the sound of the iron tub being carried into her room brought a smile to her lips. Soon, she would be lounging luxuriously in a hot bath. "What next?"

"We will travel along the Seine to Paris," Geoffrey said. "It is a great distance, but it should only take us a few days if we ride hard."

"What can we expect when we get there?"

Geoffrey frowned. "They are not going to be pleased with the news I will deliver. I suspect they will have more questions than we have answers."

"What will they think of me?" she asked, careful to keep the tremor out of her voice. It was a question that had been burning within her for several days.

"I wouldn't worry about that." He smiled, but she could tell it was forced. "We will speak with the Grandmaster himself. Robert de Sable is a hard man, but he is fair and honorable."

"He won't think of me as a danger?" she asked. "I am privy to a great secret held by the knights. I would think he would see that as a threat."

"He will know the secret holds as much danger to you as it does to us," Geoffrey replied. "Were you unchanged he might view you as a threat, but you have become one of us now." He stared at her a moment and then shook his head. "No, he will not view you as a threat, Josephine. Though others might."

A soft tap sounded from the door, and Geoffrey frowned. She realized they should not have been talking of such things even in the quiet of their rooms. He motioned to the door behind her and she retreated to her room. In earlier times, the two rooms had been used as a suite, but the inn had since fallen on hard times. Josephine was thankful they had simply installed a lock on the door. She felt safe knowing Geoffrey would be so close to her.

A maid was in her room now, pouring buckets of hot water into the iron tub. She nodded to the young girl and sat on the bed. Feeling the tension in her muscles, she closed her eyes and waited for the bath to be made ready. In the next room she could hear Geoffrey directing the men to set his iron tub in the center of the room.

She listened to the maid work and the gentle splashing reminded her of days long ago when she and her sisters would draw a bath. They would take turns fetching a bucket of hot water heated on the iron stove and comb the tangles out of each other's hair. It was the first time she had thought of her family without a deep well of sadness rising up from within her. The melancholy was still there, tempering her thoughts, but now it was only a whisper of yearning that echoed the love in her heart.

"Ma damoisele?"

Josephine opened her eyes and smiled at the young girl who gestured toward the tub, indicating the bath was ready. She only knew a little French, but what she did know would suffice for her needs. She continued to smile at the young maid, her hand gripping the delicate blade hidden behind her back. That hand trembled at the thought of what she was about to do, and she wondered what would happen if she failed to entrance the young woman. But the maid gazed into her eyes and was caught. Josephine, sighing in relief, spoke smooth words

204

that ran through the maid's mind, bidding her to relax and drift into a standing slumber.

The young woman's shoulders slumped, and her eyes went blank. Josephine held out the knife, the blade shaking, and ran it across the girl's wrist leaving a trail of blood in the wake. It was a shallow cut, but deep enough to open up the flow of blood beneath. The sight caused Josephine's whole body tremble, both in fear and in desire. She touched her lips to the soft skin, sucking in the life's blood and delighting in the pleasure that filled her body. The long week at sea washed out of her with the blood, and she felt her legs tremble beneath her. Careful not to drink too much, she lifted her head and, as Geoffrey had shown her, made a small cut on her finger to mingle her blood with the maid's.

She then wiped the blood from the girl's wrist and whispered more soothing words in her ear, bringing the maid out of her daze. Josephine scanned the bewildered expression on the girl's face for any sign that she remembered. Satisfied she would only recall becoming confused for a moment, Josephine bid the maid a good night and sank thankfully into the hot water.

The heat of the water, the steam, and the fresh blood pumping through her brought a smile of pure pleasure to her lips. She caressed her flesh and felt the tingle of her touch reach deep inside. It was the second time she had tasted life's blood, and the ecstasy washed over her in waves. She languished in that feeling, finally reaching over and picking up the washcloth to run it across her body, coaxing away the dirt and grime from a week spent on the ship.

She washed her hair and laughed out loud at the gentle tides of joy her hands brought to her face and neck. The ship, the travel, the fear of pursuit, they were all washed from her with the dirt and the grime. Her hair and body finally clean, she lounged back, closing her eyes, and let her fingers dance over her skin. The wake of her touch brought a whisper to her skin, extending the joy of the blood. She ran her hand down her side, over her hip and to her thigh, letting the sharp fingernails scrape across the flesh. She moved her hand to her breast, feeling the nipple harden as her fingers slipped past. Flattening her hand, she pressed the palm against her neck and felt the pulse of blood just under the flesh. Her hand moved up to her chin, and then her lips, sending tingles around her mouth.

A thought occurred to her, and she smiled. She lifted her naked body out of the tub and grabbed a nearby towel. Drying herself, she wrapped the towel around her body and tiptoed over to the door that separated her room from Geoffrey's. She paused, listening. She could not hear the splash of water, nor could she hear any movement from the room.

She opened the door and peeked inside. Geoffrey was sitting at a table in the far corner of the room his attention focused on the coveted book. He did not lift his head when she entered. He would have heard the door open and heard her light footsteps. But knowing who it was, he paid the footsteps no mind. He had often sat like that for hours on the ship, staring down at the words as if by

206

merely willing it, he would suddenly understand them.

A few moments passed, and he finally dragged his eyes from the book to look at her. Josephine's hand was on her chest, and she could feel her heartbeat pounding at the look of surprise on his face. Hooking her thumb over the lip of the towel, she slid it down her breast until the edge of the towel hovered over her pert nipple.

He looked away, and her heart trembled.

"If you need another towel, there is a spare beside the tub," he said. His voice was heavy, but she could detect a slight tremor in its tone. Tears welled in her eyes, and she retreated from the room. She curled up on the bed and let the tears flow.

Some time later, she became aware that he was there with her, sitting at the edge of her bed and gently stroking the back of her neck. She found comfort in his touch and the courage to turn and look him in the eyes.

"Is it because you are a knight?" She sniffed. "Is that why you don't want me?"

He shook his head. "No, child, that is not why," he whispered.

"Why, then?" she asked. "Am I ugly?"

He smiled, but there was a touch of sadness in his look. "No, child, you are not ugly. You are very beautiful."

"Why then?"

He turned to look at the tub in the center of the room. "You drank from your maid?" he asked.

"Yes," she said.

"The last week on the ship, we shared the same room," he said. "We slept not five feet apart, huddled under the covers to keep the rays of the sun at bay, and yet you never touched me with the passion of a woman touching a man."

She remained silent, not understanding what he meant.

"It is the blood in you, child," he said. "You asked why I did not want you, and there is no answer to that, Josephine. I looked at you and I did want, but I knew it was the blood within you that brought you to my room. The blood, and the pleasure of a week's travel washing from you."

"That's not true," she replied, "I do want you..."

"Josephine, have you ever been with a man in that way?"

She looked away from him. "No," she whispered.

She felt his hand caress her neck and looked back at him. He smiled at her. "You are young, Josephine," he said. "You are full of passion, and the blood brings that passion out in you. You must be strong, Josephine, and master the passion. You cannot let the passion of the blood become your master, or you will be lost."

She nodded. "But we can love, can we not?"

"Yes, we can love," he said. "The blood does not keep us from the earthly pleasures. Nor does it keep us from earthly sins, which is why we must always strive to be the master of the blood."

She closed her eyes and realized what he said was true. The ecstasy of the blood was gone, and she could no longer feel the passion that had

208

engulfed her so fiercely. She reached out and found his hand, gripping it tightly. Josephine knew Geoffrey had been strong for both of them.

"Now, if you are ready, there are some errands we must attend," he said. "Get dressed. We don't want the night to grow too late"

He left, and she grabbed a towel, drying off her hair as best she could before quickly dressing. She went to his room and watched him pack the book away. She realized what a fool she had been earlier. He was her protector, almost a father to her, and she had let herself become a slave to her passion.

He turned and smiled at her, and she felt the warmth of her embarrassment spreading from her cheeks down her neck and across the bosom of her breasts, the very same flesh she had bared to him earlier. He noticed her blushing and smiled even wider, finding humor in her humility.

She pouted, though her eyes mirrored the mirth in his, and she mouthed the words, "Thank you."

He nodded and motioned toward the door. "Shall we?"

They exited the inn, and he led her closer to the gates of the city. Just inside the gates was a stable. The scent of horse was thick in the air, and she could hear the slight rustle of horses behind the stable doors. Geoffrey stopped and turned to her. A small pouch jingled with coin in his hands.

"I need you to purchase two horses for us." He handed her the pouch. "Instruct the stablemaster to have the horses ready at dusk tomorrow. Be sure to pick out two of their best, for we will ride hard over the next few days."

Her eyes widened. "Me?" she asked. "Shouldn't it be you? I don't know much of bartering with merchants over horses."

"Sure you do." He chuckled. "It is much the same as bartering for anything. The merchant will try to cheat you, so reject the first offer and come back with a counter offer much lower than his. He will give you some excuse why that price is unreasonable and come back with another offer. You should end up paying at least half of what he originally offered. Any more than that and he has gotten the best of you."

"But surely it is too late to be buying horses." She glanced around. There were still quite a few people in the streets, but she ignored them. "The shop will be closed until tomorrow, perhaps we should just stop by on our way out?"

"Nonsense," he replied. "This is a port town, and travelers often require a steed at all hours of the night. You will find someone there to sell you two horses, and we cannot spare the time to haggle over prices tomorrow night."

"But..." She tried to think of another reason why he should be the one haggling with the merchant, but she couldn't.

"You need to learn," he said. "I will not always be with you. You must learn how to survive on your own."

"I guess you are right," she said. "Where will you be?"

"There is a small temple of the knights nearby. I need to send a message to Paris to inform them of our coming, and I also have a few other messages that need to be sent."

"Alright," she said. "Just don't be too long."

He smiled at her. "I won't."

There was a small shop next to the stable with the sign of a horseshoe in the window. She knocked timidly on the shop door and was greeted by the grizzled face of the merchant who complained that it was too late to be selling anything. But he led her to the stables and began showing her some of the horses, and she realized this was part of his show. She wasn't an expert, but she knew enough to pick out two strong horses and inquired as to their price. He gave her an amount that seemed outrageous, but she kept the surprise from her face and countered with one much lower. They haggled, the stablemaster explaining that the local duke had recently demanded many of the best horses sent to him for his army. He insisted his price was fair considering he had a full family to feed.

She thought this a lie, but the merchant stood firm behind it. In the end, she settled on a price a little over half his original offer, believing there might be some truth to his story. She made arrangements to pick the horses up at dusk the following day and thought the business finished when he surprised her with another question.

"Will you be needing saddles with those horses?" he asked. "Perhaps a bit and a harness too?"

"Of course we need saddles," she said. "They don't come with the price of the horse?"

"Oh no, lady," he replied. "I wouldn't be able to sell them to you so cheaply with the saddles included. But I do have several very fine saddles that I can part with. I think you will be able to afford them. How much coin did you say you have?"

"She didn't say."

The stablemaster jumped at Geoffrey's voice coming from just inside the door. "What?"

"Come, Lady Josephine," Geoffrey ignored the merchant's surprise. "It doesn't seem as if this gentleman wants to sell you the horses, but I know of another merchant in the city that will include the saddle with the price of the horse."

"Now, now," the merchant said. "Don't go running off too quickly. I think I might be able to squeeze a couple of saddles in with the horses, but don't you go telling others I did you this favor or else they'll all be wanting the same."

"We'll keep your secret safe," Geoffrey said, winking at Josephine.

212

CHAPTER TWENTY

Two of them followed him. They were not strangers. He knew their faces, though not their names. They had approached from a side hallway, one of them even nodding at him when he looked them over, but there was something not quite right.

Zain had learned long ago to trust his instincts. It was one of many reasons he was considered the most dangerous of the Isma'ilites. His mind could pick up details he was not aware of and point him in the correct direction. His instincts were now urging him to beware of danger, and he took the warning seriously.

Thus, it came as no surprise to hear the faint hiss of iron on leather that a blade makes when it is slowly drawn from the scabbard. The sound was faint, barely audible over the thudding of their boots walking down the hall. Those following him hoped to draw their blades in stealth before launching their attack.

Zain did not react. He took one step, then another, then a third, seeing in his mind's eye the blades crawling out of the scabbards. And then, pivoting, he launched himself at his would-be attackers. They were caught off-guard, the tip of their blades still inside the scabbards. His sudden attack surprised them, and for an instant, they did not react. Zain drew his blade and slashed through his opponent's face in one smooth action. He then lashed out with his boot, slamming the second assassin against the wall.

The assassin drew his blade. There was no fear in his eyes, though he surely knew death was imminent. Instead of fear, there was salvation. He was ready to give his life for what he believed.

Zain bowed his head toward his opponent, granting the man a gesture of respect before engaging him. The man was skilled with a blade, but unused to the two-blade style. Not accounting for the second blade, he received a sharp slash on his upper thigh.

The dance of the blades consumed Zain, as it often did. His body flowed in and out of the melee, his blades whirling about him independent of each other. Nothing existed for him during his time, not his opponent, not himself. All that existed were those two blades weaving through their deadly dance and the blade of his opponent being beaten back. The would-be assassin could not match the onslaught of strokes and took another deep gash. Another followed, and then another before he finally slipped, and received a fatal lunge through his ribcage.

The new Old Man of the Mountain hovered over the assassin, staring down without emotion while the man gasped out his final breaths. And then he bent down and used the man's shirt to wipe the blood off his weapons before replacing them in their sheaths.

It was the second assassination attempt that week. Zain did not begrudge the men he fought. In truth, he accorded them a certain amount of respect. They were willing to give their lives for something they believed, a trait enviable in any man, even if that loyalty was placed in a man seven days dead. Or, perhaps, all the more because of it.'

He rounded the corner to the great hall and whispered to a brother assassin to have the mess in the hallway promptly removed. The pause gave him time to survey the room, and his eyes went to a stranger standing near the great table. The man was talking with Nizam al-Qadmus and gesturing wildly with his hands.

It must be more bad news. He had just gotten word that the Knights Templar had deserted the monastery. Rashid-al-din, being a fool, had not dispatched enough of the Isma'ilites to properly follow the knights when they moved, and their location was lost. He knew only that one of the knights had left in the presence of two priests, and another, with the woman, had left the next night.

Zain approached the great table. "What news?"

"This is Azmed," Nizam said. "He brings word from the Knights Hospitaller."

"What?" Zain glared at the man. "I thought I forbade any contact with the Christian knights?"

Azmed stared at the ground. "Master, I am sorry, he came to us."

"Look at me when you are talking, Azmed," Zain said. "And refer to me by my name. I am not your master, only Muhammad and Allah hold that honor."

"Zain," he said. "The knight approached with hands held high and away from his weapons. I did not know what to do. We weren't under orders to slay any that approached. He called out that he had a message so I went down to receive it."

"You did fine," Zain said. "What was his message?"

"He bade me tell you the knights have left the monastery taking with them the book."

"This is known to us. Did he have anything else to offer?"

"He said the knight and the woman travel to Europe. They believe the pair hold the book and are destined for a temple near Paris. He was unsure if the pair meant to stay in Paris for long."

"Did he mention where they might go from there?"

"No, Zain," Azmed said. "That was the whole of his message."

"You have done well," Zain said. "You can return to your station. If any other knights approach, take their message. But make it clear that their presence is no longer well received by us, and we will not guarantee their safety in these lands."

"Yes, Zain," Azmed replied. He bowed, and then retreated back down the hallway.

"What do you make of it?" Nizam asked. "The knights know that we no longer wish dealings with them. Why would they give us this information?"

Zain shrugged. "They know we still seek the downfall of the infidels. And they know our reach is far and can extend into Europe if the need is great."

"Can we trust them?"

"Trust?" Zain laughed. "No, we cannot trust them, but I do believe they are telling the truth to us. They need our help to retrieve the book. They cannot be discovered acting directly against the

216

Templar, or they will come under suspicion of their church. They need us to do their dirty work."

"If this book is so precious, how do they know we won't simply keep it?"

"They know its value better than we," Zain said. "If they were worried about us keeping the book, they would never have made deals with us in the first place. Either the book can bring down the Templar without the Hospitaller's intervention, in which case we are both served regardless of who holds it, or it requires the Hospitaller's intervention, which ensures them that we will hand it over once found."

"What are we going to do?"

Zain considered. "We will go after the book," he said. "With it, the Templar will be dismantled from the inside, leaving us to deal with Knights Hospitaller in our own fashion. We will get the book, hand it over to them if need be, and prepare our blades for the blood that will follow."

Nizam nodded. "Shall I make the arrangements?"

"No," Zain said. "You will have your hands busy here."

"What?"

"I need you to take command, Nizam, if only for a short while."

"You aren't thinking of going yourself...?"

"Of course," Zain said. "The book has slipped in and out of my hands once before, I will not allow it to escape my grasp again."

Nizam shook his head. "You are needed here, Zain. There is still much work to be done. The fidais of al-Qadmus and Hadid have sworn to your rule, but the outlying fortresses are still in confusion."

"You will need to see to it, Nizam." Zain put his hand on his friend's shoulder. "This task set before us is too urgent to ignore and too important to give into inferior hands. You must see to our people while I am gone."

"It is too much," Nizam replied. "The loyalty to Sinan ran deep. There is still great division among the rafiq to your rule."

"You are well versed in diplomacy, Nizam," he said. "Far more so than me. No, don't deny it. I have great patience when it comes to my blades, but little patience when it comes to politics. Seek aid from the Imam in Alamut."

"Yes Zain," Nizam said, bowing his head.

"I shall leave with tomorrow's sun," Zain said. "If we are quick enough, perhaps we can catch them in France."

CHAPTER TWENTY-ONE

There was something different about the people in Ville Neuvu du Temple. They had arrived well after sundown, but there were still several people walking the streets, not uncommon for a small town. It took her a few minutes to recognize what she was sensing. It was reverence. No matter what the people were doing, they would occasionally stop and stare at the large, round building in the center of the village.

The temple was built in a circle out of respect for the Dome of the Rock in the Holy City, and it was one of the most influential buildings in all of Europe. In those halls, the upper echelon of the Knights Templar played friend and advisor to kings and princes. It was into those hands that great amounts of money flowed through Europe to the land of Palestine.

She felt the quiet awe too, but she also felt something else. Fear. She was a merchant's daughter from a faraway land and knew little of such stately matters. How would these great men, friends to kings, take to her, a simple merchant's daughter? And how would they feel about her sharing their secret?

Geoffrey did not lead her straight to the temple. Instead, they lingered at a small tavern just across from the main entrance. It was late, but there were still many customers in the tavern. Geoffrey called for a table near the back where they could be alone. He ordered a mug of ale for himself, a small glass of wine for her, and then waited quietly while the wench brought them the drinks and departed.

"You are nervous," he said.

"Yes," she admitted. "Do you have to tell them about me? Couldn't you just give them the book?"

He shook his head. "I have an oath to them. I will not go back on my word, but I will give you my oath as well, Josephine. You will not come to harm here. I will see to that."

He reached across and held her hand in his. She relaxed, but his touch brought a flush of embarrassment to her. He had become a guardian to her, a fatherly figure, and she couldn't help but feel shame about that night when she made the clumsy overture to him. Even now, she could see the look of disapproval in his eyes.

It was that same look, those very same actions, which bound her trust to him so completely. She knew he would stand by her, protect her, and, if need be, lay down his life for her.

"I will meet with the Grandmaster tonight," he said. "You will wait in the entry alcove of the temple. I don't know how long you will be there, perhaps a few minutes, perhaps an hour. If someone asks, simply tell them you are waiting for someone."

She nodded.

"You must avoid eye contact," he said. "And try to remain unnoticed. It will be late evening, but there will still be many people in the foyer. It is very important that no one suspect what you have become until I have had the opportunity to discuss these matters with the high council."

"What would they do?" she asked.

He frowned. "I don't know. This is important. If someone questions you and wants you to come with them, refuse. No matter how kindly or menacing the offer, do not leave the foyer. If they try to force you, call out my name as loud as you can, and I will come to you."

"Do you think that will be necessary?"

"No," he said. "I would not have you wait inside the temple if I thought that likely, but I want you to be prepared. Many people come to the temple simply to sit and pray, or to think. You should not be bothered. And if you are, simply keep your head down and your answers brief, and everything should be fine."

"What do you think the high council will say?" she asked. "When they hear about me, I mean."

"They are going to be surprised." He chuckled, but then his face grew serious. "We are forbidden to share our gift with anyone, not even other knights. It is our order's holiest sacrament, and it is carried out only under the special guidelines of the high council.

"There has never been a case like yours. In the many decades since the forming of the Knights, none other than our own have been known to be like us. You will be quite a surprise to them."

She shifted in her chair.

"You are right to be nervous." He smiled across the table at her. "But all will go well. You will see."

"Do you think we will be here long?"

"I hope not," he said. "It will not be a secret that we have come here, and I have little faith those after the book will be put off simply by the distance we have traveled. I will urge the importance of us moving on, in secret, and as soon as possible."

"And the book?"

He shrugged. "With or without the book."

She remembered the strange man, Damon, and his words to her. "I have a feeling the book will remain with us."

"I do too," Geoffrey said.

He got up from the table and led her across the street to the temple. Once again, she was amazed by the aura of power that seeped out of the walls and brought a hushed silence to those walking the streets. In a normal town, she would have expected to hear the quiet hum of conversation in the night's air, but here people spoke in whispers or, more often, not at all.

They temple opened into a long hallway covered with red carpet and lined with marble statues. There were several benches near the front doors, most of them occupied despite the late hour. They walked down the hall and came to a room shaped like an octagon with hallways branching off in all four directions. In the center of the room was a small fountain surrounded by small wooden benches.

"Wait for me here," Geoffrey said. He guided her to a bench and leaned close to whisper in her ear. "Remember what we talked about."

She nodded and took a seat. Opposite her sat a man with his head bowed to the ground. His hands were clasped in his lap, and he mumbled something under his breath. If she concentrated, she would hear the words, but she refrained from using her gifts. This was a holy place, and she would respect the man's privacy.

Geoffrey still hovered over her, and she could tell he had doubts about leaving her alone. But her own anxiety had faded when they entered the temple. It was a place of peace, and that peace had washed over her, taking with it her worries and her fears. She smiled at him to let him know she would be fine, and then turned her eyes to the fountain.

***

It had been many years since Geoffrey had last stepped foot in the temple, but he knew the look of the man he would need to see, if not the name or the face. His search did not last long, finally spotting a man with a special insignia embroidered on the sleeve of his tunic marking him as the Grandmaster's Squire, a position that even knights honored.

"Squire, might I have a word," Geoffrey said.

He could see right away that he had made a mistake. The squire barely glanced up from the papers he was studying. "Yes, knight?"

It had been too long since he had been here, and he was unused to the politics. "I have important news for the Grandmaster and request an audience with him at his earliest possible convenience."

"The Grandmaster has taken to his chambers and is likely asleep by now." He looked back down at the papers. "You will have to come back in the morning."

Geoffrey laughed. "The Grandmaster has about as much chance of being asleep as I do of being a rabbit."

The squire gave him a sharp look, and Geoffrey caught those eyes in his. He didn't have time for politics. "I need to speak with the Grandmaster." His voice was low and even. "And Robert wishes to speak to me. You will take a message to him and beg him to spare me a few minutes of his time."

The squire stood up and left without a word. He returned a few minutes later and beckoned for Geoffrey to follow, leading him to a small room down the hall. The squire tapped on the door and opened it without waiting for a reply.

Robert de Sable, the Grandmaster of the Knights Templar, sat at a table. Across from him was a knight Geoffrey recognized as Gilbert Erail. Geoffrey had never spoken to Gilbert, but knew he was an Inner Circle knight of high standing rumored to be second in power only to the Grandmaster.

Neither of them looked pleased with the interruption.

"You may go," Robert told the squire. He waited until the man had closed the door and then gave Geoffrey a penetrating stare. "Geoffrey Furnivall. We had word you were on your way here from Paris."

Geoffrey nodded.

"We did not have word that your mission was of such importance." The Grandmaster frowned. "Important enough to use your parlor tricks on my squire, it seems."

"I'm sorry, sir."

"It is the craft of the Devil, Geoffrey," Robert said. "We have been given great power, but we have also been given great temptation. And, just as Jesus was tempted by the Devil, so shall the beast tempt us."

He had forgotten how superstitious even the Knights were with regard to the power they held. In the Holy Land, the knights used what power they had to defeat their enemies, but here in the civilized world, there were certain rules that must be followed, and Geoffrey had carelessly broken one of them.

Geoffrey bowed his head. "Forgive me, sir."

"What is this news that brings you back to civilization?"

Geoffrey had planned to begin with the day Josephine came to the temple, but his mistake had cost him favor with the Grandmaster. He knew his lord's patience was stretched thin. "I traveled here with a woman," he said. "She is one of us."

"What?" Gilbert Erail halfway stood from his chair. He glared at Geoffrey, clenching the side of the table with his fists, and then pulled himself back down. "How did this happen. What knight disobeyed our highest order?"

"It was not a knight," Geoffrey said.

"How can that be?" Gilbert asked.

Robert folded his hands on the table and leaned forward. "You have begun your tale in the middle, Geoffrey," he said. "You have our attention now. Please start at the beginning."

Geoffrey glanced at one of the chairs. "May I?"

"Of course."

225

Geoffrey sat down. "A few weeks ago, a young girl, the daughter of a merchant from a nearby village, came to us for sanctuary. Her family had been foully murdered, and she had been chased to our very doorstep before her assailants finally relented.

"They were Isma'ilites."

"What did the Isma'ilites want with a poor merchant's daughter?" Gilbert asked.

"At the time, we did not know, but we were certain of their interest in her. They left agents near the monastery and watched us closely. We questioned her, and she said one of the assassins spoke of a holy book during the attack. Hoping to find out more, we took her to the site of the murder, and, finding nothing there, we continued on to her uncle's home a half-day's ride from the village.

"On the way, something happened. A strange man approached the camp, and he used the power on us. There were several of our knights there who are not yet chosen, and they fell under his spell. His power also extended to Gerard and Edward. With a single blow, they fell before him. But it was not the force of the blow that felled them, though, but the power."

"How can that be?" Robert asked. "I am not as well versed in these matters as you, Geoffrey Furnivall, but does not the power only work when used against those that have not shared of the blood?"

"So I believed as well," Geoffrey said. "And yet, this man used it against two of our own. At the time, I thought he had come for the girl. But that was not his intent, he simply came to give me a message."

"A message?" Robert asked.

"He said it was important for us to retrieve the book and keep it safe. He hinted that it contained information about us."

"And did you find this book at the uncle's house?" Gilbert asked.

Geoffrey nodded. "We did. And no sooner were we out the door when we were attacked by the assassins. We lost three of our own, including Edward."

Gilbert's eyes darkened. "Edward Conyers? It would take a small army to overcome him!"

"Or one very dangerous Isma'ilite," Geoffrey said. "He was cut off during the skirmish, bravely holding his position while we prepared the retreat. He was set upon by one of the assassins, different than the rest, and bested."

"Different?" Robert asked. "You don't mean...?"

"No," Geoffrey said. "He was, simply, dangerous. He carried himself in an almost regal fashion, and his eyes bespoke a confidence in his own abilities. He looked upon us without fear, but with a burning hatred."

"If he was able to defeat Edward, then he is truly a dangerous man," Gilbert said.

"We rode from the house, and just before dawn, we met up with the stranger once again," Geoffrey said. "He urged us to give the girl, and the book, into his care and he would carry them to the monastery during the day while we slept."

"But, if he was one of us, how could he carry on with the sun in the sky?" Robert asked.

"I am just as bewildered by this riddle as you, Robert," Geoffrey said.

"You didn't give this stranger the book, did you?" Gilbert asked.

"I didn't see that we had much choice," Geoffrey said. "We were certain the assassins would not give up their chase so easily, and the man who stood before us... I stood before him, my lords, and I felt his power. It was immense, awe-inspiring, and I knew that we had little choice in the matter if he had set his mind to this action."

"You were cowed by him, man," Gilbert said.

"No, I think not," Robert said. "I have known Geoffrey for many years now. His courage and leadership are beyond reproach. He is a leader among the Inner Circleand has fought long and hard in the Holy Lands. He did not earn his place among us because he is easily cowed, Gilbert Erail, of that you can be certain."

Geoffrey smiled at the compliment, but it was short-lived. He continued. "We woke the next night and rode to the monastery. The book was there, as was the girl, but the strange man was gone and the girl was... changed."

"He shared blood with her," Robert said.

"Yes," Geoffrey said. "He gave her the gift of his blood, first asking if she would accept its curses, and he then left her with the book. And there is one other thing I should mention."

Robert raised his eyebrows.

"On the night that he took the girl, the stranger mentioned that the Knights Hospitaller also searched for the book. He said that a troop of knights rode out with hopes to aid the Isma'ilites in its recovery, and that he took care of them."

Robert exchanged a glance with Gilbert. "We have heard that a troop of Hospitaller were lost in battle to an unknown enemy. They gossip in Rome that we had something to do with the defeat."

"We were visited by two priests from the church asking questions," Geoffrey said. "It was then that I felt the book would be best moved out of the Holy Land."

"You have brought us important news indeed, Geoffrey," Robert said. "I wonder if you have thought what our course of action should be?"

"I don't think book should not stay here long," Geoffrey said. "Nor I or the girl. I hoped to travel to England at the earliest convenience."

"Surely the book is best guarded here," Gilbert said. "And this girl who is now one of us, we can't simply..."

"What are you suggesting we do, Gilbert?" Geoffrey asked.

"She's a threat," Gilbert said. "She knows of the secret, and yet she is no knight, she has sworn no vows."

"Calm down, Gilbert," Robert said. "Geoffrey, what do you know of this girl?"

"She's not a threat," Geoffrey said. "She has strength of mind and she is, after all, in as much danger from the secret as are we. I do not think we need a vow from her that she won't give her life willingly away."

"She could make a mistake," Gilbert said. "Someone could find out."

"She is under my care," Geoffrey said. "I have trained many knights in these matters. She will make no mistakes."

Robert sighed. "I can hardly see how we have much choice in the matter. She will be your responsibility, Geoffrey. If she breaks one of our oaths, we will view it as you breaking our oaths. Is that understood?"

"Yes, sir," Geoffrey said.

"Alright, the girl goes with him," Gilbert said. "But the book should remain here, in our most sacred shrine far beneath us, next to the bottle. Here, it will be safe if any place we hold is safe."

Robert looked thoughtful.

"Sir?" Geoffrey asked.

"Yes?"

"The world does not know what we hold in the deepest recesses of our temple. The world does, however, know about the book. And they know of its coming here. I do not think it wise to draw too much speculation about such items to our temple."

Gilbert shook his head. "If the book holds information about the chosen, then we must keep it here and study it."

"The book is old," Geoffrey said. "Ancient. I have seen many languages, but the script in its passages is one unknown to me. It would take a scholar to unlock its mysteries. Do we trust letting one of the learned men in here to study the book, not knowing what it contains?"

"Geoffrey may be right," Robert said. "But I would have a look at this book, and this girl, before I make my decision."

"She is here in the temple."

"Then, please, fetch them here," Robert said.

CHAPTER TWENTY-TWO

Her peace was gone. She watched people walk past her spot in front of the fountain, but she couldn't put her finger on the uneasy feeling brewing inside her. It had been some time since Geoffrey had left her to wait, but this feeling was new. She remembered when her father was first teaching her to ride. The horse had scared her. It was just a pony, but she worried she would fall and be trampled underneath those powerful hooves. She felt the same now, only this time there was no name for her fear, and her father wasn't here to comfort her.

Where was Geoffrey? He said the wait might be long, but surely he should be back by now. She fidgeted and stared around her. The man who had been sitting across from her was gone. There were a couple of knights down the hall, but they weren't paying any attention to her. She could hear voices coming from behind her, but fought the urge to turn around and stare. Geoffrey had told her to sit still and keep from being noticed, but her body was telling her to stand up and move around.

She clenched her jaw and stared through the fountain. It was just anxiety. She knew she should try to relax, but her body was tense. She tried to think of the peaceful feeling the temple had given her just moments before, but it was now a faint memory. Where was Geoffrey?

"Can I help you?"

The voice startled her. She had not heard him approach, but her thoughts had been so far away that a herd of cattle could have stomped through the temple and she would not have noticed. She looked up and saw a man dressed in a fine tunic with a curious expression on his face.

"No, thank you," she said. "I am just waiting on someone."

"Ah," the man said. "Perhaps I can track this person down for you, who did you say you were waiting for?"

"Geoffrey Furnivall." The man's stare made her uncomfortable. He looked at her like he recognized her, though she had never seen him before.

"Hmm." The man stroked his beard. "I am not familiar with a Geoffrey Furnivall."

"He has just arrived from the Holy Lands," Josephine said. "He shouldn't be long."

"Just arrived, did he? Perhaps I can be of assistance to you. If you would follow me down the hall, I can get someone to check on this Geoffrey Furnivall for you."

He wouldn't be easily persuaded to leave her be, so she raised her voice. "Is it not allowed to sit here and wait?"

He flinched. "Well, of course it is."

"There are plenty of others here." She pointed down a hall where a man was walking toward them. "Are you questioning each of them about their business?"

"Why, no," the man said.

"Is it because I'm a woman? Are women not allowed to sit alone in a house of God?"

"Certainly," the man said. "I just..."

233

"You just what?" Geoffrey's voice came from over Josephine's shoulder. "Is this man bothering you, Lady Josephine?"

Now that Geoffrey had arrived, the man looked uncomfortable. "No." She stood up. "We were just talking."

"Good," Geoffrey said. "If you are done talking with him, the Grandmaster will see you now."

The man's eyes widened, and Josephine choked down a smile that threatened to engulf her face. "Good day to you, sir." She curtsied, and then followed Geoffrey down the hallway.

When they turned a corner, Geoffrey smiled at her. "Not exactly what I would call keeping a low profile."

"I'm sorry," she said. "The man was persistent. He wanted me to follow him down the hall. He said he would help find you, but I don't think that was his intention. There was something about him that felt different."

"Yes," Geoffrey said. "And do you know what that was?"

"No."

"We know one of our own," Geoffrey said. "It is something we can sense. No doubt, the man sensed it in you and was curious."

"Then he...?"

"Is one of us," Geoffrey said. "He sensed something odd about you, but you are a woman and could not be one of the Inner Circle. No doubt he is even more confused now knowing that you go to meet with the Grandmaster."

Josephine grinned at him, and a sudden memory came to her. She was knocking on the door of the monastery, begging for help, and just when her prayers were answered and the door opened, she felt a sudden jolt of dread enter her.

"I felt it that night," she whispered. "When you answered the door, I had the same feeling of uneasiness, though I did not know what it was at the time."

"Interesting," he said. "It is rare for someone not of the blood to have those feelings. Yet, it does sometimes happen. Usually, they are simply dismissed. People will often dismiss what they cannot explain, even before questioning it."

"What do you mean?"

"You were with us for several days in the monastery," he said. "Did you always have this feeling around us?"

"I had the feeling that first night." Another memory came to her of Geoffrey walking into the dining area and feeling a chill brushing against the back of her neck. "And the second night," she added, "But not after that."

"Your mind had grown used to the feeling," he said. "You still sensed it, but because you had felt it before and had no explanation for the feeling, you dismissed it. There were others things as well. You stayed with us and yet never saw us during the daylight and never saw us eat. You were with us when Edward called to the wolves, you traveled beside us to your father's house and your uncle's house, and you watched us move with unusual strength and speed during the ambush of the assassins. Did you ever question any of these things?"

She shook her head.

"You had all of the clues to the mystery before you, and yet you never questioned," Geoffrey said. "The mind has two parts, what is on the surface, and what lies inside, and a veil separates the two. We cannot see through this veil to find what our innermost mind is thinking, but we can hear its whispers. It is into this mind that we use our voice to implant suggestions that will be obeyed without question. And it is this same inner mind that can sometimes sense our unusual nature, but having no explanation it shields us from those thoughts."

"It sounds as if we are simply slaves to this inner mind," she said.

"We are slaves to it," he said. "And it is a slave to us. Before, when you felt our presence, you dismissed it because there was no rational explanation. Your inner mind sensed it, but it was a slave to what was on the surface. Now you know us for what we are, and know the feeling for what it is, and you will be able to use this sense to detect others like us."

She nodded. "Then that man, he knew?"

"He sensed something," Geoffrey said. "But not all of the Inner Circle are well versed in these things. And even if he were versed in this knowledge, he would hardly believe that a woman with the blood flowing within her would be patiently waiting out on one of the benches. Remember, the knights believe they are the only ones with the gift of the blood. The idea that there are outsiders with the blood is unheard of."

He smiled at her. "But enough of this for now. Robert de Sable is waiting and we do not want his ire brought down on us for keeping him too long."

He didn't immediately move, however, instead leaning down to her and putting his mouth close to her ear. "We will be meeting with Robert de Sable and Gilbert Erail. When we enter, take a seat and place the book on the table. You must be strong, Josephine. These men are unused to dealing with women, and may seem harsh, but remember my oath. You are safe, and you will always remain safe so long as blood pumps through these veins."

She nodded and followed him into a room at the end of the hall. The room was decorated with ancient wooden crucifixes hanging on the walls. And, for each crucifix, there was a weapon of war hanging below it. In the center of the room was a small round table carved from marble the color of ivory.

Her eyes were drawn to the two knights sitting at a table. The knight on the left was surrounded in a quiet power. His hair and mustache were neatly trimmed and he regarded her with calm, blue eyes. He seemed more a prince than a warrior. She knew without needing to be told he was Robert de Sable, Grandmaster of the Knights Templar. Geoffrey had described the man in detail but even without the description, Josephine would have known from the regal air about him.

The other knight was shorter in height and rounder in girth. His eyes darted between her and

Geoffrey, and he wore a frown like a permanent fixture. She felt uncomfortable under his stare and was glad when Geoffrey guided her to one of the chairs so that she might avoid those penetrating eyes.

Following Geoffrey's instructions, she took the book from her handbag and placed it on the table. The book appeared quite mundane, but the effect it had on the Grandmaster was immediate. Robert de Sable reached for the book with eager arms, stroking the cover with a finger and gazing at it as if mesmerized. He opened the book and peered at the unknown script.

The Grandmaster spent several minutes examining the book in silence before passing it on to an eager Gilbert, who took hold of it with the same awe and reverence. Josephine recognized the ritual, for she had watched Geoffrey do the same for many nights on their long voyage. There was a strange power emanating from the book that couldn't be seen, but could be felt.

"I agree with you, Geoffrey," Robert said. He barely glanced at Josephine, his eyes still drawn to the book. "The Knights Hospitaller have long attempted to turn Rome's favor against us, and the threat of the book seems great. I would not have suspected it before seeing it with my own eyes. But there is a power here, and I suspect there is danger as well."

"I feel this script is very old indeed," Gilbert said. "We will need to consult with the scholars to see if they can decipher the meaning of these words."

"Do you think that is wise, sir?" Geoffrey asked.

"We must know what secrets the book contains," Gilbert said.

"We know that the Hospitaller wanted this book enough to enlist the aid of the Isma'ilites," Geoffrey said. "If what the stranger says is true, it contains secrets we would rather remain hidden from the world. Are there any great scholars within the Inner Circle?"

Gilbert frowned. "No."

"Do we dare let someone not of the Inner Circle try to decipher its meaning?" Geoffrey asked.

"You are right, Geoffrey," Robert said. "There is too much that we do not know about this book. Until we know more, we would do well to keep it hidden away from eyes that might recognize that script."

"But we must not dismiss the book so lightly," Gilbert said.

"Nor do I plan to," Robert replied. "We will discuss this more at a later time."

Geoffrey and Gilbert both nodded, and then Robert de Sable turned to Josephine. "I did not mean to ignore your presence," he said. "Please excuse my rude behavior."

"There is nothing to excuse, m'lord," she said. "My family died because of that book. I did not think it rude that it gained your full attention."

"I am sorry for your loss," he said. "Do you think you could you tell us of this stranger?"

She told him the best she could of the events that transpired after she awoke in the monastery. In truth, there wasn't much to tell. She had spoken to Damon for most of the morning and well into the afternoon, but much of their conversation had been about her family. He came back to her that evening, and they talked some more before he offered her the gift.

"And you accepted," Robert said. "What happened when you agreed?"

"He said that I must trust him. He looked at me with those eyes and bid me remain calm, speaking in that low voice that implants suggestions within our minds. He then took my wrist and made a sharp slash on it. He drank from me and my vision blurred. I don't know how long he drank of my blood. The next thing I knew, he had his wrist pressed against my lips and bid me to drink from him. I did, and the world seemed to come apart."

"Yes." Robert smiled, and Josephine saw understanding in his eyes. "And, afterward, did he mention anything about the book?"

"I did not realize the book's true importance then," she said. "I did not think to question him on it. He said it was important for it to remain safe. He said its journey had not come to an end yet and, until that time, there would be much danger."

"Did he say where the book must be taken to?"

"No," Josephine said. "I got the feeling that it wasn't that type of journey. I don't know; it's hard to explain. Perhaps it was simply the blood newly flowing within me, but I had a sense that it wasn't so much of a place the book must journey to as a time or a person."

Robert glanced at Geoffrey.

"The stranger often spoke in riddles," Geoffrey said. "It was almost as if he didn't want us to know too much about the book, only that it was important for us to keep it safe."

"We need to find this man," Gilbert said. "Did he say where he was going when he left you?"

"No," Josephine said. "I don't even remember him leaving. He was there, and then he was gone, but, for some reason, I did not question it."

"The power," Geoffrey said. "He implanted suggestions within your mind. Either before he shared his blood with you or after. It seems he wanted to avoid such questions."

"If what Geoffrey tells us is true, I'm not sure we want to find him," Robert said. "He seems to bring danger with him, and we have all the danger we need at the moment."

Robert's eyes rested on Josephine for several tense moments. "What are we going to do with you, Josephine?"

She was surprised at the question, and a little afraid.

He smiled at her and shook his head. "No, not that," he said, soothing her fears. "I think something quite different. The only ones like us that we know of, besides this mysterious stranger, are of the Inner Circle. We normally choose new initiates carefully, studying them as squires, and then allowing them knowledge of our secrets as knights. We watch them for many years before finally deciding on them, but it seems our decision about you has been made for us.

"Will you join the Inner Circle, Josephine?"

241

She glanced at Geoffrey who nodded. "Yes," she said. "If that is what is demanded of me."

"It is still your choice," Robert said. "We cannot, of course, make you a knight, nor can we scribe your name officially in our books, but we can perform the ritual of the blood and make it known to the Inner Circle of your special status. But, it is still your choice, Josephine. We will not do you harm if you choose not to take our oath."

She nodded. "I know of no others like us," she said. "You said the choice had been made for you, and so it seems that it has been made for me as well. I will take the oath."

"Good," Robert replied. "We will need to gather those of the Inner Circle that are within the temple, which will take some time, but all available members are always present at the ritual."

"Perhaps we can make an exception in this case," Geoffrey said. "Josephine is already the focus of much attention by those wishing her harm. It might be in the best interest of all if we keep her status a secret for now."

"I agree with Geoffrey on this," Gilbert said. "The three of us can be the witnesses to her oath. She is already a special case, it seems natural to make some exceptions in the ritual for her."

"So be it," Robert de Sable said.

***

In a room far beneath the surface of the temple, Josephine knelt in the midst of smoke rising from lit candles. She stared reverently at a pedestal that held a small bottle of what appeared to be wine, but Josephine knew otherwise. The knights were there, now dressed in white robes and bearing golden crucifixes about their necks. Geoffrey and Gilbert took their places on either side of the pedestal. Robert held a bible in one hand and a wafer in the other. He stepped in front of the pedestal.

"Lord, give us the strength and the wisdom to choose your champion here on Earth so that we may rise in strength defending your faith in the Holy Lands. We pray you infuse this champion with the same strength and nobility that graced your Son when he championed those same lands long ago, and we ask you to guide the hand of the champion to do your will and your will alone.

"Josephine, you have been chosen to become a champion of the Lord, to uphold the values and morality he wishes upon us, to not fall to the temptations of the Devil and to ever act in his name and his name alone. With this pledge, you will be tied to us in faith and in blood, acting to serve the Lord while the power of the Son's blood flows in your veins."

He placed his right hand on her shoulder. "Do you accept this offering?"

"I do," she whispered.

"Whoso eateth my flesh, and drinketh my blood, hath eternal life," Robert chanted.

He held out the small wafer and placed it upon Josephine's waiting tongue. She swallowed and watched the bottle be taken from the pedestal by Geoffrey, handed to Robert, and finally placed in her waiting hands. She clasped the bottle and felt a

243

tingling sensation run up through the palms of her hand. She could feel the power and the holiness infused within the bottle and trembled in its glory.

"This is the cup of my blood," Robert said. "The blood of the new and everlasting covenant. It will be shed for you and for all, so that sins may be forgiven. Drink. And feel the power of the Lord raising you up from the mortal plane and transforming you into a champion in his service."

Josephine knew the blood contained within the bottle was precious. Her hands shaking, she put the tip of the bottle to her mouth and allowed only the barest drop to stain her lips. The blood was surprisingly warm. She felt a tingle where it touched her lip and a strange warmth pass over her mouth.

She handed the bottle back to the Grandmaster and bowed her head.

"Go forth, Josephine, and serve the Lord with his blessing."

***

Later, back in the initial room, the four gathered around the book once again. Josephine still felt the strange warmth in her lips and had trouble concentrating on the words being spoken. She knew that Gilbert still wanted the book to be kept within the temple, while Geoffrey was insisting the book should remain with them.

"Enough," Robert said, finally. "I have heard what I needed to hear. I agree with you, Geoffrey, there is too much interest in the book right now. Already, the Hospitaller spread a new web of rumors in Rome. If they mention a sacred book being held secretly within this temple, we might find the priests banging on our door demanding to see the book."

"We cannot simply let the secrets of the book ride away from us," Gilbert argued.

"The book will not be forgotten," Robert said. "I will trace a few words from the book onto a parchment. These words will be chosen at random so that their meaning will not be clear to the one that looks upon them. This parchment can be given to our scholars to deduce the ancient language. In the meantime, we can search for any references to a mysterious book in hopes of gaining a clue to those secrets

"In time, the book will be forgotten or, at least, will not be the focus of such an active search. We can then safely bring the book back to us and study it at our leisure. Hopefully, by that time we will have learned more of the book and the strange language in which it was written."

Gilbert frowned, but finally relented. "I agree," he said. "We will gather what knowledge we can in the book's absence."

"Geoffrey, the book will be left in your care until such a time as it is deemed safe for its return," Robert said. "I would hear of your plans."

"We will leave when the sun sets on the morrow," Geoffrey replied. "Officially, I am still here at the temple, researching an artifact found in the Holy Land. Have a squire travel frequently to Paris and retrieve books on holy artifacts and ancient cultures. Perhaps you can search for clues to those secrets in these books but, if asked, the official word is that a strange knight from the Holy Land has returned and is deeply involved into some secret research.

"After two weeks' time, send out word that I travel to Rome. The Hospitaller and the Isma'ilites will think I go to continue my studies in hopes of unlocking the secrets from the book, which should draw attention away from the temple and away from us.

"By the time they realize their mistake, it should be too late. Our trail will have grown cold, and they will find it difficult to follow in our tracks. They will not be sure who has the book, and I don't think they will risk spreading such rumors without knowing the book lies within the temple. Already, the Church grows tired of investigating rumors that lead to nothing and further such failed inquisitions would hurt their cause."

"Agreed," Robert said. "We will make the arrangements. Be ready to ride at dusk."

CHAPTER TWENTY-THREE

Sir Jonathan Alderson sat in silence. His hair was neatly cut and combed to the side, his clothes clean and recently pressed, but the red, tired eyes betrayed his appearance. The muscles in his lower back clenched into a tight ball of pain which radiated out and washed over his shoulders. He had been up late the night before, as he had every night that week, and his exhaustion showed through his neat hair and fine clothes.

Despite these feelings, he remained motionless and patient. He stared up at the men before him and waited for the proceedings to begin. Everard de Montbard looked down at him and smiled. Jonathan took some comfort in the gesture. He knew the proceedings would not go well, but the mere fact that Everard showed him that brief sympathy suggested there was still hope. Had he already been condemned, his judge would remain emotionless, not wanting to show any connection with the guilty.

Sir Edgar Berard sat to the right of Everard. Jonathan did not have to look into Edgar's eyes to see how he felt. Edgar had already questioned his actions in the past. The old knight did not approve of his methods and had been furious at the loss of twenty seasoned veterans.

The man sitting to Everard's left was unknown to Jonathan. He had seen the man several times in the past few days, but had been busy with his own plans and paid him no mind. He should have been more attentive to the talk going on around him. As it was, he did not know if the man would sit in judgment for him or against him.

"Sir Jonathan Alderson," Everard said. "I wish, first, to inform you that this is not a formal inquisition by the knighthood. It is not, however, a light matter before us today, and we do hold some power over disciplinary action that may be handed down to you.

"You have been brought here because of the increased rumors of dealings with the Saracens, our enemies, and against our brother-knights, the Knights Templar. We will hold you to question about these charges and, should we find warrant, will open up an official inquest on the behalf of the knighthood. Do you understand?"

"Yes, sir."

"Good," Everard said. He glanced at the knights on either side of him and then turned back to Jonathan. "Let us, for the moment, dispense with formality and speak plainly to each other. These are the official charges, but well we all know that it is the failure to complete your special assignments that have brought us to this pass.

"In the recent weeks, you have made contact and allies with the Isma'ilites, a group of Saracen assassins of questionable character and allegiance. You have used them in pursuit of a mysterious book. During the course of these events, an entire troop of our knights was defeated at the hands of an unknown enemy."

"The Templar," Jonathan said.

"Yes," Everard said. "We are familiar with your theories of who attacked our troops. Those very same theories brought two priests to us questioning our actions on that night, questions we would rather not have to answer I might add."

"We have long tried to stir the tide of rumor against the Templar," Jonathan said.

"True, but we have not always been so actively involved in events against them. We can little afford to have our actions uncovered by the Church or, as you well know, it will be us facing the flames of the Church's ire, and not the Templar."

Jonathan nodded.

"We are all aware of your recent failures, Sir Jonathan," Everard said. "You have been given much latitude to accomplish your goals, but have thus far been unable to get your hands on this book you claim will put an end to the corruption of the Templar. The three of us have gone over the facts of these events in great detail, and what we wish to hear from you today is why you think this book is so important. What makes you think this book, which we have paid for in the blood of many of our own knights, will accomplish our goals?"

Jonathan had always evaded direct questions about the book and his discovery of what it may contain. Until now, he had never been pressed on it. This time there would be no evading.

"Well?" Everard asked.

"I first heard about the book from an old merchant in the bazaar." He thought back to that day. There was no way to describe the old man to them. He had a strange quality that drew Jonathan to him. He had eyes that bespoke of knowledge contained therein that all people sought but few obtained, and his words had the rhythm of truth.

"Do you visit the bazaar often?" Everard asked, and the strange man to his left chuckled.

"Not often, sir," Jonathan said. "I was just passing through, but something the merchant said must have intrigued me because I stopped to take a closer look at his wares. Most of it was common stuff, old artifacts, some pendants. He even claimed to have rock straight from the Dome.

"I was about to walk away when he grabbed me by the arm and said he had something that might tempt a knight such as me. I asked him what he meant by that, but then he stepped back and gave me a hard look." Jonathan did not mention the chill that ran through him when the merchant stared at him.

"He then said the oddest thing. He looked at me and said, why you aren't one of those Templar, you probably wouldn't be interested in this book anyway. It doesn't have anything to do with knightly things, it contains the secrets of the blood.

"I was, of course, surprised at his words and inquired further, but he said he didn't have the book anyway. He'd sold it to a fellow merchant that was interested in such things and, since I wasn't a Templar, he didn't think I was worth the trouble of searching down this merchant on a fool's errand.

"At first, I didn't think much more of it. The Knights Templar have been in these parts for decades and they haven't spent all that time under the light of the moon without attracting many different rumors to their name. I thought the old

250

man was just repeating some tavern tale he had heard, hoping to trick me into buying something."

"But I could not seem to get his words out of my head. The next day, I went back to the bazaar and tried to find the old merchant, but he was gone. I asked around and many the merchants were well aware of the old man. They called him a Traveler, one of those from the nomadic tribes that roam these lands, and whispered that he held the secrets of life and could read the future within the stars.

"I continued to look for the man over the course of the next few days and finally spotted him late one afternoon standing near a tavern. I took him aside and questioned him further, but he seemed uninterested in selling me this book. Not worth his time, he repeated. He'd already sold it to another merchant, and it would take too long to track it down. I asked him who this merchant was and he told me."

Jonathan stared up at the knights in front of him. He could read in their eyes they were not pleased at where this tale was taking them. Nor could he blame them when the blood of fellow knights had been spilled over a tale from an old merchant. He would not have believed it either had he not been there, had he not stared into the old merchant's eyes and felt the shiver swimming up his own spine.

"I asked him why he thought the book would be of interest to one of my brother-knights." Jonathan looked at each of the knights in turn. "The old merchant gave me the strangest look, grabbed my arm, and said, I think you know why, Jonathan. I

251

found this odd because, up until this point I had yet to mention my name."

"He could have found out your name from someone else," Everard said.

"True," Jonathan said. "But I have to wonder why he would go to that trouble. It had been several days since I had last seen him, even though I was a frequent sight in the bazaar during that time. Had he wanted to trick me, I would think he would have searched me out sooner, instead of forcing me to search him out."

"And this is why you have spent so much of our time and effort?" Everard asked. "Because of some words spoken by an old, probably drunk, merchant in a seedy bazaar?"

Jonathan frowned. There was no way to make them understand. They had not been there. They had not seen the old man.

"He spoke of other things," Jonathan said. He shrugged, knowing his explanation would do him little good. "He said the book would not interest me because it was old, very old, and written in a long dead language. I asked why it would appeal to the Templar, and he said that it told of their beginning. I laughed. I told him the Templar had not even been around even a century and asked what language had died in that time."

"He gave me another of his strange looks and said the Templar have been here far longer than that. They have been here since the beginning. They weren't always called the Templar, but they were always both holy and demonic, and the same blood flowed through them now as then."

252

"Certainly, he knew what words to use to strike our interest," Everard said. "But still, this is no proof of what the book contains."

"It was enough to pique my interest," Jonathan said. "I tracked down this merchant and questioned him about the book, but he claimed to have never heard of it, or the old man. I described the book to him in detail, for I had gotten a description of it from the old merchant, but the man denied knowing of it. But I could tell from his expression when I described the book that he lied. He had the book, but for whatever reason he denied it.

"I couldn't rightly barge into his home and search for it myself, so I enlisted the aid of those who could. I didn't expect what would happen next. I never told the Isma'ilites to harm anyone, simply to retrieve the book."

"You should have expected what would follow," Everard said.

"Perhaps," Jonathan said. "We had worked with them in the past, though, and they had proven reliable. It was, however, apparent after the incident that the book held some interest with the Templar, for they immediately put the girl under their protection and went after the book."

Everard nodded. "The merchant may have been intending to sell it to them, which would explain his lie to you."

"There's one other thing," Jonathan said. "I've spoken to you plainly of things that I have not told another, I might as well speak to you of this."

"Go on," Everard said.

"After the incident with the merchant, I went back to the bazaar to find the old man and gather more information from him. I was unable to locate him, so I went to the same merchants I had gone to before and inquired after him. This time they said they had never heard of the old man. I was angered by this, telling them I had been there not two weeks before and they had certainly known of him then. But they claimed to have never seen me before. And, just as I knew the merchant was not telling me the truth, I knew that these men were."

Everard glanced at Edgar and then leaned back to whisper to the strange man on his left. After a few moments of conference, he turned back to Jonathan.

His voice returned to its official tone. "Sir Jonathan Alderson. I must inform you that as of this moment you are hereby stripped of your knightly rank and privileges until such time as a further inquest can be held into the events we have spoken about this day."

He stared long and hard at Jonathan, and then added, "Until then, you are free to make use of your own time in any way you see fit. But you are not to involve the Knights Hospitaller in any investigations."

Jonathan nodded. He was being told, in no uncertain terms, that he had better produce results soon. It was what he expected, what he hoped for, in fact. They could have stripped him of his knighthood and forbade him further investigation into any knightly matters, which would have sealed his fate.

This was why he had been up late every night for the past week. He had been planning, studying everything he knew about the Knights Templar, especially the knights Gerard de St. Amand and Geoffrey Furnivall. He already knew Geoffrey was headed back to Europe. He had also arranged for the Isma'ilites to learn of his departure. If Geoffrey still had the book, he would have to hope the assassins would find it for him. He was not going to be able to stretch the leniency of the verdict into allowing him travel back home. Instead, he would need to focus on those left behind: Gerard de St. Amand and the strange monk that stayed with the knights.

He was dismissed, but he didn't return to his room. The castle air seemed stale, the walls too close together. And the thought of another night spent in his room studying old tomes for some clue did not appeal to him. Instead, he left the castle and wandered into the village. It was an hour after dusk, and a cool wind swept through the streets. He walked aimlessly, the night air clearing the haze from his mind, and the beginning of a plan came to him.

It had been made clear he was not to call upon his fellow knights to help him in his investigation. Yet, he could do little alone. He thought about the two priests that had recently visited the Knights Hospitaller. They were in the company of a Templar, though this knight was low in rank and not yet among their Inner Circle. The priests had just come from the monastery and brought word that Geoffrey Furnivall and the merchant's daughter would be traveling back to Europe soon.

He needed to get inside the monastery, but he knew the Templar would never allow it. If he could find the priests, he might be able to convince them to return to the monastery with him. He would need an excuse for them to return and for him to accompany them. The cardinal had mentioned that Geoffrey suffered from a strange sickness while they were there. Jonathan knew the truth, but perhaps the sickness could be used as a reason for them to return?

He smiled. Yes, it might work. He looked around and noticed his mindless wandering had led him to an area of the village dominated by taverns. He could hear the sound of raucous laughter drifting into the streets, and became aware of a man standing half in shadows between two of the taverns. The moonlight betrayed the man, and Jonathan found his gaze drawn to the man's eyes. There was something familiar about that stare, something youthful and yet ageless. They reminded him of the old merchant. He, too, had the eyes of a child in the body of an old man.

Jonathan crossed the street and approached the man. There was something very familiar about him, but Jonathan could not place it. The man stared at him as if he was waiting for something. "Can I help you?"

The man twitched, and then smiled at him. In his hand, he was holding a dagger, and Jonathan could see blood dripping from it. Jonathan opened his mouth to demand an answer from him, but for some reason, he could not force the words from his throat. He choked, unable to breathe, and felt a warm liquid flowing down his chest. Gasping, he put a hand to his neck and felt the same warmth plashing through his fingers.

His vision blurred. He fought it. With all his might, he struggled to clear his vision, and for one brief moment, the world around him became clear. The man still wore a curt smile, and in that moment, Jonathan recognized the man. He had only met him on a few occasions, but he had read much about him recently. It was Gerard de St. Amand, Knight Templar. And, with that thought, Jonathan Alderson fell over dead.

CHAPTER TWENTY-FOUR

A steady flow of rain fell from the sky, as it had for the past several nights. Josephine might have expected booming thunder and flashing lightning, but there was none. It was a light but steady flow that stopped only for a short time to gather itself before drenching the land again. When asked about it, Geoffrey had jokingly welcomed her to England.

The rain obscured her vision, which could normally cut straight through the shadows of the night. It confused her hearing, which could pick up a bird settling on a tree's limb in the far distance. It left her feeling very alone. Months ago, the feeling would not have bothered her, but now, she was accustomed to her heightened senses. She knew her life might depend on picking up that stray sound or spotting a slight movement within the shadows.

They reached a small village, and her heart lightened. Their destination was near. The drizzle continued, but they would soon be out of the miserable weather. They rode through the streets, and Josephine peered into windows trying to spot a face within the shadows. Unlike London, where they had so recently stayed, the people of the village took the darkness of the night as a sign of the day's ending instead of the night's beginning.

London. She had never been in such a place. In France, they had come close enough to Paris for her to see the outlying villages sprawling their way toward the city, but they had detoured to the small village around the temple and never set foot into the city proper. She had been in port towns and small cities in their winding travels through Europe, but none of these prepared her for a true city.

The first thing she noticed was the smell. It was the stink of body odor and waste riddled by the faint scent of death and decay. She gagged at the gates, and it was only at Geoffrey's urging that she forced herself to ride into the city. He assured her that she would get used to the smell, that she would learn to filter out the bad and focus on the pleasant, but she was unsure whether she would ever be able to ignore a stench that rose up from the very ground to fill the air of the city with its noxious gasses.

She finally succumbed to grabbing a patch of cloth from her saddlebag and covered her nose to filter out the smell. The sights that greeted her were not much better. It was well past dusk when they entered, but the city streets were alive. People were everywhere, some traveling on business, others on their way to the theatre, some huddled next to buildings searching for a scrap of food, and others passed out drunk in an alleyway.

They rode through the poorest quarters in the city, and the small, decaying homes slowly gave way to arching stone buildings that crawled up the sides of the streets to hover over the passer-by. The smell of death receded, if just by a little, and Josephine was able to drop her hand from her face to survey the new landscape. The rain had stopped, and she could see into the distance where building after building stood guard over the streets.

They finally came to a small inn that suited their needs. Josephine had expected most of the occupants to be asleep -- it was well into the night after all -- but the main room was still crowded with those wishing to spend the night's hours in blissful drink. She clung to Geoffrey, avoiding the stares of those in the inn, and was thankful when they finally made it up to their rooms.

Not for the first time in the past few weeks, she felt lost and alone, cut off from everything she had ever known. Her life had shifted so dramatically in the past weeks she barely recognized herself, as if she really had died with her family only to be born again a week later by the blood of a stranger.

"We're here." Geoffrey's voice called her back to the present.

They had passed through the whole of the village, a small town that Geoffrey called Southwork, and come to a small estate on the outskirts of town. The rolling lawn was dotted with trees, and the house was not much larger than those in the village. The house was dark, and Josephine wondered if anyone was home.

Geoffrey gave her a reassuring smile and tapped on the door. If anyone was home, they were surely asleep. How would they hear such a light knock? She was about to urge Geoffrey to knock louder when the door opened and a great expanse of man peered out at them.

Josephine took an involuntary step back. The man was half as wide as he was tall, and hefted a huge wood ax over one shoulder. His mustache, gray with age, twitched around his lips. He took a step forward, and Josephine stepped back to keep as much distance as possible between her and this menacing figure.

"Geoffrey?" The man's bushy eyebrows came together in the center of his forehead. "By the gods, it is you, Geoffrey."

"Thomas." Geoffrey clasped the arm of the giant. "It's been a long time."

"A decade if it has been a day," Thomas said. "And who is this you have with you?"

"Thomas Navarre, may I present to you the Lady Josephine."

She curtsied. "How do you do, sir."

He bowed back, but there was a strange look in his eye. He looked at Geoffrey and cocked his head to the side.

"Yes," Geoffrey said.

"Well," Thomas replied. "It seems you have quite a tale to tell. Come inside; no need for us all to remain out in the rain when a warm, dry house awaits us. I expect you are the author of the cryptic message I received a week back?"

"That I am, friend," Geoffrey said. "I am sorry I could not be more clear, but we had reason to obscure our travels."

Thomas led them into the back of the house and broke open a bottle of wine, pouring them each a glass. "Your message spoke of having a need you hoped I could meet?"

"We need a place to stay for a few weeks," Geoffrey said. "Or, perhaps, longer."

"And you want to stay here?" Thomas asked. "I wondered why the message had me out to these estates. Wouldn't you be more comfortable in the city?"

"It is our aim to keep our presence here as little known as possible," Geoffrey said.

"I see." Thomas nodded. "But to hide too much is to point out where you are hidden."

"True," Geoffrey said. "We will be seen in the city, but I would feel more comfortable away from the noise where we can at least hear the approach of any enemies."

"I would think we would want to keep away from London altogether," Josephine said.

"There is nothing that will get talk started faster than strangers keeping to themselves," Geoffrey said. "If we were to hide out in the house, rarely seen by those in town, we would quickly become the objects of scrutiny. And if we go about in the village but not to the city, people will wonder why a knight behaves as such and think us, perhaps, criminals."

"If you truly wish to hide, you must seem as normal as possible," Thomas said. "Granted, for us such a thing seems difficult at best. There will be enough suspicion at two newly arrived strangers that are only seen when the sun has vanished from the sky. These suspicions can be calmed, though, by making an effort to appear normal in all other respects."

Josephine nodded.

Thomas turned to Geoffrey. "If I may ask, how does a woman come to hold the blood within?" He chuckled. "I don't expect the knights are letting women in these days."

"It's a long tale, but one that you have every right to hear," Geoffrey said. He quickly filled

262

Thomas in on the events of the past few weeks, omitting any references to the book.

"Assassins, you say?" Thomas said, amazed. "The Old Man is still up to his old tricks, huh?"

Geoffrey smiled and glanced over at Josephine. "Can you believe this pile of flesh used to fit on a horse and actually ride out with us knights? They even made him one of the Inner Circle, though how he managed that one I'll never know."

"Don't believe his talk, Josephine," Thomas said. "I knew him when he was fresh to the field, still wet behind the ears and probably still missing his momma. Why, I wouldn't be surprised if he cried himself to sleep after we sacked our first city."

Josephine laughed. The thought of Geoffrey crying at anything seemed absurd.

"If I cried myself to sleep, it was because I realized I'd be spending the rest of my life with the likes of you," Geoffrey said. "It's good to see you, old friend, it has been much too long."

"How are the knights these days?" Thomas asked. He winked at Josephine. "I gave up that knightly stuff long ago. Though I expect they'll be calling me back any day now. They can't seem to run things properly without me."

"Don't listen to his nonsense," Geoffrey said. "He's as much a knight now as he ever was, or rather, half again more by the looks of him."

"I knew there was none that could match me." Thomas rubbed his belly. "So I figured the more of me the better."

"Are you really going to go back there?" Josephine asked. "To the Holy Land, I mean."

"Aye," Thomas said. "In a year or five, I'll be back there. Those of us that are of the blood are rotated out every decade or so. It wouldn't do for those we associate with down there to go noticing how we don't seem to be getting as many gray hairs as the others. Though why they bother that nonsense with me I don't know, I have as many grays as I'd likely have ever had."

Josephine nodded. She hadn't thought of it before, but it certainly would appear strange for a legion of knights to never age. She would have to live her life much the same, occasionally traveling to some place new to keep suspicions from arising about her, perhaps even taking on a different name.

She eased back in her chair, holding her wine glass close to her, and let the two old friends carry themselves away in their conversation. They were soon reliving old tales of battle and accounting the deeds of knights whose names she had never heard. She was glad for the respite, and sunk down into her own thoughts of what life may hold in store for her in the future.

CHAPTER TWENTY-FIVE

"The book is in play."

Damon kept his attention on the three men in front of him, but he was well aware of a fourth set of eyes watching from a crevice high above his head. The cavern was two hundred meters high and covered in shadow, but Damon got a clear look at the man when he had entered. He was curious; he didn't recognize the man. Odd, considering he had spent so many centuries here. He have might suspected the stranger was new to their ways, but he felt great power from the opening in the rock.

"You have done well, Damon. We have watched your progress intently. The book will do its work, winding its way through the land before finally making its way back to us. And with it will come a fresh set of initiates."

Damon bowed his head.

"You question?"

He smiled. There was no keeping secrets with them. "Only involving the Hospitaller. The Templar are like us, though young in our ways. The Hospitaller are not, and they have involved the Isma'ilites in their game."

"It is as we planned. You still cling to your covenant even after these many centuries here with us. Your brothers and sisters have long since died, and yet their laws live on in you. But we don't hide the truth from them out of fear, we hide it because they would not understand. The book will leave a trail, and those ready for the knowledge will find it. And that trail will eventually lead them here, to us."

"I don't understand."
"You will."

CHAPTER TWENTY-SIX

It was a month since they had arrived in Southwork, and it had rained almost every night. They spent the hours of twilight trapped indoors, reading books and keeping each other company. Thankfully, Father had taught her to read. He collected books among other trinkets, and having no sons, he insisted she learn his trade.

"You may very well get married and spend your days raising your man's children," he would say. "But it doesn't hurt you none to learn a few things before then."

It had seemed a needless chore. There were no libraries where they lived, and Father was not wealthy enough to own more than a few books. Now, she blessed him for it. Thomas had a treasure trove of books stashed at the estate, and she spent her nights reading them.

The few times it had not rained they visited London. Josephine was growing accustomed to the city. She learned to filter out the odors and even came to appreciate the throngs of people. They certainly made quenching the thirst easier.

Tonight, the rain had not come. She could tell by the moisture on the grass that it had rained that afternoon, but now the sky was clear and the moon unobstructed by clouds. They rode to Thomas's estate just outside of London, one of three estates the big man owned. The other was in the city, but Geoffrey said it was rarely used.

This estate, like the other, was simple and eloquent. Small bushes lined the recently cut lawn, and the trees on either side of the house showed the brilliant colors of the season. Thomas was waiting for them on the porch, whittling a piece of wood.

"What are you making there?" Geoffrey peered at the big man's handiwork. "Is it a pig?"

"Bah, it's a horse." He held it up for Josephine to see.

"I think it is a fine horse," she said.

"And I think you are a fine liar," Thomas replied, smiling. "But I thank you for it."

"I still think it is a pig," Geoffrey said.

"Now why would I be out here on this fine night carving myself a pig?"

"Why did you start up a poker game during a siege?"

"I did no such thing," Thomas said. "You don't believe him, girl, he'll only tell you lies about me."

"I only tell lies about you because no one would believe the absurdity of the truth."

Josephine laughed. It was good to see Geoffrey in such a good humor. He was different here, in England. He was relaxed.

"Don't worry, Thomas," she said. "I would never dream of believing you would play cards before a fight," Josephine said. "Why, if what I have heard is true, you'd be too busy in the outhouse fighting the strong drink from the night before!"

Thomas slapped his knee. "If that ain't the truth of it!"

"Are you ready to go, my friend?" Geoffrey asked.

268

"Aye," Thomas said. "I don't imagine I will be staying late tonight, though. I will just make a brief appearance and then be off."

"Business?" Geoffrey asked.

"Business, or pleasure, however you want to look at it," Thomas said.

"We could stop by somewhere on our way to the party?" Geoffrey asked.

Thomas shook his head. "I have an excuse to leave the boredom early and I plan on taking it. I'll leave you two to deal with the nonsense those nobles spew at these things."

Josephine sighed. Thomas had a way of making these events almost bearable. She had been excited, even flustered, at the first party she attended. But she soon found it to be a bore. The people were peacocks, each one trying to outshine the rest. It was tiring to watch, but Geoffrey insisted they take every opportunity to be seen in the city.

"If you don't want to stand out, be seen," he would say.

"Can't we be seen in a tavern?" They were certainly a lot more entertaining.

But he would just laugh. "People don't talk about who attended the local tavern."

This night's party was at a lavish mansion just inside the section of the city that housed those higher born. The estate could not be more different than the one they left. Plentiful gardens and great marble statues gave way to marble columns and stone fountains. The decorations looked impressive, but they were packed so tightly together that each had to fight the other for attention.

"Geoffrey, so good of you to have come." Robert Poynings greeted them at the door. Robert was not high born. He was a wheat merchant who had made his fortune during a great drought several years back. When Geoffrey had told her about the man, she didn't believe it. She couldn't believe this place could ever be without rain for months straight.

"Thomas, you are looking well," Robert said. "And you must be Josephine. I have heard so much about you."

They exchanged pleasantries with Robert and were then ushered inside where his wife took charge of them. She made a few comments to each and then led them to the back of the estate, where people were gathered around a large fountain. The servants wove through the area holding trays of food and glasses of wine. Thomas, catching one of them with a full assortment of drinks, nimbly grabbed glasses for the three of them.

Josephine sipped on the dry white wine and played the part of thoughtful observer, nodding her head and occasionally replying to a direct question but letting Geoffrey and Thomas lead most of the discussions. She was unaccustomed to dealing with people in this type of environment. She was happy to simply listen and learn, but she also did not want to appear too reliant on the knights. Eventually, she left them and drifted over to where several other ladies stood.

"Why, Josephine, we didn't know if you were going to show at this late hour," Margaret Paston said.

"The men got to talking and we were late, as usual," she replied.

"That is an interesting dress you have on, Josephine," Helen Berry said.

Josephine refused to be baited. "It is just something I found hanging."

"It must be difficult to find good help out there."

"We manage."

"I wonder what you do all day way out there in Southwork," Helen said. "It must be terribly dull to pass the time."

"It's peaceful," she said. "It gives me time to catch up on my reading. Oh, but living this close to the shops must wreak havoc on your reading time."

She was being bad, and Geoffrey would disapprove. It was rare for a woman to read, noble born or otherwise. It did the trick; she was promptly ignored.

She hovered around the edge of the discussions for some time, though her mind was often elsewhere. She had little interest in the current fashions of London or what nobleman was chasing what noblewoman, or any of the other gossip at court that seemed to predominate most of the discussions. She was relieved when she caught Thomas's signal that he was departing, and used it as an excuse to break away from the catty women.

"Don't let them get to you," Thomas said. "They are just a bunch of old hags, really, even the young ones are just old hags waiting to have their age catch up to their mentality."

"I don't pay them much mind," she said. "Honestly, I would rather spend an evening at your estate talking with you and Geoffrey than an evening in the city, but I suppose we must be seen now and again."

He winked. "It is part of the price we pay for being so dashing."

"We'll see you in a few days." She squeezed his shoulder. She envied him. He would soon be enjoying a quiet evening at home while she must, once again, brave the boredom of her betters.

She didn't return to the circle of noblewomen. She was out of patience with their chatter, so she joined Geoffrey. He was talking with several men, so she took up a position just within hearing range, but not so close to be noticed.

"There are some that say the Sultan cannot be pushed back," David Argoth said. "The failure of the campaign of Hattin and the disaster at Nazareth weakened our cause more than many know. If Redfort had heeded the council of the Hospitaller, we might not be in the mess we are in today."

Josephine's ears prickled at the mention of Redfort. Geoffrey and Thomas had been drilling her on the history of the knighthood, knowing that it was important for her to be knowledgeable in all areas of the Templar. Gerard de Redford was the Grandmaster of the Templar before Robert de Sable.

In Nazareth, Redfort went on a tirade, accusing the Hospitaller of being cowards for not charging into battle against the enemy. His cajoles worked, and the two groups clashed with their foe. In the midst of battle, the Horsemaster of the Hospitaller turned up dead, presumably at the hands of the enemy, and the Christian forces were driven back with heavy losses.

"There are some that say the Templar have grown too close to the Saracens," David said. "There are some that say the Templar have brought the worship of their heathen god into the house of our Lord."

Geoffrey grunted. "And there are some that say that nobles can hold their liquor no better than commoners."

This was met with laughter from several of the men, but Geoffrey did not stay around to enjoy it. He spotted Josephine at the edge of the crowd and joined her.

She smiled. "He doesn't look too happy with your comment."

"He's probably still trying to think of a reply," Geoffrey said. "Besides, some would say he's just getting a taste of his own medicine."

"And some would say he doesn't appear to like it." She giggled. "You've behaved just as poorly as me."

"Are you getting yourself into trouble?"

"I won't be invited over for afternoon tea," she said. "But I'll manage. So, this is how the highborn spend their time here in London?"

"Rather droll, isn't it?" he said. "It's much like a tavern on any given night, except people dress nicer."

"It smells better too."

"Yes, that too." He sniffed the air. "If only barely. I'd almost say I prefer..."

His body tensed, and his eyes searched the crowd behind her.

"What is it?" she whispered.

"It seems we did not do a good enough job in obscuring our trail here."

CHAPTER TWENTY-SEVEN

Josephine glanced over her shoulder, searching through the crowds. Her eyes passed over people, faces that were both known and unknown to her, but she couldn't pick out what had caused his sudden change. And then she saw him. He was carrying a plate of hors d'oeuvre. He glanced her way, and she recognized his eyes.

She shivered. "It's him, isn't it?" she whispered. "The one who killed Edward."

"Hush." Geoffrey grabbed her by the arm and led her through the house. "We ride straight to the estate."

"Shouldn't we go to Thomas's?" she asked. "It's closer, and he should be home by now."

"We have to get the book."

The book. She wanted to tell him to forget the book; it didn't matter. They should be safeguarding their lives, not a book. But the book was more important to him than his life. Or her life, for that matter. It presented a danger to the entire knighthood, and he would do anything to keep it safe.

She should feel the same. She was a knight now; she had sworn the oath. But, given the same choice, she would choose life. The book had already caused enough death.

Their horses were quartered in the stables, and a servant stood by ready to assist them. Geoffrey didn't bother with the man. He brushed past him and released his horse from the stall. "Can you ride bareback?"

"No." She hated the delay, but it was better to take the time now than for her to be thrown from the horse later. He grabbed a saddle from the wall, and she went to the door to watch for danger. At any moment, she expected dark figures to swarm the courtyard wielding curved blades and murderous intent. But it was strangely quiet.

Geoffrey finished with the clasps, and they mounted. The courtyard was still empty, but she could feel the danger in the air. They galloped through London, ignoring the angry accusations of those forced to scramble out of their way, and left the city.

The roads were clogged with mud, so they rode in the fields. It was faster to go overland, and Geoffrey knew the land well enough not to need the roads. Josephine's horse was well-trained and followed Geoffrey's lead without direction from her. She kept her eyes behind them, scanning the land for an unusually dark shadow, or the glint of moonlight on metal.

They approached Southwork, and Geoffrey slowed his horse to a trot. He motioned her to pull up beside him. "When we get to the estate, go retrieve the book. I will check the house for assassins and meet you out front. If we see any sign of them, do not delay. Head straight for the horse and be away from here. If needed, I will hold them off."

"I can't leave you," she said.

"The book is more important."

"I can fight."

"You will do no such thing," he said. "I gave you my oath once, Josephine, that you would come to no harm so long as I might protect you. And you gave an oath too, later that night. Do you remember your oath?"

She frowned, but nodded.

"Protect the book at all costs," he said. "If we fail in that, then all of us are lost."

***

Geoffrey didn't wait for her reply. He spurred his horse into a gallop and skirted the edge of the village. It would not do to attract too much attention. The Isma'ilites might not know where they stayed, but a tale of a man and a women racing through the village would get back to them. And from here, the assassins could pick up their trail.

How did they track them to England so fast? His mind flashed through their travels trying to pinpoint where they made their mistake. But it didn't matter. It was better to focus on the now and worry about the how later.

They reached the estate, and Geoffrey rode right up to the door before dismounting. There was no point waiting to check for the enemy. Thomas had picked this house well. It stood on a hill and anyone approaching would be noticed long before they caught sight of anyone inside. Besides, it didn't matter. They had to get into the house anyway. The book was well hidden, but given time, the Isma'ilites would uncover it.

He paused just inside the entrance and held onto Josephine's arm. It was dark, but his vision could pierce the shadow. The house was as they had left it. He sniffed the air and picked up a strange scent, but it was faint. Pushing Josephine toward the stairs, he went to check the main room. It would not do to be caught unawares because the enemy had recently bathed. He prowled through the house, focusing on every sound, each sight, and any smell to detect anything out of place. He heard Josephine upstairs retrieving the book, but all else was quiet.

Geoffrey relaxed. If the assassins had been here, they were gone now. But they were sure to have an agent in town watching the house, and Geoffrey wanted to be away before more could arrive. He was just lucky to have caught sight of the Isma'ilite posing as a waiter at the party else they might have had more time to set up an ambush.

There was something strange about that. Saracens were not unknown in England, but they were not common either. It was a mistake for him to have gotten so close. Or was he just as surprised to see them? He might have donned the outfit of a servant to overhear dinner conversation in hopes of catching a stray morsel that would lead him to his prize.

But still, it was a mistake for *him* to do it. Surely, he knew he would be recognized. He should have sent another to the party. He was too smart to risk everything in the name of ego.

Geoffrey cursed. Of course he wanted to be discovered. They had already searched the house and found nothing. The assassin decided to let his prey lead him to the prize, and Geoffrey had played the fool and walked into the trap.

The door creaked open. Josephine! He had been so preoccupied he had lost track of her in the house, and she was already at the door. "No," he whispered. He didn't dare give a louder warning, and prayed her sensitive ears would pick the word out of the air.

He rushed through the house, cutting a corner too tight and knocking a table into the wall. He barely noticed. Josephine's figure was hovering in the doorframe, the moonlight shining on her hair. She had not heard his quiet warning. And when he reached her, she was already falling.

Dark shadows crawled across the lawn like little ants surrounding a dead mouse. There was a dagger sticking from Josephine's shoulder, and another flying through the air. He stuck out his left arm to block the throw, but he wasn't wearing his armor, and the knife thunked into the meaty flesh of his hand.

Geoffrey jerked the dagger loose and threw it, but his aim was haphazard. He didn't bother with Josephine. He could better protect her now by making himself the target, so he drew his sword and launched himself at the closest shadow. He trusted she would remember her oath.

He made short work of the first assassin. The man's attack was frenzied, but he was no match for the power of the Inner Circle. Geoffrey batted the sword aside and felled the man with a kick to the groin.

Two approached from the side. They were cautious, forcing him to engage. He leapt between them, giving them the advantage in order to turn them away from Josephine. He was patient, exchanging blows with them, but then he saw another shadow climbing up the hill and knew he had to be quick. Josephine was just then standing up, and the assassin was already between her and the horses.

Geoffrey let his sword drop too close to the ground. The assassin saw the opening and lunged, but Geoffrey was too quick. He stepped aside and then impaled the man. He immediately dropped to the ground, avoiding the second assassin's attack. His sword was buried in the first assassin, the hilt resting against the man's belly, so he pivoted and threw the man into his companion. They both went down.

He glanced at Josephine. She didn't have a weapon, but she was fast. She rushed the assassin, avoiding his sword and knocking him to the ground with the force of her body. She stumbled, but didn't pause to finish off the man. Instead, she kept her promise by running to the horses.

Geoffrey reached over and broke the neck of the assassin trying to untangle himself from his dying companion and then retrieved his sword. He expected the other assassins to be chasing after the girl. They could clearly see she had the book in her hands. But they were running back down the hill as if they were retreating.

Horses. They couldn't intercept her before she reached her horse, so they would go back for their own. They might not be fast enough, but he was. Not bothering with his own horse, he took off in their direction.

He was halfway down the hill when he spotted a single assassin standing in the middle of the road. This one wasn't going for the horses. He was waiting for Geoffrey. Had it been anyone else, Geoffrey would have dashed past, perhaps taking a swipe at him as he passed, but remain fixed on his goal. But this was no ordinary man. Geoffrey had seen this assassin defeat Edward. This one was too dangerous to leave at his back.

The assassin held two swords, one long and curved, the other short and straight. It was difficult to wield two blades at once, and most used the off-hand weapon mainly to parry and for the occasional strike. But this assassin could use them both with deadly precision.

Geoffrey stepped forward and engaged his enemy. He had often practiced swordplay with Gerard and was not intimidated by the two blades. He feinted an overhead slash and then swiveled the blade so that it would come up from beneath the man's belly. But quick as he was, the man he faced was faster. The curved blade parried his broadsword while the shorter blade grazed his shoulder.

Geoffrey danced back to evade a wicked backslash from the scimitar. It was too bad he didn't have time to put on his armor back at the house, but fighting without the encumbering metal had its advantages. He lunged forward, forcing the assassin to step to the side, and then dropped to a crouch.

Whipping out his foot, he knocked the assassin's legs out from under him.

He dove forward with his blade, but his enemy rolled away and flipped back onto his feet. They exchanged blows, neither cutting through the other's defenses. He needed to give his enemy something. He pressed forward, slashing at the assassin's shoulder, and leaving his leg exposed. The assassin parried his attack, and pinned his thigh with the shorter blade. Geoffrey shifted his weight to that same leg, pivoted, and kicked the man in the gut.

The assassin anticipated the move at the last second. He was unable to avoid the blow, but twisted enough to miss the full brunt of it. The assassin danced to the right and twirled at him, sending one blade after another, and Geoffrey was forced back. It took all his concentration to keep the dangerous blades away from his flesh.

He took another hit to the thigh, this one deeper than the first, and a cut to his right forearm. It was a shallow slash, but the blood was seeping down his wrist and into his hand. The blood mixed with sweat making it difficult to keep a firm grasp on the hilt of his broadsword.

The assassin pressed his advantage. He feinted to one side then sprung to the other, forcing Geoffrey to put the weight of his body on his injured leg. Geoffrey took a step back, and the assassin surged forward. The calm demeanor was gone. The assassin was now raining down blows one after another, his face twisted into a snarl of utter hatred.

The precision was gone, but the speed of the attack kept Geoffrey on the defense. The attack amounted to little more than wild slashes. They had great force, but little accuracy, and Geoffrey's blade continued to deflect them. He was patient. He did not return any of the attacks with one of his own. The assassin was in a fit of rage, and he would soon make a fatal mistake. Geoffrey waited for that opportunity.

And then his grip slipped.

The force of the blow sent his broadsword tumbling out of reach. Geoffrey cursed himself for a fool. His enemy had not been filled with rage. The powerful slashes were meant to rip the sword from his slippery hand. He took a cut to the arm, and another across his side. His blade was three steps to his right, but the assassin would expect any move toward it. Instead, he rushed forward, hoping to slip between the blades. He was fast, but the assassin was faster. The scimitar tore through the side of his throat, and Geoffrey lashed out with his arm, clubbing the assassin to the ground.

He couldn't breathe. Blood flooded his windpipe. He put his left hand to his neck, stifling the flow, and scrambled to his sword. His foot slipped on his own blood, and he came crashing down to his knee, but he got his hand around the hilt of the sword. He turned around, but the assassin was there, his blade slicing into the other side of his neck.

CHAPTER TWENTY-EIGHT

Josephine had broken her leg when she was seven. She had been playing a game with her sisters, and her foot got twisted under the rug just when her oldest sister jumped on her back. She still remembered it like it had happened yesterday morning. There was a loud pop, but she didn't feel anything for several seconds. She even tried to get back to her feet, but the pain hit her when she stood up.

That pain was nothing like what she felt now. The knife sticking out from her shoulder burned as if it had been heated in a forge. She rode at full gallop, and the tip of the blade scratched against the bone with each stride of the horse. This sent tendrils of excruciating pain shooting down her arm and chest like someone had reached into her wound and was ripping out chunks of meat and bone with their fingernails.

She knew this would end if she removed the blade, but she didn't dare. She would have to use her right hand to yank the knife out of her shoulder, leaving only her left hand to grip the reins. That hand was already weak from pain, and she needed her grip to steady herself on the back of the horse.

She looked behind and saw riders in the distance. They were still far away, but they were gaining ground. And her horse was still winded from the ride from London. It wouldn't be able to continue at a fast pace for long. She dug her heels in and urged it to use what strength it had to keep the riders at a distance.

But she knew there was no hope of losing the assassins. When she had escaped to the Templar, they had let her go. They wanted to see if she would lead them to the book. She had the book now, and they knew it.

The path ahead was covered in mud, so she sent the horse galloping through the open fields. She needed time. Time to think. And time to get the knife out of her shoulder. The rush of blood flowing from the wound had slowed, but it still oozed. She could feel it wet against her blouse, sticking to her breasts.

Could she make it to London? No, it was much too far away. Her horse would be spent before she crossed half the distance. It would also be a mistake to ride into London with a knife in her shoulder and assassins on her trail. There would be too many questions. They would also want to tend to her wound. She might protest, but she was just a girl, they would think her hysterical.

There was danger in that. The blood gave her extraordinary powers of healing. It might take a day, or two, but the wound would heal. And it would heal far faster than an ordinary person. What had Geoffrey said? That he had seen a babe killed just for having a strange mole on its body? She could hear the voices accusing her of pacts with the Devil.

No, she couldn't go to London. She must head for Thomas's estate, but that was still much too distant for her horse to travel at this brisk pace. She needed to lose the assassins first. But how? Their horses were fresh, and there weren't enough trees to provide her with cover. After all, she couldn't simply circle around a farmhouse and then disappear.

She glanced behind her. The assassins had covered half the distance between them, and she could now clearly make out their silhouettes against the moonlight. There were three of them. And *he* wasn't one of them. She would recognize the one that killed Edward, even at this distance.

And Josephine knew she couldn't lose them. Her horse was almost spent. She had to do something, and she had to do it soon. She searched around for anything that might provide some cover and her eyes went to a farmhouse in the distance. It wasn't perfect, but it would suffice for what she had in mind.

The house was dark, but she couldn't tell if it was from being abandoned or if the occupants were simply asleep. She hoped it was abandoned. There wasn't time to find a different spot. She galloped past the house and raced to the barn. The barn door wasn't open, and she didn't want to risk it being locked, so she steered the horse around back and jumped off.

She jerked the dagger out of her shoulder and a rush of blood came with it. The horse backed away, nervous, but it was battle-trained so it didn't bolt. She huddled at the corner of the barn trying to ignore the pain lancing down her arm and silence the thud of her heart beating in her chest.

The first rider raced past and yelped in surprise at seeing her horse. This warned the second rider who slowed to a trot and leapt off his horse.

Josephine could hear the gallop of the third rider's approach, but she concentrated on this one. He drew his blade, but he hadn't spotted her yet. He was looking down the rear of the barn, perhaps thinking she'd made a run for it.

She sprang at him. He turned, trying to get his sword between them, but she was too fast. She plunged the dagger into his chest and heard the loud crack of bone as she buried it to the hilt. She expected a scream of pain or anger, but his eyes just widened and his legs went limp. He fell backward, and the weight of his body tugged the dagger from her hand.

Damn. She should have kept a better grip. But it was too late now; the first assassin had circled around and was now off his mount. She charged. He lunged at her with his sword, but his blade seemed to move like it was stuck between two moments in time. She batted it away, ignoring the pain erupting from her forearm where the side of the blade bit into flesh, and clubbed him in the neck with her fist. There was a crackle of bones snapping, and he collapsed to the ground.

The third rider was off his horse and approaching from behind her. She grabbed the dead man's sword and whipped around, holding the curved blade awkwardly in front of her. The last time she had held a sword in her hands, she was eight and had taken her grandfather's sword down from its place of honor over the fireplace. The sword was almost as big as she was at the time, and her mother had yelled at her.

The assassin saw the clumsy way she held the blade, but there were two dead Isma'ilites that warned she was not to be underestimated. She defeated those two by surprise. They did not expect her attack, and weren't prepared for the speed at which she executed it. This one was cautious.

He tapped the tip of his blade against hers, and she flinched. He didn't press the advantage. He circled to the left and tapped her blade again. She jerked her blade to the side, anticipating an attack, but it didn't come. Was he toying with her? No. He wanted her to let down her guard, and then he would attack. It would be swift. A lunge. He wouldn't want to warn her by raising the sword for a slashing attack.

He tapped her blade again, and this time she didn't react. She would watch, wait for his move, and be ready for it. The ritual repeated, and the assassin circled her. Is he stalling for time? She listened, but she couldn't hear the approach of horses. No, that is what he wants.

And then the attack came. She easily dodged to the side, but was too flustered to take advantage with an attack of her own. He dropped his game, and came at her with his blade twirling and twisting in the air. She was fast, but he was deceptive and the blade scraped against her ribs. She managed to parry two swings, but almost walked into his next lunge. She leapt away at the last moment, the blade teasing her flesh enough to draw blood again.

She could not keep up with him. He'd let her parry those two attacks to set her up for the third. Next time, she might not be fast enough. She might

288

have the advantage in speed, but that could not make up for her lack of experience with a blade. Had she even a few lessons, the blood could have made up for it, but as it stood, she was as much a danger to herself as to him.

She could not best him with a blade, but she was fast and strong. He came at her, and she dove to the ground, rolling. He leapt over her easily, but she did not intend to trip him. She sprung, closing the distance between them before he could whirl around and get his sword in place. She bowled him over and landed on top shredding into his face and chest with her fingernails.

She lost control. Weak in mind and body, the scent of blood strong in the air, the thirst took over. She hissed and drove his head back into the ground, baring his neck. Holding him in place, she sank her fangs into his flesh and felt the warmth of life's blood flow into her.

She drank.

Time lost all meaning to her, and the fury of her thirst lasted until the man's heart stopped, finally ceasing the flow of blood. She rose from the ground, the front of her dress covered in blood. It dotted her lips, soaked her hair, and dripped down her cheeks. She stood over the body, staring at the moon and reveling in the ecstasy. She could feel the strength returning to her body. Even now, the pain in her shoulder had receded to a dull ache. Soon, the pain would cease, and the wound would close. It might take a few nights to heal completely, but it would no longer encumber her.

Josephine looked around. The assassins' horses had fled, the stench of blood too much for their training, while her own horse was trained by the Templar and remained where she'd left it. She stood still and listened, but couldn't hear anything out of place in the night.

Slipping out of her dress, she used the backside to clean the blood from her face and tore off a strip of cloth to wrap around her wounded shoulder. The flow of blood had stopped, but the ride to Thomas's might cause it to start again.

She stood there, naked, staring at the dead men in front of her. She knew what she had to do, and it was revolting. But there was no getting around it. She went to the man she'd clubbed in the neck and undressed him. His pants were too big for her, so she had to take his belt as well. She also had to roll up the sleeves on his shirt else they cover most of her hand.

She tossed her bloody dress on the ground and walked over to the horse, but then thought better of it. It was better not to leave any evidence of her presence. She grabbed the dress, and also the sword. She might not know how to use it, but she felt safer with the weapon strapped at her waist.

She mounted and tapped her heals against the horse, but she didn't steer it towards Thomas's estate. It would be foolish to ride straight there. The assassins might find their fallen men, and she didn't want to make it easy for them to track her, so she rode off in a different direction. After a while, she picked a new direction and headed for the road. It was bogged down with mud, but she let the horse

290

trot for a fair distance before going back overland. She continued this winding path, never heading straight for Thomas's estate, but always in the general direction.

Finally, after an hour of winding back and forth, she abandoned the meandering path and urged the horse into a half gallop. She had covered a fair distance and it wouldn't be long before she reached Thomas's estate.

Would Geoffrey be there? He had told her to get the book and ride off if there was trouble, but he hadn't mentioned where they should meet. But if he survived, he would surely meet her there.

If he survived.

She could not imagine anyone defeating Geoffrey. Not even the one who had killed Edward. But she didn't know how many had stayed behind to fight him. Three had followed her, but how many had been at the house? She tried to think back, to count them, but she was unsure. It had all happened too fast.

She knew her horse was exhausted, but she couldn't wait any longer. She kicked it into full stride. Geoffrey would be there when she arrived. She'd spent a lot of time covering her trail. He would be waiting for her.

But what if he wasn't?

No matter how she tried, the thought nagged at her and wouldn't let go. Geoffrey was her anchor in this new life. He taught her to feed and how to travel. On the trip to Paris, he taught her how to dig a hole in the ground and bury herself if she could not find shelter for the day.

"The trick is to pile the dirt on a blanket," he had said. "And then lie down in the hole and slide the blanket over you. But the real trick is in the breathing. If you let it, the mind will become panicked with the idea of suffocation. You must breath through your nose and into your belly, not your chest. This will help keep you calm and relaxed."

She followed his directions now, hoping to dispel the sinking feeling in her gut, but it didn't work. She could still see him bursting in front of her and putting his hand in the path of a knife meant for her. She saw the blade sticking through that hand, and felt the blood trickling on her ankle.

He would be at Thomas's. He had to be there. She still needed him.

She slowed the horse to a trot when she reached the edge of the estate. The assassins had tracked them to England and discovered the house in Southwork; did they know about Thomas's estate too? She thought not. They had only rarely traveled out because of the near-constant rain, and they had only been to Thomas's a few times. But she kept her eyes out for anything out of the ordinary as she approached.

The house was dark, but Thomas had little need for lights. He might light a lamp to read, but otherwise, he could exist just as well in the dark. She jumped down from the house and was halfway to the door when it opened and Thomas came barreling at her with his axe raised over his head.

Josephine had spent several evenings with the knight, but she did not recognize the towering

292

menace racing toward her. There was death in his eyes, and it happened so fast she could not think of anything to do but just stand there.

Thomas stopped. "Josephine?" He dropped the axe and shook his head. "My world, girl, what are you doing here at this hour dressed as one of them damned assassins?"

The clothes! She'd forgotten about them. "My dress was bloody," she said. Her heart was beating so fast that she was having trouble breathing. "Is Geoffrey here?"

"What's happened?"

"Is he here?"

"No, girl, I haven't seen him since I left the party." He grabbed her by the shoulders. "You must tell me what has happened. Why are you dressed as one of them?"

"The assassins," Josephine said. "They attacked us at the house. And Geoffrey stayed behind to hold them off."

"They followed you here? To England?" He shook his head. "That doesn't make sense. Why are you so important?"

"Not me," she said. "It's something I have."

"Tell me the whole story," he said. "And quickly."

"We don't have time," Josephine said. "Geoffrey stayed behind."

"I know what is in your heart," Thomas said. "Believe me, it is in mine as well. But whatever occurred has already happened. No matter how fast we are, we cannot beat time. Now, tell me your story."

"But Geoffrey..."

"Is either alive or dead," Thomas said. "What we do now will have little effect on the outcome of his life. But it may have an outcome on yours. Now speak."

Josephine stepped out of his grasp and went back to the horse. "It's this." She pulled the book out of the saddlebag. "This is what they are after."

He took the offered book and flipped through it. "I can't read this."

"Neither could Geoffrey." She wished now that they had told Thomas about the book. "But that book is what the assassins are after. And it seems they are willing to track us here to get it. Whatever it is, Geoffrey believes it represents a danger to the Templar."

Thomas stared off in the direction of Southwork. "You rode straight here?"

"No," she said. "Three of them followed me. I knew my horse couldn't make it here at full speed, so I set up an ambush for them."

"I take it from your strange garb that you made a good account of yourself."

"They are dead," she said. "I..." She remembered the feeling that came over her when she pounced on the last assassin. "At the end, I..."

"The blood took you."

She bowed her head. "Yes."

"It happens," he said. "Battle is a strange mistress. I've seen knights still green behind the ears take a sword for a comrade, and veterans of many battles weep before an onslaught."

"It felt awful," she said. "Only, it didn't. It felt wonderful, like for the first time in my life I was truly alive. But, now, thinking back, it was awful."

He touched her shoulder, and she looked down to see a spot of blood. Her wound must have bled during the ride and seeped through the cloth.

"You were wounded?" he asked.

She rubbed the shoulder. "A knife."

"Geoffrey explained what happens when you don't feed? It is much the same with wounds. If you lose too much blood, you can lose control. It is something you must guard against, because the need to feed will consume everything. What you felt was only the beginning. If left unchecked, you would not care who the blood comes from, only that you must have it."

She nodded.

"It is too dangerous to go back to the house," he said. "I know, I know, you want to save Geoffrey. I do too, but that battle is well over by now. All we can do is wait, and plan what to do next."

"Next?"

He stared at her. "I know you don't want to think about this, but we need to be prepared if Geoffrey doesn't arrive."

"I understand." And she did. Suddenly, it was clear. She knew what she had to do, and she would not let Geoffrey down. "If he doesn't arrive within the hour then I must get out of England."

CHAPTER TWENTY-NINE

There was a thump outside her door, and Josephine came awake. Her heart raced, and she lay very still, listening. There was another thump, this one further away. She sighed. It was just someone walking down the hallway.

Her sleep was often troubled. She would wake to any strange noise outside her door and was greeted by heat and sweat and the soft motion of the sea beneath her.

It had been different on the passage to France. Geoffrey had been with her. Then, as now, she spent her days in the cramped quarters wrapped in several blankets to keep the sunlight from her flesh. Her body sweltered inside the protective cloth. But he had been with her then, and she had felt safe.

Not so now. Each sound brought with it fear that someone had come to check on the strange lady that never left her room during the day. She sometimes left her room at night, but she kept it brief. She longed to exult in the night air, but it was too dangerous. Instead, she would feign sickness, and retreat back to her room.

At least this time she didn't need to bother with clothes. Geoffrey had been amused at her modesty, but she noticed he did not strip down under his blankets either. She rolled over, her sweat-soaked body sticking to the blankets, and tried to go back to sleep.

There was another thump outside and loud footsteps pounding down the hall. What was going on? She lay very still and listened. There were more footsteps, and these seemed to stop just outside her door. She held her breath and prayed the next sound she heard would not be knocking at her door. There was a bump further down the hall, and the footsteps followed it.

And then came a loud crash above her, followed by several men cursing. She strained to hear, but couldn't quite make out what they were saying. Nervous, she slipped her hand out of the covers and grabbed her dress. If there was some type of accident, they might require all the passengers on the deck. But, it was still midday. She didn't know how long she could survive under the glare of the sun, but she knew it wasn't long.

More footsteps outside her door, and a woman called out, "Johnny, get back here!"

"But I want to get up to the deck. Tom and Beth said to meet them there."

"You can play with your friends after you have packed."

"But mom!"

Packed? Josephine smiled. They must be near the port. That was the cause of all of the commotion. Soon, she would be able to walk under the stars and feel the wind brush against her cheek without worrying about looking suitably nauseated and disoriented. She lay there and listened to the sounds of people preparing for departure.

The noise outside her door died down, though she still heard the occasional bump and crash from above. The ship flowed back and forth atop the waves, but it was no longer moving forward. She pictured the mass of people departing the ship, and the sailors packing up the stores to transport them to town.

A loud knock came from her door.

"Miss Josephine? This is the Captain. We've arrived at port. Are you all right in there?"

"Yes," she called out.

"Do you need some help packing your things?" he asked.

Damn. She hadn't thought about what to do when they finally got to port. She had just assumed everything would be fine. Resigned to what she had to do, she gathered her strength and raised herself off the bed. She kept the blanket wrapped around her and opened the door a crack. "Captain." Her voice was scratchy. "I am not feeling well. I was up most of the night with the sea's tides and I'm exhausted. Do you think it would be all right if I slept a few more hours and disembarked later this evening?"

"Miss Josephine, you look awful," he said. "Perhaps I should get someone to take a look at you."

"No." She shook her head. "It's just the heat from this blanket, but huddling within it keeps my stomach somewhat settled. I will be fine. Just a few more hours, Captain, please, I beg of you, I'm too tired to leave just yet."

"A few hours won't hurt me none, Miss Josephine," he said. "We are going to be up late unloading all of the supplies anyway. I just hope you can sleep through all the racket. If you need any help with your bags, just give me a holler and I will send one of the boys down to help you."

"Thank you, Captain."

The light of the sun, even muffled as it was in the depths of the ship, pressed against her skin. Just beneath its touch was a burning sensation like a mosquito's bite begging to be scratched. She wanted to dash to the bed, pounce on it, and cover herself deep within her blanket to ward away the painful light, but it wouldn't do for the Captain to hear such activity coming from her cabin. She shambled to the bed, walking like she imagined someone dizzy from the sea would walk, and when she finally reached the bed, she sank into it and pulled the blankets tight around her.

Josephine huddled there for the rest of the day. The Captain had been correct about the noise -- she was unable to get back to sleep. But even if the ship had been quiet, she would have been unable to find rest. She was too anxious to be rid of the cabin, so she spent the time imagining the feel of the night air dancing through her hair and picturing the moon glowing in the sky.

It grew dark, and she was finally about to pack up her things. She was careful to stagger when she reached the main decks. It wasn't difficult. Weeks spent in her cabin had left her weak and disoriented. She wanted to rush out onto the dock, but fought down the urge. Instead, she made her way to the Captain.

"I wanted to thank you for your kindness, sir." She held out a few of the coins Thomas Navarre had given her.

"Miss Josephine," he said. "I was just doing my duty, and it was my pleasure to look after you."

She reached out and squeezed his arm. "You have gone far beyond the call of duty, Captain. You made sure that my dinner was brought to me each evening and my days were undisturbed." She slipped the coins into his hand. "I cannot tell you how difficult it is to travel when the sea disagrees with me so, but you have been absolutely wonderful in making me as comfortable as possible."

"Thank you, Miss Josephine." He tipped his head to her. "And I know you want nothing more than to leave this ship. Here, let me help you."

He took her arm and escorted her to the dock. What she wanted more than anything was a nice room at an inn and a hot bath, but she stayed on the dock and chatted with him for a few minutes. Finally, she thanked him again for his kindness, kissed him lightly on the cheek, and went in search of her desire.

She arrived at the inn a huddled mass, her hair wet with sweat and clinging to her head. An hour later, she emerged, clean from a long bath and dressed in fresh clothes. She carried a large bag in her hand and made her to the small building near the gate. A sign out front marked it as an outpost of the Knights Templar.

She entered and spotted a squire sitting behind a large desk. He looked up, studied her a moment, and went back to writing. "May I help you?"

"Yes." She rifled through her bag and produced the note Micah had given her. "I am just in from England and would like to withdraw this money."

The squire looked down at the paper and studied it a moment. He glanced back up at her, and she could see suspicion in his eyes. The squire may have thought nothing of a man holding the same document, but a woman?

"I'll need to check this over with my commander," he said. "I hope you don't mind?"

"Of course not," she said. "Sir Geoffrey Furnivall might mind. He was very insistent that I would have no problems with the note. You do recognize his signature down at the bottom, don't you? He might not be pleased to hear of the confusion when I drop in to see him. But I don't mind, please, take your time."

"Geoffrey Furnivall, you say?" He frowned. "When did you say you saw Sir Geoffrey?"

"I didn't say. But it was a couple of months back. I was called home for a time, but I am gladly back in the Holy Land and so looking forward to sharing dinner with him. He made me promise to stop by on my way back, and I never fail to keep my promises." She gestured at him, letting her wrist hang limp as she had seen some of the women in London do.

"Sir Geoffrey was called back to France," he said. "I don't believe you will get a chance to dine with him soon."

"Oh," she said, feigning surprise. "I do hope that Gerard de St. Amand is still at the monastery, then. I had been looking forward to stopping by and seeing how Micah has kept up the gardens."

"I believe Gerard is still there," he said. "But I don't know of anyone named Micah."

"Micah is the monk that stays there with them." She shook her head at his ignorance. "He's truly delightful to hold conversation with, and he does a wonderful job with the garden. I do hope he is still there, I will miss him if he's not."

"Ah, the monk. Well, I'm sure he's still there, Lady..." He glanced back down at the note. "Lady Josephine. Let me just get you what you need. How much were you looking to withdraw?"

She smiled, gave him an amount, and watched him scurry away to fetch the money. Thomas had warned her that she might run into problems using the note. He had assured her that the knights would make good on their payment, but she might be subjected to more scrutiny than a man. And it was dangerous to attract too much attention. But the mention of Geoffrey and Gerard did the trick. The squire returned with the money and gave her a new receipt with the adjusted balance.

Her body yearned for her to stay the night. Weeks locked in her cabin had left her muscles stiff, but she was too anxious to make it to the monastery. She still hoped that Geoffrey survived, though she knew Thomas had serious doubts. His hopes had faded when his friend failed to arrive that night, but Josephine would not so easily give up. Perhaps Geoffrey had been forced to retreat, but didn't want to lead the assassin to Thomas's estate?

He might be on a ship right now. He might even be at the monastery. Her ship had stopped in several ports on the way, and it was entirely possible he could have arrived before her.

These thoughts kept her from staying overnight. She only had one task left, and then she could set off to the monastery. And this task was easy to fulfill. Geoffrey had taught her how to feed, and there were plenty of people about in the port town.

***

It took her two nights of hard riding to reach the monastery, but when it finally came into view her hopes sank. There were two torches outside the monastery, one to each side of the great doors. Normally, these torches would be lit during the dark hours of the night signaling a safe sanctuary to any in need. Now, the torches were cold and dark.

Josephine struggled to keep tears from her eyes. Had she traveled all this way only to find the monastery empty? She steered her horse toward the building. Even if it were empty, she would have to stay. It was too deep into the night to find another place for shelter. But, the idea of staying in the empty monastery was almost more than she could bear.

She rode past the entrance to the stables. Geoffrey had always insisted on prompt care for the horses. "Treat your horse well," he would say, "And it will treat you well in return." She dismounted and was about to open the door to the stable when she felt a strange sensation wash over her. She had left the sword at Thomas's estate -- it would not do for a lady to be seen carrying such a weapon -- but she had a small knife hidden by the folds of her dress. She held on to the hilt and searched the night.

"Josephine?" A figure emerged from the shadows, and she recognized the voice.

"Gerard!" She rushed into his arms. "It is good to see you. I saw the torches not lit and feared the place empty."

"We haven't lit them for weeks. We are not open to travelers, or at least, not just any traveler. Where is Geoffrey? We did not expect the two of you back so soon."

She trembled and held him tighter. "I don't know if he lives," she whispered. "The last I saw..."

"Hush," he said. "We'll talk about it later."

She clung to him, the tears she had fought against now rolling down her cheek, and he held her. She had been strong through weeks of travel out of necessity. But here, in his arms, she felt safe. And with that safety came feelings long kept buried deep inside. She wept, and then let him lead her into the monastery.

"Tell me what has happened," Gerard said. He smiled, but it wasn't reflected in his eyes. He feared for Geoffrey too.

She began her tale when they had left the monastery and left out no detail until finally coming to the night of the attack. She paused then, building up strength. He put his hand on hers, and she felt his strength moving into her, giving her the courage to go on. She spoke of that night, of the surprise attack, of her wild ride and her eventual fight with the assassins. She told him about Thomas, and the ship, and finally coming back to the monastery hoping that Geoffrey would be there.

When she got to the end of her tale, she looked at him. And she could tell by the deep look of sadness in his face that he knew Geoffrey would not be coming back. He clenched his fist, the sadness replaced by anger.

"This assassin, he was the same one that fought Edward that night long ago?"

"Yes," she replied.

"His name is Zain," Gerard said. "Six weeks ago, he assassinated the leader of the Isma'ilites and named himself Old Man of the Mountain. Soon afterward, he disappeared, and I had not seen him since, until a few nights ago. I was keeping watch on their stronghold, as I often do these nights, and I spotted him riding through the gates. He looked as if he had just come from a long journey."

He paused and looked like he was about to add more when the door opened and Micah, looking worn and tired, stepped into the room. The monk stopped when he saw her, his eyes going wide. "Josephine, you are back!" He stepped forward to greet her, but then stopped. "Where's Geoffrey?"

"He's..." Josephine glanced at Gerard.

"No," Micah said. He took a step back and shook his head. "It can't be." Tears began streaming down his face. "It just can't be."

Josephine had not realized how deep the strange friendship between the knight and the monk ran. She went to him, putting her arms around him and trying to give him the same comfort he gave her in her time of need.

"I just can't believe it," he whispered. "Sir Geoffrey was so smart, he was so strong. I've seen many knights come here and then go off to battle not to return, but Geoffrey always returned."

Josephine squeezed his hand, but her eyes were on Gerard. The knight's eyes burned, his entire presence sizzling. They were both reeling from the loss of their leader, each in his own way. She thought of the knight that had come to her rescue on that day long ago, of the unwavering trust she had come to have in him in their travels. And she thought of the assassins ambushing them at the Southwork estate, and in her heart, the grief took on the same rage that smoldered in Gerard's eyes.

"What are we going to do?" she asked.

Gerard looked at her and she felt him measure up the woman she had become in the past weeks. "We are going to teach you how to use a sword," he said. "I can't turn you into a master swordswoman in a matter of days, but I can teach you how to hold your own. And, with your strength and speed, that will be more than enough for most opponents."

She nodded. "And, after that, what then?"

He smiled. "And then, we play..."

CHAPTER THIRTY

Zain entered the hall. Nizam al-Quadus had received word from one of the fidais that he had arrived, but he wasn't prepared for Zain's appearance. Normally neat and kempt, the man walking toward him now was a chaotic mess with wind-blown hair and skin smudged with the dirt of weeks on the road. He marched through the hall in a fury, and the fidais he passed shrank away from him.

He'd failed. There was no other explanation for his leader's appearance. Zain stalked to the table and fell into the great chair in the center, his brooding stare gazing beyond the stone walls to sights unseen.

"It has escaped me again." He clenched his fist. "It was within my grasp. I could actually see it dangling from her hand, and yet, still, it escaped me."

"Your mission did not fare well, then." Nizam set his glass on the table and turned to his friend. There were many pressing issues that needed the Old Man's attention, but he would not bring them up until Zain was ready to hear them.

"We tracked them to a small town outside London," Zain said. "They stayed not far from the city in a small estate near a village. We waited for them to leave and searched the house, but came up with nothing. They would hide it well, we knew, perhaps in some secret passage, or behind a seemingly solid rock, or some other place that would make it hard to find.

307

"I knew that we could search the house over and over for days on end and come up empty handed, so I decided to press the issue. The knight was the real danger, so I arranged for them to lead me to the prize. The plan worked perfectly. I let them spot me in the city, and they flew back to the house, running straight for the book and hoping to flee before we could catch them.

"That was my trap, and they fell right into it. We jumped them when they exited. We circled the house, forming the jaws of the trap. The knight, as predicted, stayed behind to fight, while the woman and the book fled. I had three men, good, solid men, stationed at the edge of town waiting for her to ride away so they could close the jaws and retrieve my prize.

"I dealt with the knight personally, it was my pleasure, and I never thought for a moment the woman stood a chance against trained Isma'ilites. I was wrong. If I had only accounted for *that* it could have been dealt with, but I never expected it of her..."

He lapsed into silence, his angry stare flowing off into the distance.

"What didn't you expect of her, Zain?" Nizam asked.

"She is one of them," he hissed. "They changed her into one of their own. I don't know what unholy rites they perform to bring the devil inside them, but they performed them on her. Three of our brothers were found dead near a farmhouse. She, a mere woman, had killed all three of them and fled with the book."

Nizam sucked in a breath. "She killed all three of them?" he asked. "Even with the devil's blood in her, I can hardly believe a mere merchant's daughter would be capable of taking on three Isma'ilites."

"It seems she was more than capable," Zain said. "She killed the first with the very same dagger I sent into her shoulder. She killed the next with her bare hands, and the last... I don't know how she killed him, but his throat was torn through like a wild animal had savaged him.

"That is what we are dealing with, old friend. We fight men that turn into beasts, that have the strength of several men, the speed of the wind, and can kill with weapon or bare hands. They have hell's fire within them and, if we are not too careful, that fire will be unleashed and will consume us all."

"What will we do?" Nizam asked.

"We must get that book," Zain said. "The other knights, the Hospitaller, believed it would turn their church against the Templar and destroy them from within."

Zain bent forward, bringing his lips close to Nizam's ear. Whispering so lightly Nizam had to strain to hear the words, he said, "I never thought I would say this, old friend, but perhaps we do need those Christians. We need to find out where the girl has fled."

"I fear that will prove difficult, Zain," Nizam said. "We have had word from the Hospitaller. The recent failures to obtain the book have caused them to lose faith in the mission. The knight, Jonathan Alderson, has gone missing and they assume he is dead. The other knights seem unwilling to spend more effort on this cause."

Zain leaned back in his chair, his eyes sweeping the hall with a murderous gaze. "Perhaps it is for the best," he said. "Our past dealings with the infidels has only brought us to defeat. It is time for us to act on this matter in our own way."

"What do you propose?"

"We need to find out more about this woman. We still have men watching her uncle?"

"Yes, Zain." Nizam nodded. "He left the house and stayed with another for several days after the attack, but then returned. He did travel once to the slain merchant's house and transferred some possessions back to his own home."

"It is time for us to pay him a visit and reap the rewards for allowing him to remain alive," Zain said.

"Should I assemble some men?"

Zain shook his head. "I will handle this myself. I cannot accept any more unexpected events. I must ensure this is done properly."

"There are pressing matters that need your attention," Nizam said.

"I am sorry," Zain said. "I have not asked you how all has fared since I have been gone."

"Not as smoothly as we hoped," Nizam replied. "The fortresses of al-Qulaia and al-Maniqah are still out of our control. A rafiq in Masyaf named Nasr al-'Ajami has spoken out against you. He spreads doubt that Sinan is actually dead."

"I know Nasr," Zain said. "He is a fool."

"Fool or not, he has the Imam's ear," Nizam said. "I was unable to win the support of Alamut."

Zain was silent for a moment. "Nasr must be dealt with. His foolishness divides our people and weakens our strength."

"And the uncle?"

"I can wait to deal with him," Zain said. "If the man had a mind to flee, he would have done so by now."

CHAPTER THIRTY-ONE

"Are you ready?" Gerard asked.

Josephine nodded. It was a week since they'd started the training, and the sword felt more comfortable in her hands. She only knew the basics, but just knowing how to stand and how to hold the sword was more than she knew a week ago. He taught her how to parry thrusts with a small shift of the blade and how to spot an opponent twisting his blade under hers. But she was still a novice, and she would need to rely more on her strength and speed than her skill.

Gerard glanced at the monastery. "I'm worried about Micah," he said. "I have a bad feeling that something will happen here. It might be best if you stayed here to protect him and guard this place."

He was lying. He wasn't worried about Micah; he was worried about her. But he had little chance of surviving without her. Zain would require all of his attention. Someone had to be there to protect his back.

"I am ready," she said. "I may not yet be a master of this blade, but I am stronger and faster than those I will face. I won't let you down."

Gerard smiled. "I know you won't."

She did have her doubts, but it wasn't in her ability. She had already faced three of the assassins. Her doubts were of another kind. She looked up into the sky and stared at the stars. "I do wonder if he would approve."

"I can't honestly say," Gerard said. "Geoffrey and I were always different in our approach to

312

problems. I prefer simple and direct. I don't live for violence, but sometimes fighting must be done. Zain will never stop searching for you, and he will never stop searching for the book. There is nothing that will persuade him from this task. So, there is only one solution that will stop him."

"You make it sound simple."

"It is simple," he said. "It just won't be easy. There are few men alive that could have bested Edward, and fewer still that could have bested Geoffrey. The task we face is difficult, it is dangerous, but it is also inevitable. The only thing we can decide is when we will do it and if it will be on our terms or his."

"Well," she said. "We might as well face it on our terms then."

He handed her a black cloak. "Put this in your saddlebag."

"What's this?"

"I went out at dusk to ensure we would not be observed leaving," he said. "The Isma'ilites have continued to watch the monastery closely. Two of them were kind enough to loan me their cloaks before they died."

She smiled. "That was nice of them."

They mounted the horses and left the monastery. Their destination was al-Kahf, the hiding place of the Old Man of the Mountain. Josephine had been surprised to learn how close it was to the monastery and equally surprised the assassins controlled nearly a dozen fortresses. Gerard referred to al-Kahf as the Castle of the Cave. The castle was built at a junction between three narrow valleys, and Gerard had told her it might be the most impregnable fortress in the Holy Lands.

But she didn't think about that on the ride. Gerard wouldn't be undertaking this mission if he didn't have an idea on how to get into the fortress. She reviewed what she had learned in the past week. Along with basic swordplay, he taught her how to walk on the sides of her feet to reduce the noise. It was not difficult, but required concentration. He also taught her how to scale the wall of a sheer cliff. It had been surprisingly easy, and even fun. The strength of her blood allowed her to easily hold her weight using only her fingertips. Once she gained some confidence, she was able to scramble up the side of a cliff like it was a ladder.

Of course, a week was not enough to make her a master of any skill, but her blood would allow her to do more than most. She had faced down three assassins with the strength of that blood alone. She would do better now.

"From here, we go on foot," Gerard said.

She hopped down, and they led the horses to a ridge running alongside the road. They followed the ridge until they reached a small crevice that led to a small opening. An old, battered tree stood in the center, and Gerard looped the reigns of his horse around a small limb.

"Will that hold?" she asked.

"No," he said. "But they are well-trained. They will be here when we get back."

She nodded and tied her own horse to the same limb.

"From this point forward, we only talk in whispers." He led her back through the crevice. "We will pass near an Ismaeli village on our way."

"We weren't really talking much anyway," she said.

He smiled at her. "No, we weren't were we?"

She reached out and clasped his hand, the heat of his palm feeding the confidence she had in their mission. She squeezed the hand and then released it, nodding with her head for him to lead onward.

They had already traveled most of the way to al-Kahf, but the last leg of the journey took time. They walked down into deep ravines and wound their way around a mountain spur. The Ismaeli village sprung up in the bottom of a valley, and Gerard took special care to give the village a wide berth. Their movement slowed at this point, Gerard careful of any unwanted observers, until they finally dropped down onto a ridge. Rising from the junction of three valleys, the castle stood atop the low cliffs ahead of them.

Josephine stared at the imposing sight. The moon hovered behind the castle, and its gentle glow created a soft shadow on the land. The castle rose from those shadows as if created from them. At the base of the cliff, she could see the mouth of the tunnel illuminated by the flickering light of torches. She could just make out the small shadows standing guard over the tunnel, and she knew others were spread out around the fortress.

Gerard tapped her on the shoulder and motioned for her to follow. He led them around to the side, frequently stopping to stare at the fortress before continuing. He was searching for the perfect place to cross. They moved past the middle of the outer wall before he stopped and nodded his head.

"Leave the packs here," he whispered, "and put on the cloak."

She opened the pack and took out the cloak. Now that it was upon them, her hands shook. But whether it was from fright or excitement she wasn't sure.

"When we ascend and reach the point where the cliff gives way to the walls of the castle I want you to hold that position," he said. "I will continue up the wall and make certain the top is clear of guards and then signal for you to follow."

She nodded, and he took off across the valley. He moved fast, but his footsteps were silent. She tried her best to mimic his grace, taking special care to step exactly where he did to avoid the added sound of a snapped stick or crackling leaves.

At the base of the cliff, he turned and pointed up. He smiled at her and then scrambled up the side of the cliff. Josephine took a deep breath and followed. It was easier than she imagined. The small ridges Gerard had taken her to on the last few nights were very sheer and proved difficult to grip at points. She found no such difficulty here. Soon, she topped the cliff and stood on the small ridge in front of the castle walls.

Gerard was already ascending the wall. He disappeared over the top, and she waited for his signal. It was critical they gain access to the courtyard unnoticed. There were guards posted at each corner, and others walking the walls. They couldn't risk silencing one of the guards because he would soon be missed. So they had to time it just right.

Gerard signaled, and she began to climb. It was even easier to scale the castle wall than the cliff. The wall had a pattern where the stones met. The small crevices between the stones were only deep enough to fit the very tip of her finger, but that was enough. Had she not had the strength of her blood, the climb would have been impossible no matter how much training she had. But with that strength, she scaled the wall with ease.

Gerard helped her over the battlement. He signaled for her to wait, and then hopped over the side, landing neatly on his feet. Her drop was less graceful, and she was forced to tuck and roll as he taught her. Gerard was already crossing the courtyard, but she did not hurry after him. It was just as important to be silent as quick, so she concentrated on stepping with the sides of her feet like he taught her.

He reached the building and slipped into a small pocket of shadow between two flickering torches. She was still at the halfway point, and she kept her eyes on him, expecting at any moment for the alarm to sound. Could they fight their way back out? She didn't know, and didn't want to find out. She was almost to the building when he waved to her, and she abandoned stealth for speed.

She hugged the ground and waited for the alarm to sound, sure the pounding of her footsteps had been noticed. Gerard reached over and squeezed her hand, and she relaxed. It was a fair distance from the building to the wall, and any sound she made had been swallowed by the wind.

They watched the guard march past them along the wall. When he was out of sight, they moved. The entrance was well lit by torches. The flickering light created dancing shadows across the front of the courtyard, but not enough for them to hide. They crept to the edge, and then Gerard stepped into the light. He transformed from a man of stealth to a man of noble bearing and approached the entrance with purpose.

Josephine trailed after him, walking a step behind and to the right as if ready to attend to his any need. Her heart was beating so loud she could barely hear her own footsteps. She wrapped the cloak around her to conceal her bosom, and kept her eyes on the ground.

There were two Isma'ilites posted at the entrance, and both watched their approach with interest. Gerard waved one of them over when they were still a fair distance away. The guards exchanged glances, and one of them shrugged before jogging over to meet them.

Gerard kept the man between himself and the other guard. He raised his hood, and Josephine could see the guard's eyes widen in recognition. They might be able to pass a casual inspection, but not a close one. The guard opened his mouth, but his eyes lost focus before he could raise the alarm.

Gerard closed the distance between them. "We are messengers traveling long and hard from the knight's monastery." His voice was a whisper, and he used fluent Arabic. Josephine could only understand a few of the words, but they had gone over this part in detail. "The knights amass a small army at their temple. We fear they are preparing for an attack and I have been sent to give this urgent message to Zain, Old Man of the Mountain."

"You are messengers," the man said.

"You will take us to the great hall," Gerard whispered. "And we will deliver the message to Zain."

The assassin frowned, and Josephine fought an urge to slide her hand to the hilt of her sword. He was likely disturbed at news of a possible attack, and was only acting accordingly.

"Come with me." He led them to the entrance, and when the other guard took a step toward them, he waved him away. "Messengers from the monastery." They passed through the entrance, Gerald holding his head high in confidence, and Josephine's lowered in obedience.

Once inside the building, Josephine's nose wrinkled at the sweet smell of incense in the air, the scent so powerful she almost sneezed. She breathed out of her mouth to relieve the pressure building in her nose, and she could taste the incense on her tongue. The assassin guided them through several small rooms before they entered the great hall. He paused before one of the guards at the entrance. "Messengers," he informed the guard, and motioned for them to follow.

Josephine could feel eyes on her when they entered the hall. Would they see through the ruse? Her heart trembled. At any moment, she expected to hear a shout of alarm. This was the center of the

319

assassin's power. They couldn't just walk right in the front door, could they?

When Gerard had unveiled his plan to her, she had accepted it without a word. After all, Gerard would not have suggested it if he didn't think it would work. But now that they were here, she began to doubt. She stared at his booted feet tapping the floor in front of her, and dismissed the sinking feeling in her stomach. Why would she doubt now if she did not doubt then?

It was fear. And it was fear that was her enemy, because it was fear that would cause her to make a mistake. A nervous glance. A hand on her sword. These were the actions that would give them away. But fear did not exist in the world; it only existed inside of her. It wasn't real -- it was conjured.

She would be strong. Gerard depended on her, and she would not let him down. She lifted her head slightly and peeked through her hood. The Isma'ilites seemed distracted, too busy with their own problems to pay much heed to a couple of messengers. A few glanced their way in curiosity, but paid them little attention.

Why should they? This was their stronghold. If an attack came, it would be from outside the walls, not inside.

At the end of the hall was a great table where several men gathered and talked in hushed tones. The men at this table marked their presence, one of them turning to peer at them in curiosity. The others merely glanced over and went back to their conversation, except for the man in the middle. He did not look up at first, but when he did Josephine felt a stab of recognition.

It was Zain. Would he recognize them? She didn't even breathe, fearful the air coming from her mouth was enough for him to see through their disguise. He turned back to the men around him, resuming the conversation, but then he looked back up at them, and this time his stare was intense. He detected something amiss.

Gerard did not waste any time. He drew his swords and the man leading them collapsed to the ground with two deep slashes crisscrossing his back. Gerard leaped to the side and impaled an assassin before the man realized what had occurred and rushed to engage another.

Josephine was just as quick, if not as eloquent. She dashed to the side opposite of Gerard and ran her sword through the nearest assassin before he could get his weapon out of his sheath. She pounced on a second assassin, chopping at him, but her clumsy blow was easily parried. She slashed at him wildly, and again the man parried, but this time she ended with a neat lunge that slipped under his defenses. His mistake in thinking her unskilled was his last, but that trick would not work again.

Gerard finished off his man, and there was no one between them and the table. There were four men at that table. One was still sitting, stunned by the attack. Another stood and reached for his weapons. A third was coming around the sign and the fourth, Zain, had both swords drawn and was leaping over the table.

Gerard ignored Zain and rolled under the table. He thrust his sword into the man still staring wide-eyed around the room, and rolled back out from under the table. Zain pounced on him, but Gerard was ready, and the two squared off, exchanging blows.

Josephine hesitated only long enough for Gerard to pick his victim. When he rolled under the table, she dove over it, hoping the ferocity of her attack would catch the man off guard. The man was quick and got his sword in front of him, but she batted it to the side. Lowering her shoulder, she rammed him in the chest, and he bounced against the wall. He slashed at her, and a burning sensation ripped up her side from his blade raking her flesh, but she ignored it. She grabbed him by the hair, and slammed his head back into the wall. His head cracked against the stone, and Josephine rushed around the table to cut off the third assassin before he could flank Gerard.

The alarm had been raised, and soon the hall would be filled with assassins. It was her job to keep them away from Gerard. He would need to focus on Zain, and she must stall the rest until he was done.

She would have to make short work of this one. She attacked, her sword darting in and out with blurring speed, but he parried the blows and returned one of his own. He was fast, and she was barely able to keep it from her flesh. She attacked again, and this time his riposte pinned her shoulder.

He was fast, but she was faster. She sent a flurry of blows his way, but he knew how to use her speed against her, and she took several more cuts in return. He came at her, the tip of his sword flirting around her blade, baiting her one way while he delivered a wicked slash on the opposite side. He hadn't scored a deep wound yet, but he could wear her down with many small ones until, in pain, she made a crucial mistake.

She was beaten. Sooner or later, her guard would come down and his blade would slip through. He might best her, but she could still win. She concentrated on parrying his blows, and waited for just the right one.

It came. He lunged at her, his blade aimed just to the left of her belly. This one she didn't parry. Instead, she stepped through it. A surge of pain unlike anything she had ever felt ripped through her body. She could see the look of victory reflected in the assassin's eyes. And then she brought her own sword up and through his throat.

Blood splattered against her face. He clawed at his throat, and fell to the ground. Josephine staggered, the pain so intense she almost fell with him. But she was determined not to let Gerard down. Not now. She had given him her life, and now she would give him her death.

She put her free hand around the sword that impaled her and yanked it out of her body. The blade cut into her palm and fingers, but she could not feel anything besides the fire in her belly. She dropped the sword, and it clamored against the stone floor. And then, holding her own sword defensively in front of her, she turned to the assassins fanning out in the hall.

They were poised on the edge of attack, but when she stepped toward them, they stepped back. She read the thoughts in their eyes. How could they defeat this demon that had just taken in death and was now turning to meet them?

She smiled at the irony of it all. The strength was leaving her body. Even now, she could barely keep her sword in her hands. Her vision blurred, but she knew so long as she had the strength to stand, they would not approach. So long as she had the strength, Gerard was free to focus on Zain. She didn't hope to live long, but she would live long enough.

***

It was a dance. Zain executed an intricate combination of thrusts, slashes and lunges, and Gerard parried. And then Gerard unleashed his own series of attacks, but Zain matched him. They went back and forth testing different strategies. Gerard first tried using his speed, but Zain was too quick. Zain countered with guile, letting one of his blades dip enough to create an opening, but Gerard anticipated the trap.

They were evenly matched, each mirroring the other, and neither able to gain advantage. Gerard was fast, possessing the speed of the blood, but Zain was just as quick. He was strong, but Zain knew how to use his balance to maximize his own strength. He was skilled in the sword, and Zain matched that skill. They exchanged blow after blow,

324

and the only marks either had to show were stains of sweat.

But in one area Gerard was Zain's superior. He could continue to fight for hours upon hours without tire, his endurance never giving way to exhaustion. Zain was in peak condition, but would still feel the slow weight of their battle. Gerard used that to his advantage, conserving his energy and forcing Zain to remain on the offensive. With each pause in the attack, Gerard punished his opponent with a fury of strokes delivered with the strength of many men.

A clatter of a sword hitting stone alerted him to Josephine's victory. He could smell fear, and he knew the other assassins were holding back. They would not be interrupted. Zain realized this too. Gerard could see the frustration in his eyes.

The assassin launched a blistering series of attacks. His sword danced high and then dipped low, feinted to the right and appeared on the left. His body twisted and contorted, the clamor of metal on metal echoing off the walls. The viciousness of the attack ebbed, but Zain pressed forward. He danced with his enemy, falling into a comfortable rhythm. The sound of their swordplay rang out like music in the hall. And then, like a lute player breaking a string in mid-song, Zain dropped to the ground, rolled, and brought his sword up into his opponent's groin.

But Gerard was no longer there. He expected the gambit and was waiting for that string to break. When it did, Gerard hopped over his enemy, twisted in the air, and swung his sword down through Zain's neck. The clash of his sword against the stone floor was followed by the light thump of the assassin's head rolling across the ground.

Zain was dead.

Gerard stared at the body, watching it convulse as if it hadn't yet realized it was dead. There was no joy. There was no satisfaction. The fury that had welled up into him upon learning of Geoffrey's death ebbed, and Gerard took no pleasure in killing. In many ways, they were similar, and not just their skill with the blade. Their ideals and beliefs were different, but their relentless pursuit of them was the same.

Finally, the body lay still, and Gerard knelt down beside to perform the Last Rites. What would Josephine think? He was giving solace in death to the same man who had killed her protector. She must think him a monster, but it was no matter. He did what he thought was right.

Gerard looked up at her and sucked in a breath. He saw the blood dripping from the wound in her back, and knew it went all the way through. He noticed what the assassins, in their fear, did not. The slight tremor of her arm, and the way her back arched as if a slight bend would cause her to come crashing down. She was only minutes away from losing the last of her strength and collapsing to the floor. And, should she lose that strength, she would never rise again.

She had paid this price for him. To give him time to deal with Zain. She had reached deep down and found the strength to remain standing throughout the fight despite the blood draining from her body.

326

Gerard flowed forward and ran the blade of his sword across his wrist. He came up behind her, looped his uninjured arm around her to give her strength, and brought his bloody wrist to her mouth. He paid no heed to the Isma'ilites. Many had fled the hall at their leader's death, others were prostate on the floor, praying. He held Josephine and beckoned her to drink deeply of him, hoping his strength would be enough to heal her wounds.

EPILOGUE

The old man followed Josephine into the room. She showed him to a chair at the table across from Gerard and then stood behind him. Gerard noticed that she kept her hand protectively over her side where the sword had impaled her. It had been over a month, and yet still the wound pained her.

It would heal in time. All of their wounds would heal, but hers ran so deep it might take many more months for them all to heal, and not all of her wounds were physical. He smiled at her, and then turned to the old scholar.

"You are said to be an expert in ancient languages," Gerard said.

"Yes." The man nodded his head. "I've studied long and hard these many years and come across languages so old few recognize their script, and fewer still can translate the script into words."

Gerard nodded. The old scholar was not the first to pay them a visit, and would not be the first to examine the book. Each time, the scholars had talked of the ancient languages they knew, and each time they had been unable to read the words.

"I wonder if you might take a look at something for me and tell me if you can read it," Gerard said.

The man glanced from Josephine to Gerard, and then shrugged his shoulders. Gerard could tell he was annoyed. People came to him to ask their questions, he did not come to them. But he was also curious, or else he would not be here.

Gerard smiled. He reached into the bag lying at his feet and produced the book. He watched the man's eyes follow the book's progress to the table and allowed him to just enough time to become curious, and then put his hand over the book, obscuring it from sight.

The man looked at him, annoyed, and Gerard caught the old man within his gaze.

"You will read the words on the cover and tell me if you can understand them." His voice hummed like a song.

He turned the book to face the man and slid it across the table. The man glanced down, his lips mouthing the words from the cover. "The Vampiric Bible." He looked up, his eyes still glazed over from the power of Gerard's voice. "An odd title..."

Gerard glanced at Josephine who shrugged and nodded her head.

"Open the book and read from the first passage,"

The old man laid a withered hand on the cover and opened the book. He reached out and stroked the words on the page like the touch of a mistress. "In the beginning..."

Gerard reached across and slammed the book shut. "That is enough."

He grabbed the book and deposited it back into the sack. The man dully followed his movements and remained staring at the bag waiting for the book to emerge again. Gerard placed his hand between them and snapped his fingers drawing the old scholar's attention back to him.

"How long have you walked upon this earth?" Gerard asked.

The man's eyes were still glazed over, and his response slow. "I will see my sixty-third year this spring."

Gerard was surprised. It was rare for a man to live to such an old age without aid of the blood. "And do you fear the death that slowly creeps toward you?"

"A man as old as I am does not fear death. He has lived with death many years and comes to expect its visit."

"And, when death approaches, will you welcome it, or will you ward it away?"

"I will say my prayers hoping that death has merely come for a glance and will pass me by sparing me for another few days, or another few years."

"And if I were to give you life unending, a chance to stay for all of eternity with the books you love, would you accept my gift?"

The man's eyes flashed, the haze in his vision replaced, for a moment, with a burning light. And Gerard had his answer.

THE END